# EVOKING MIRA

## Erica Chilson

# EVOKING MIRA

Wicked Reads
PO Box 29
Nelson, PA 16940

www.ericachilson.com/wicked-reads

Printed in the United States of America

First Printing, 2021

ISBN: 9798706602598

# EVOKING MIRA

With a single glance in the mirror, the reflection gazing back evokes Mira's sense of self.

Struggling to rearrange the broken fragments of her psyche, Mira attempts to piece her memories together into a survivable landscape.

Once, twice, a dozen cycles, Mira is forced to experience memories plucked from time, over and over again until they finally take root, as if they're happening in the now.

One misstep.

A chemical-induced amnesia resets the cycle, where she is destined to repeat her own history.

Instead of naturally spreading the events over a lifetime, Mira must face the traumatic demons of her past in agonizing bursts.

The pain.

The joy.

The sorrow.

Will it be one time too many?

That last traumatic nudge propelling Mira over the edge of the abyss into lucidity, or will she be stuck in an endless rotation where her memories lock her away from reality?

# Mistress and Master of Restraint

Restraint
Unleashed
Dexter
Dalton
Queen Omnibus*
Jaded*
Queened*
Checkmate*
King
Faithless
The Hunter
Integrated
MASSacre
Hero
Thief
Dirty Laundry

# BLENDED

Good Girl
Wildly Wedded Wife
Widow
Wanton
Warped
Woven
Wager
Wicked
Wonder
Wexler

# RUSTY KNOB

Rusty Knob
Tarnished
Stainless
Polished
Tied Knots

# FOLLOWILL

Followill
Followill Loyalty
Followilled


## EVOKING MIRA

Dear reader,

Perhaps you wonder what inspired such a bizarre story. Perhaps not, but I'll attempt to explain it anyway.

With only a snapshot of an idea, I sat down to write, and what was meant to be a few pages to appease the muse, turned into five days of around-the-clock writing. The story quite literally wrote itself, my sanity the cost, written in one session from start to finish.

During the writing process, I generally go back and rewrite large portions before moving forward: expand scenes, clarify motivations, add setting, deepen emotions, and evolve the world building, as I now have a firmer grasp on the ending. A heavy lesson learned from the M&M of Restraint series. This process happens during rereads as well, which I've dubbed rewrites. It's part of the editing process, but more so the rewriting process.

Evoking Mira is the only novel where I've never changed anything, not even the sentence structure. No mulling over passages. No rewrites. After a dozen times reread, I've changed nary a word. Each time I reread the novel, I felt what was on the pages was as it was meant to be. The entire novel written during an odd moment of inspiration, the emotions evoked left unnamed.

Honestly, I have no idea where the story came from, why it was written, but had an undeniable desire to get the words on paper. But there is a method to my madness, the refusal to change a word that was written during an intense inspiration session… the vibe would be different, altered from what was meant to be on the pages. However imperfect, it is as it was meant to be, in its original form.

Written as a standalone, I have no idea if I'll ever revisit this odd world I've created. I've left openings for me to work from, while also leaving it in a way that the reader can use their own vivid imagination as to what happened next.

If you were intrigued by Mira and her family, leave a review or drop me a message. Nothing inspires the muse more than communicating with readers. Suddenly inspiration will strike, and the undeniable urgency to put words to paper will overcome me, and a new novel will be born.

Over the months since I completed the novel, in the quiet hours, Mira revisits my thoughts. Even I, its creator, am not sure how I feel about the novel. Not quite sure how it made me feel. But one thing is for sure, I doubt I'll ever forget Mira. Other characters fade over time– just as Mira attempted to explain recollection –they fade into the background, a trigger easily reminding me of their existence. Mira is different for me. She ghosts into my thoughts, her story never shifting, leaving as softly as she arrived.

*Edited to add at a later date:* While preparing Evoking Mira for publication, after reading my beta notes, where I contemplated adding their questions and my answers to the end of the novel, knowing readers would have those same questions too, another bout of inspiration struck.

What I thought would be a simple passage from a reliable narrator, used as a vehicle to answer questions, ended up adding a significant amount to the overall story.

Thank you for reading Evoking Mira.

May you all experience rare bursts of inspiration.

–Erica Chilson.

# AWAKENING

"Her heartrate just elevated," a whisper flutters to my right. Fogginess dilating around the edges, eclipsing all clarity. "Should we sedate her again before we continue on with the examination?"

There's the blackest of nights, where you can't see your hand before your face. Then there is the darkness of wakeful sleep, where you can sense light pouring around you, naturally attempting to tear you into consciousness.

The light intensifies, even though I can't actually see it. It's a sensation deep-rooted in primal instinct. My skin flushes, even though there is no heat.

There's the realization that something isn't right within my thought process. There are instincts that defy all laws. You just know who you are. Your name. Your age. Your appearance. Your gender. Where you're from, where you've been, and where you are in the present.

Muscles at rest, skin lax, vision quiet beneath the darkening blanket of eyelids. The fight or flight reflex not engaged. No necessary cocktail of endorphins, hormones, and adrenaline. No chaotic emotions, the median between sociopath and empath, a forced sense of safety, comfort, and calm, induced by psychotropic drugs.

Mind swirling, heartrate monitor picking up to a screeching buzz saw that assaults my ears. The sudden reality that what I should know doesn't manifest upon waking as it has since the first breath I took after being expelled from my mother's womb.

Zero sense of self.

Held captive by my own mind.

The scarier revelation is the fact that I know everything but who I am and how I got to be here. Brain supplying a plethora of information, right down to the proper titles for body parts but not my own name. A fully grown, educated woman, but I know naught of the most important of facts regarding myself.

The whispered touch of air fluttering from a vent nearby alerts my sense of touch that I am fully exposed, laid out naked and vulnerable, with no way to protect myself. The screeching beep draws out in a loud panic, heart fluttering in terror.

Waiting for a sharp bite to accompany that sedation comment, all I sense is a soft tug on my arm. A catheter rooted into my vein, pierced sharply, releasing a flood of toxins to induce a false sense of safety and security.

"The scars are lighter than last week," comes sluggish and nearly inaudible as my ears struggle to process sound.

"That's the first time she's awakened in nine days," is the only part that is computed by my brain, the rest trailing off into nonsense.

Floating, soft and light and dreamy. "We need to consult the log to properly judge the sedation schedule. She's not ready."

The shadowy darkness of natural sleep is replaced by the terror of forced unconsciousness, the panic causing the siren screech to flatline.

"Miraculously she healed more than expected. Far more." Partially alert, consciousness swimming to the surface, fingertips are clinically prodding at my nether regions.

Lying unnaturally still, held hostage by a cocktail of drugs someone has injected into my system, I have no idea who I am, where I am, or what I even look like, but I instinctively understand which parts of my body are being touched without my consent.

"I had worried," voice breaking, the male's voice is off toward my side, not the female whisper examining me between my legs. The scritch, scritch, scritch of a pen dragging against paper.

How can I understand what is producing that sound, when I have no concept of time before thirty seconds ago?

"Me too," is a breath barely understood. The ghost of a touch drawing cool sheets to cover my vulnerable flesh. "I feared we wouldn't survive if we didn't repair our patient into working order."

"Working order was the bare minimum to keep breathing." The scratching sound stops, the presence shifting a step or two. The light placement of a soft-soled shoe loud enough for my ears to understand. "You did exemplary work on her breasts and labia."

A shuddered sigh alerts me to the female shifting her position on the other side from where the male is standing. Cool fingertips lightly prod my left breast, drawing a line near my armpit.

Wrong.

A sense of wrongness descends. Wrongness because what my body instinctively recognizes is different than what I feel beneath what I can only assume is the fingertip of a female doctor.

While I might not remember anything prior to a minute ago, my own fingertips understand that what the doctor is feeling is not what I've felt since puberty onward.

The violation. The rape of autonomy. Laid out on a table, skin sliced, muscles yanked from bone, body irreparably altered without my consent, never to be what once was. My breasts, just the weight of how they sit upon my chest, they are not *my* breasts. The arch the fingertip made on my nether regions, that is not the arch I have known since I learned what it meant to be a woman.

Sliced. Torn. Penetrated. Reshaped. Violated from the inside out. Natural form stolen.

The constant, steady beep confuses my senses, because I'm not in a panic. Not fully awake, yet coherent enough to understand the injustice is only lessened by the fact that a female physician is performing the examination while the male takes notes.

"Miracle," is whispered at my right, while at my left the doctor prods at my breast. "Your feat should be published, but your reconstruction will never see the light of day."

"If my performance ever sees the light of day, I never will again." Panicky, the doctor doesn't need a heartrate monitor to tattletale on her.

Eyelids shuttering my vision, the image affixed in my mind is of me floating above near the ceiling, a downward view of the body lying on a hospital bed, two white-coat doctors flanking the sides, heads bowed in concentration.

Disassociation disorder, my brain supplies for the question I demand of it. Why am I not emoting what human nature dictates? Why am I more cued into what the doctors are feeling?

Amnesia. Detachment.

Dissociative amnesia: memory loss, centric to sense of self. Fully aware of everything learned throughout a lifetime, with the exception of self.

Depersonalization-derealization disorder: observation of oneself from a distance, where emotions felt are muted. Detached. Life taking on a dreamlike quality, but perhaps that is due to the sedatives coursing through my veins to alter my brain chemistry.

Why do I know these things?

Do ordinary people just naturally know complex diagnoses.

"Her breasts are pure perfection." The doctor tries and fails to hide the undercurrent of lust coursing through his voice. "Seated naturally, the size complementary to the width of her torso. The height is impeccable, the droop landing just above the crook of her elbow. She can either have plump cleavage in a bra or a natural curve when braless."

"Elian–"

"I'm just commenting that he will be pleased with the results," the male doctor charges right over the female doctor. *As if anything is new with that dynamic* is thought sarcastically.

I'm sarcastic?

"The man has paid over a million dollars for her reconstruction, we need to feel proud that we managed–"

"My only reward is waking to see the next dawn." Unnerved for me, a woman's need to protect overpowers prideful tendencies. A sheet is drawn up higher, competent fingertips tucking it around my shoulders. The touch is foreign, numb, as if it's happening to someone else.

"The vaginoplasty was a success. The labia minora is safely tucked beneath the majora." Again, that lusty note enrages me, yet nothing but a hot wash though my veins occurs, not even the heartrate monitor accelerating. "It looks better that way. Pure and clean. It looks filthy and slutty when the inner lips hang outside. Now it's just a plump little palmful, the scars hidden along the apex of her thigh and majora. Pretty in the seat of her panties or bikini bottoms. No humungous fat bitch bulge or bubblegum tramp pussy."

Movement occurs around me, instinct providing what is occurring, since my sense of sight is absent, the drug firmly taking hold but not enough to fully render me unconscious. The female doctor places herself between me and her male colleague.

"You disgust me, Elian," flows with such ferocity that it's a miracle the heartrate monitor doesn't explode along with my actual heart.

"*I disgust you?*" is accompanied by a sharp scoff. "We work in a facility filled with Jane Smiths who have zero recollection of who they once were. Men provide us with an image on how to design their purchases. We allow our patients to go home with these men. You allow it without a second thought, spending your paycheck at the cost of your soul just as I do, yet you lecture me because I am merely complimenting both your skill and his design? *You disgust yourself, Sabrina.*"

Brain recalibrating. Perhaps it wasn't an event that stole my memories, but rather a drug.

Purchased?

Redesigned.

Sent home with a strange man who paid over a million dollars for his designer amnesiac– a hostage to both my inability to remember and his captive.

Even still, the detachment is still there, forced amnesia or not, unless that is a biproduct of the drug. Blinded. Paralyzed. Reshaped. Incorporeal.

"Not every single one of our patients are trafficked," the female doctor defends herself and their soulless practices.

Trafficked?

Me?

Whoever the fuck I am, I instinctively know I am the last person who should be subject to human trafficking. Can privilege be marrow deep, to where you know on a genetic level that you are somebody? Not only are you a somebody, you're somebody important, at least to someone else.

Stolen. Trafficked. Hospitalized. Drugged. Sliced. Altered. Sold.

"What leads you to believe this one isn't?" Another sharp scoff, where at least the male doctor acknowledges his own sociopathology and accepts it as fact. Nothing is worse than someone who is blinded by their own faults, judging others, while committing the same acts.

The momentary blindness of women's empowerment fizzles quickly, as I assess how the doctor doesn't see herself with clarity. Worse, I blame her more because she is a woman, committing the most egregious crimes against her own kind.

When... when will my emotions come back online? I don't know if I should pray for it or rue its reemergence.

"She is in her own wing, where he visits numerous times daily, needing nonstop updates– that's why." Movement swirls around me, causing the sheet to rustle. It tickles at my numb skin, and the inability to scratch at myself is inexplicably maddening.

Mind focused on the dueling doctors, I ignore the insanity of not being able to scratch an itch. "Yeah, and Jane Smithson on Level Four is currently getting a pair of Size-H tits that will bop against her chin– it's a good thing it's not pointy, because she'd pop herself."

"You sick fuck–"

"I'm the sick fuck? I'm a realist, sweetheart." Oh, the good guys always pull out a sweetheart to hammer home the insults. "Jane Smith the fifth is currently being turned into a chick with a dick, since he couldn't locate a bonafide intersexed person to kidnap, because his fetish is to rape and slaughter her during climax. So keep telling yourself you're not as evil as the rest of us, sweetheart, because the money you earn spends just the same as the rest of ours."

A nearly inaudible hitch in her breath is the only telltale sign that her colleague is getting to her.

Fuck her– after everything I just heard. Seriously, fuck her. She should be on one of those tables, getting altered without consent. Carved and strung up like a succulent goose, drooled over and devoured by gluttonous fiends. Used and abused. Life drained. Digested, shat into a commode, and flushed.

Two things I've learned about myself during this momentary reprieve of lucidity. I'm sarcastic and ruthless.

How the fuck did I get here? When did I get here? Who the hell am I? How the hell am I getting out of this?

*You're not* is readily supplied by my overactive mind, the only part of me still properly functioning, even if at a low capacity.

*Get to praying, because your survival rate is directly tied to whomever purchased and designed you.*

Outlook grim. No man purchases a woman for her intellectual abilities, then alters the state of her breasts and vulva.

Speaking of intellectuality, I know without a shadow of a doubt, I cannot get out of this. I'm not ignorant enough, nor naïve enough to honestly believe I can stave off the effects of whatever drugs are pumping through my IV. But I'm not hopeless, because eventually I will be well enough to be of use, and once I'm of use, I will see how I can use that to my advantage.

"I don't want to hear about any of this, Elian." Voice soft, manipulation hitting hard, what was her name? Oh, yes. Sabrina. Sabrina is playing the helpless female card now.

God, I loathe Sabrina even more than Elian.

"I just do my job. Their sins are not mine. I'm not the one who steals these women, nor orders their surgeries. I sleep well at night, knowing I'm only paid for medical care."

Oh, goddamn you, Sabrina.

"Keep lying to yourself, sweetheart." Another scoff, this one so sharp it's a bladed slash. "The only reason I sleep well at night is because it's on a mattress fit for an actual king, and I accept the fact that I'm a monster too."

A flash of movement shifts against the side of my bed, then fingertips are adjusting the sheet over me. The flutter yet again aggravates my skin to the point of tickling where no one can scratch.

"Did you plot all the data?" Sabrina plays pretend. If given the chance, I'm sure I could diagnose her with a plethora of psychological disorders next. "What is our projected time to re-administer the sedative?"

"Less than two hours." Elian mumbles absentmindedly, and the image inside my head is of him bowing over a medical file, pen ticking off what he had written earlier. "Four months is four months longer than the others."

"As I said," Sabrina suddenly sounds perky, and it raises my hackles. "She's different. The others are only sedated during pre-op and post-op, then they go home once recuperated."

"Well, those women didn't come in here the same way this Jane Smith did," Elian sounds impressed, and I begin to question what the hell that even means. "She was in bad shape. A lot to damage was done–"

"Think it was during the capture?" Sycophant Sabrina.

"Gods!" Elian drawls out long and low, breath whistling between his front teeth. "No wonder she keeps tossing off the sedatives. To fight that hard, only to become some wealthy man's property. Pray to the Gods!"

A sharp knock jars them both, my file clattering against the handrail on the hospital bed. A hip bumping into the side of my hand, blissfully scratching at that maddening itch caused from the fluttering sheet.

"How's my patient?" that voice. *That. Voice.* I recognize that voice, deep inside my head. Everything is alert on me, but the monitor doesn't shift its steady beep.

Feet scuffling– the doctors. Feet perfectly placed with deliberate care– my new owner.

"She is due for another sedative in ninety-seven minutes, sir," Sycophant Sabrina announces. Elian is utterly silent, but I can sense him ghosting toward the door, hoping to be unseen.

"No more sedatives." That voice. Why do I recognize that voice?

*Probably because you've heard it several times daily for the past four months!*

"Are you sure?" Elian announces his presence far away from me, where it's a strain to hear him at all. "She is almost at one hundred percent, but what about her mental competency."

"My children need a mother– *I'm sure.*" Annoyance mixed with grief, the tightness and strain in that deep voice draws moisture to creep out the sides of my eyes.

"Your children?" Sabrina croons in a false voice. Sure, it's genuine to her, but it rings false to me. Sarcastic. Ruthless. Cynical. "Did they lose their mother? How many babies?"

"Three," is whispered as fingertips walk up the length of my hand, deftly tucking the sheet away, taking that dastardly tag with it. Instant relief. "My son just turned seventeen– the twins are eight."

So close. He's so close. Those words elicit emotions, to the point I want to beg for another sedative, just to shut my mind down. I can't. I can't become property.

I can't…

"Ah! I see," Elian's voice rings loudly in my ears in comparison to the soothing brush whispering beside me. "You designed your children a new mother who looks like their lost mother–"

"Out!" is a fierce bark, an order that must be heeded, causing me to jerk on the mattress, the beep a siren screech of panic. "Now! Both of you!"

Shuddering on the mattress, the urge to piss myself is overpowering, if not for the catheter jammed inside my urethra, emptying my bladder as I make urine.

"Shhh…" is a comforting croon, fingertips whispering across my cheeks to capture my tears, a captured as I am. "My Mira."

# MUSCLE MEMORY

"I've made sure your muscles didn't atrophy during your stay." My captor is always so agreeable, comforting, with a strong desire to please, but there is always an undercurrent of grief. "But you have lost some of your muscle tone. I won't lie, it will take more work rebuilding it than it did to maintain it."

Competent hands sculpt along my calf muscles, with long sure movements, as if he knows every inch of my body better than his own. Perhaps he does, since he just admitted to touching me twice per day for the past four months. But I only know it's four months because the incompetent doctors let it slip when they thought me unconscious.

Proprietary movements, as if he owns every bit of flesh on my body, voice calm yet assertive, the man had the good sense to make sure everything but my legs are covered by a sheet.

He doesn't speak nonstop, maybe because I'm struggling to keep up. But the quiet isn't strained. The massage seems to relax him, tapered fingertip digging in slightly behind my knees.

It could be days, weeks, or even an hour since I was last coherent. Things have changed since I woke this time. I remember filtered conversation, but I don't know how long ago it took place. There is no longer a beep in the room, my body free of all the wires and tubes sustaining me during sedation.

While I haven't yet tried to form words, my eyes finally drink in my surroundings. Before me stretches a pair of long hairless legs. The dark olive tone familiar, instantly recognizable as my own. My gaze darts to the side, catching sight of my arm. Also dark olive, but there is a spiderweb of fading scars radiating from my fingertips to the middle of my forearm. Instantly, I know I am lefthanded– it just seems right.

My mind supplies facts, doling them out even if they are of little consequence.

"What's your name?" comes from a rough, dry voice that doesn't sound like my own. Yet again, my mind computes that it's hoarse from disuse, that's why it sounds odd inside my own ears.

"Ramsey," he answers without hesitation, and that sound right too. "Is this going to be the final time we have this conversation?" The amusement in his voice causes my gaze to flick in his direction. Skin tone exactly the same shade as my own, somewhere bordering the Mediterranean, either north or south. A map overlays my mind to highlight the possible locations of my origin.

"This is the nineth time in the hundred and seventy-four days since you were admitted, but I think the details will stick this time." There's a slight accent forming from lips curled with amusement.

Greek, yet again my mind supplies. It's light, as if he's the first generation to learn English as his native tongue, around parents and grandparents who learned English as a second or even possibly a third or fourth language. The few words I've spoken, the sarcastic narrative running through my brain, the accent is mine as well, but mine is deeper, more ingrained. English is not my native tongue.

Intelligent. Privileged. Sarcastic. Ruthless. Cynical. Mira. Lefthanded. Greek.

I shouldn't be the one in this hospital bed, but nothing will change that fact.

"Your psychiatrist diagnosed you with Dissociative Amnesia, so I'm not to give you too many details, because your mind is meant to heal on its own." Nimble fingertips tuck the sheet over my legs, then reach for a bottle of lotion on the side table.

"Miranda," Ramsey utters, as if he's said it thousands of times in the past few months, trying to get it to stick. Mira must be the shortened form of Miranda– it sounds natural inside my head. "Depersonalization-derealization disorder."

"My mind supplied those diagnoses earlier, whenever earlier might have been," is barely a breath of a sound ejected from my raw throat. "Must be because I heard my doctor say them?"

"Sure," Ramsey breathes right back, hands reaching out to cup my wrist, then they begin to draw upward in a twisting motion, massaging the muscles in my arm. "You've been overhearing things for months, interrogating me when you're lucid. Only to forget the conversation took place, where we have it again as if it never took place dozens of times before. Dr. Petra said that's how it would be, until it finally stuck."

"Why me?" pops out, and I add brazen to my list of facts. "Why traffic me? Why choose me out of everyone? What happened to your wife? Why me to be the mother of your children?"

"Let me guess, those idiot doctors let that slip too?" Snorting, a sound so familiar that it curls my own lips, when it should terrify me because of the subject at hand. "Not one single person in this facility is trafficked."

"A human trafficker would say that–"

"In time, your memory will return, then we will revisit this conversation, and I hope it sticks, just as I hoped the last eight conversations stuck, so I could tease you for thinking what you're thinking."

"They're doctors, why lie?"

"Are doctors suddenly exempt from being idiots?" My gaze is drawn upward because of that wry as fuck tone. I avoided everything but looking at his hands on my skin, fearing I wouldn't recognize Ramsey.

As I suspected, I don't recognize Ramsey. But this non-emotional state of being allows me to read deeper, more primal instincts, to where I'm not fearful of the man massaging my arm as if it's his own. I listen to my gut, instead of illogically panicking.

That dark olive skin is flawless, but not cosmetically so. There are fine lines bracketing the corners of full lips, as if Ramsey has spent a lot of time laughing. Deep-set eyes hidden beneath heavy brows. The caramel glowing with humor down at me is more yellow than brown. It's unique, and I'm suddenly hard-pressed to gaze into a mirror to see if mine reflect light the same as his.

Gathering. Gathering. Gathering. Gathering details to organize inside my mind. Being observant, discerning facts when my memories are absent. Even if my memories return, how reliable are they, as human nature always has us rewriting history, especially our own. The mind is the most fragile, easily to wound part of the human body.

Dressed as impeccably as his smooth hairstyle, not a single dark hair out of place. Slim-fitted charcoal trousers. That teal dress shirt is a risk, when most businessmen wear muted colors to not draw attention to themselves, but the hue looks obscenely delicious against his flesh. Oh, how this man loves attention, that is clear to see. Oh, how he no doubt deserves it and gains it whenever he walks into a room.

Peacock.

Primal. Alpha male. Leader. Man in charge. The boss. Testosterone pumping into the air with every heartbeat, reminiscent of a whirling purr.

The warmth in my chest and the moisture to my altered parts, I like this about Ramsey. It makes me feel safe and secure, as if everything is being taken care of the way it should, because people depend on me, and in my absence someone else needs to be in charge.

Shapely forearms are covered in thick fur, cuffs rolled up to almost his elbows. The only thing he's missing is a suit jacket and tie, but I don't need to gaze around the room to know they are somewhere nearby, stowed out of my reach.

Gazing down at me, Ramsey waits as I drink my fill of his person, aligning all the facts I uncovered. "I highly doubt my doctors are idiots," is murmured wryly, eyes lighting on the back of the door, exactly where I knew his jacket would be hanging.

No man such as this one would employ idiots because he would suffer *my* wrath.

"Surgeons have the highest rate of alcoholism per capita. A medical degree doesn't absolve anyone from making a train wreck out of their lives. Look at psychiatrists and therapists, their personal lives are always a mess, their relationships a toxic stew. Your attending physicians, just as the nurses and surgeons, they're told the human trafficking anecdote to keep their lips sealed. If you can't keep loyalty due to respect, then fear works best."

They were both so confident, the male doctor sure of his evilness while the female lived in LaLa Land where everyone but her was to blame. "So no one here is trafficked?" I may have amnesia, but I do not dwell in LaLa Land.

"No. *No one.*" *Not here, at least* is what isn't said.

Ramsey turns his back to me, the shirt stretched taut over muscles, where he selects something on the tray table. When he turns back to me, I catch sight of skincare products, all as familiar to me as the sight of my own legs.

Hmm… something just doesn't add up, and if it doesn't, then there is a lie hidden in there somewhere. "Why the alterations?" The disgusting commentary by my doctor has bile rising in my throat, the breast implant heavy on my chest, the oddness between my thighs tingling with awareness.

"Ask yourself that after your memory returns, Mira." What does that even mean? With a pump, a small dollop of moisturizer lands on a fingertip. Ramsey comes closer, the moisturizer cool and soothing on my cheeks.

"Am I your wife?" My mind is struggling to put the pieces together. Ramsey and I are similar– he's as familiar as my own body. He touches me with intimacy, looks at me as if there isn't anything we don't know about one another. "Your sister?"

"Neither yet both, in a way," Ramsey mutters noncommittally, scrambling everything my mind is trying to place in order. "I'm not allowed to explain, Miranda. Your mind has to heal itself, and it would harm you more if I did the work for you."

"I know that." Hesitating, I don't understand why I'm so sure on things, the comments just popping out of nowhere, then the confusion settles over me in a darkening fog.

"I know you do," follows my hesitation, trying to fill the silence of my confusion with as much truth as he can supply.

"I heard you say you had a seventeen-year-old son and a pair of eight-year-old twins. Did you lose your wife? The mother of your children?" It's the story the doctors were fed, whether it was the truth is another thing.

Panting roughly, Ramsey's chest rises and falls at a rapid rate. Teal shirt pulling taut across his muscles, nipples beaded tightly, meaning he doesn't have on an undershirt. That visceral reaction is telling. There are definitely three children, other than that, I don't know what to make of it.

"We haven't had this conversation before, never making it this far. I'm not sure if you're ready." Ramsey turns his back on me again, picking up a hairbrush. "If this conversation sticks, and the one after, then you will be ready."

Hairbrush pulled through the strands slicked to my forehead. This feels foreign. Not having my hair brushed, but how the bristles flow through. It should be longer... much, much longer.

Amnesia or not, muscle memory is something that cannot be forgotten. The memory of my hand drawing in a downward path, clear to my waist. Over and over again, for the entirety of my existence. Thick, glossy inky strands of midnight, cascading perfectly straight to my waist.

Steady strokes, my father speaking in foreign language, a complex alphabet that spawned the phrase, *It's all Greek to me*, but completely understandable to me. Words of promises, wisdom, and loyalty.

"What happened to my hair?"

Movement stilling, the rough gasp from Ramsey's throat has my eyes flicking upward to watch his expression. Wide-eyed surprise is overwritten by extreme agony. Refusing to look elsewhere than the brush in his hand, Ramsey barely breathes the words.

"That's something only you can answer." Unfreezing from his tortured state, Ramsey becomes animated again, hand slowly drawing the bristles against my scalp, sensation neither pleasure nor pain. Numb. "I can take an educated guess– I was there but not. I'm surprised you realized your hair was different."

"May I ask something?" Unsure, when I come to realize there has never been a time that I haven't spoken my mind, even as a child. My voice was one of importance. Always.

That realization, along with the others. Intelligent. Privileged. Sarcastic. Ruthless. Cynical. Miranda, nicknamed Mira. Lefthanded. Greek. Outspoken. Important.

No, I would never be a victim of human trafficking, no matter what the doctors think. This man is not treating me as an object, nor a subservient, lessor being. While he is treating me as a patient, he maintains my dignity by respecting my autonomy. Somehow, in life, he and I are equals at the very least. At the most, I am Ramsey's superior.

The money funding my care flows directly from me.

If I ask, I know without a shadow of a doubt, I will receive, within reason.

"May I gaze at my reflection in a mirror?" Mind instantly supplying a plethora of facts. "I think I need to look at myself. It will help evoke my sense of self."

"If you believe you're ready, you probably are, Mira." A palm smooths down my arm to cup my elbow, steady and sure. "I must warn you, you're naked. You'll have difficulty navigating without my help. You have taken this trek many times, but never with this level of lucidity. We had to keep sedating you, because once your memory returned, you would end up doing yourself harm."

"I don't…" voice drifting as I struggle to find the strength to shift on the mattress. The sheet bunches beneath my palm, rolling as I move. I hate the scratchy sensation, but I don't focus on it, because it's not important. "I don't believe I'm the suicidal type."

"You're not," is whispered gravely, palms settling on my hips to help me place my feet on the cool tile. "You would become enraged, the violent movements pulling at your sutures. There was no calming you, as you had one goal, and nothing could break you from that focus."

"You won't tell me," is more statement than question, feet feeling hollow and numb, other than sensing the temperature difference as I place a step. Foreign. Walking as a newborn colt.

Ramsey is unusually quiet, and it confuses me as to why I thought *unusually*, as if I know he is a chatty sort. My path is slow, knees barely supporting my weight. The coolness hitting my bare flesh doesn't create embarrassment, not that I think my body worthy of immortality on canvas, when I have no idea what I even look like. I'm a patient. He's treating me as a patient. My nudity is not lustful nor humiliating– it's of little consequence.

The path may be slow, but it's familiar. Muscle memory, can it be built in only a few short months? Everything my eyes light upon seems familiar, as familiar as my own legs and arm, minus the spiderweb of scars.

Clinical but welcoming, soothing and calming, the sage green walls aren't bordered in white or metals, which would come off as cold and institutional. I recognize the bamboo, as if it were my own signature touch.

I know all these things, except who I am and how I came to be here. The frustration is bubbling up, heating and flushing my skin, causing my muscles to tighten and sweat to bead, but I push it downward and away. If I'm overcome with panic, all progress will be lost. Again.

This is not the first time I've walked these steps, thought these thoughts, or had these conversations with Ramsey, but it will be the last leg of this journey. I'm not built for insanity.

"I'll await you out here, but the door must remain opened, just in case I need to help you." Cautious, as if on a previous time I lashed out like a wounded animal, Ramsey's back goes flush with the wall, shoulder butted up against the doorframe near the hinges.

"I..." I have no idea what to say, but I'm not a coward, so I step forward into the serviceable bathroom, prepared to meet myself, probably not for the first time.

# CREFLECTION

My surroundings are of little consequence to the ghost standing in the mirror. She is me. I am her. Yet we are not the same. Who I used to be is not the reflection in the mirror, and I doubt I'll ever regain her. I doubt I want to regain her.

Is there a diagnosis for when you compartmentalize who you used to be against who you are now, as if you're two separate entities?

DID. Dissociative Identity Disorder. Multiple personality disorder, where you believe yourself to be two or more identities, but it goes deeper than that. As the person you are in the current frame is a singular being, because you recognize that who you used to be is a ghost riding in your memories, because you cannot handle events or behaviors that took place.

Peridot glows from the reflection, seductive lips forming words spoken in Greek, voice unmistakably my own, belonging to both the ghost and the present. "Your doctor did not render those diagnoses, Miranda Livas."

Those lips in the mirror release a gasp of shock, spiderwebbed arm reaching out to grab the sink basin. Mind swirling, a fog descending, I struggle to hold my weight, as a memory resurfaces.

*"You will be our Kyrios, daughter mine." Father stood before me, elder enough to be my great-grandfather. The product of his fifth wife, all of my siblings met a similar fate as their mothers, as my mother did when I was a small child of three.*

*A wash of violence spattered across textiles. The assassin held captive by my gaze as I sliced his thigh open with my blade. Vengeance sought, balance regained.*

*Alessandro was the first born, gone fifty-four years prior to my birth. Father moving our Oikos to the states changed nothing. Ninety-seven years, five wives, and nine children, and father and I are the only two left standing.*

*"Uncle." A palm presses on my shoulder, steady and calm, supportive from a height a foot farther in the sky. "What shall my role be?" Cyrus is part of our Oikos, the last of our blood. A distant cousin, kept safe, treated as a servant for his protection. For my protection.*

*"No male shall rule while our queen still draws breath." Father educates Cyrus, the words firm but not chastising. "Cunt or no, our Miranda has larger balls than any male. She will be our Kyrios."*

*"Of course, Uncle." Head bowed, peridot gazing through the fall of inky strands bleached the color of wheat. "I just need to know my role in keeping our Oikos safe." Loyal. Trustworthy. Not a single hitch in his breath to betray treacherous thoughts.*

*Grown large and strong, mind almost as cunning as my own, Cyrus is my only playmate, the only one Father trusts. The only one outside of Father that I've ever trusted. Two years my elder, neither Cyrus nor I have left our Oikos. No cost spared, years advanced beyond our peers, educated by the finest of tutors kept loyal by fear.*

*Gazing down at me with utter devotion, Father is struggling to hold on long enough for my mind to mature, for my body to strengthen. It's harder and harder to protect our king, especially as they try to reduce him by taking out his queen. Seed too decrepit to produce another child, with my death, our reign falls.*

*The boy standing beside me is just as important as I, more so, because no one knows of his existence. If I fall, Father will fade, but Cyrus will shoulder the fate of our Oikos on his broad shoulders. It's not what Father or I wish to happen, but Cyrus is our contingency plan, as every other drop of Livas blood has been exterminated from this earth. Father and I may not be the strongest, but we are the most cunning. It doesn't take brute strength to survive, just the fortitude and endurance to be the last one remaining, mangled bodies worshiping at our feet.*

*"Chess, my sweets." Father palms my cheek, other hand reaching up to brush the hair away from Cyrus's forehead, loathing the color as much as I. We three share the Livas similarities, hidden to protect his identity. That immense build draws the attention from the eyes, but the hair would be a dead giveaway.*

*"When playing chess, the combatant's sole focus is on the king. Arrogance seeing the pawns, rooks, knights, and bishops as easily removed from the board. While their focus is on the king, they are terrified of the queen."*

*"Whatever you suggest for our safety, I will do as you wish." I am not known for behavior befitting my given name. The definition of Miranda is amenable, which I most certainly am not. Our family name, Livas, it quite literally means obstinate, which I most certainly am the embodiment. There is only one man who earned the right for me to behave as my given name, Father. The rest receive the full wrath of my surname.*

*"My life is at its end, my sweets." That palm cupping my cheek quivers, my eyes focused on the man gazing upward at Cyrus. Father and Cyrus have a silent conversation, the words only understood by them, words shared between men.*

*"We need a new focus to keep our Oikos safe, my sweets." Father's words strike a fatal blow in Cyrus, the boy gasping in pain, body bowing to lean against mine.*

*Assumptions were made that he and I would rule together.*

*"Nephew, I will make no apologies. This is for our protection. The king is the sole focus on the board, the queen the most feared, the knight the most ignored. I must protect us by choosing a disposable king."*

*"Sleight of hand," is murmured with pride, heart swelling for the man who has taught me all he knows. There are times Father surprises me, and I try to learn from what he reveals.*

*The fact that I must marry and bear a child with a man I will never love nor trust is of little consequence. Whatever is best for the Livas Oikos is all that matters, as it's the heart and breath and life running through our veins.*

"Cunning, Father. Very cunning. They will assume me a lightheaded female, clingy and terrified. Hiding behind my husband, encompassing little power of my own, when I will be the one in charge. The king a figurehead, easily replaceable, the same as your past queens."

"They were never my queens." Father's sickly breath flutters against my nose, the dusk of his life coming soon. "You will be a more ruthless Kyrios than I ever was, Miranda Livas."

ML

The only similarities I now share with the ghost in the mirror are the peridot gazing at me from the reflection, the olive skin tone, and the thick midnight tresses falling around my ears. Little else. Even the emotion blazing out in fury from the peridot is distinctly different.

The ghost frowns from her captivity inside the looking glass.

Fingertips tugging at my hair, only five inches or so in length. Confusion slams into my brain, the force nearly knocking me off my feet. An ache builds behind my eyes, cautioning me to step away from that discovery, as I am not ready yet.

Past moments of déjà vu create a slideshow through my mind, a half dozen events where the examination of my body created a mental breakdown, where I ended up sedated on the floor, the looking glass shattered to rain down to my bare feet, spattered crimson mixing in with the shards.

Raised before me, I inspect the spiderweb of scars interconnected along the top of my hand, down my forearm, all the way to my wrist. Fading paleness stark against the warmth of my skin.

Is the mirror the cause? Eyes flicking between my arm and the mirror, I know without a shadow of a doubt that I broke it every single time I entered this bathroom. All progress lost. One step forward, half a dozen steps back.

The aching throb behind my eyes goes from cautioning me to outright warning me to back off. No, the mirror didn't cause the scars. They are from much earlier, caused during the event that trapped me here.

Peridot winking out, eyelids slammed shut, fisted palms pressed against my forehead, I fight off the alarming migraine, refusing to continue this psychotic cycle of insanity. Mind stronger than my body, I will prevail.

The ghost and I communicate through the reflection. There is sense of no devastation and loss. No grief or mourning. No bitterness. No embarrassment. Only rage. Unadulterated, fire-eating, oxygen-sucking, decimating rage.

"Hello, Miranda Livas," is spoken to the ghost in the mirror, both our lips moving. "I am Mira," is stated with conviction, this nickname more suited to who I've become, as I'm not sure I want to return to who the woman in the reflection embodies.

"What was done to you that will affect me for life?" The blame is thick, lodged deep in my throat. suffocating. I didn't do it to us–she did. "Did you lose a bet?" I ask the ghost while tugging on a strand of hair. "Cut it with hedge clippers?"

"No, a double-bladed letter opener," the ghost replies. "My hair was my shining glory. It was a punishment."

"What did you do to deserve it?"

"Who said I had to do anything to deserve it?" she replies, upper lip pulled away from her teeth in a fierce snarl. "You know naught of our life. Don't judge. Don't blame. We are but the same, you and I, but do whatever you must to take leave from this place. Stay away from the mind-altering sedative combo that you yourself devised."

Eyes flicking away, I focus on the mosaic tile backsplash, because I'm even starting to confuse myself. It helps to talk to the ghost in the mirror as if she isn't me, but the fact that she is replying makes it hard to retain my sanity.

Smooth dark skin covering long, lean muscles. The scarred hand slides from my shoulder down to my other palm, noticing that the definition isn't what it used to be after recuperating for months on end in a hospital bed. I prided myself on training my body, not because of vapid appearances, but due to coveting strength. This I know without a shadow of a doubt, easily supplied from the locked cabinet drawers in my mind, drawers unlocking to reveal files of information they deem pertinent.

Both breasts hang as they ought to, after thirty-eight years on this planet. The same yet different. The ghost in the reflection keeps eyeing the right breast, tears of horror and loss glistening in her eyes.

Taking that as an important cue, I cup the left one. Finding it pliant and supple, skin smooth with some give, as if it were larger at one time. My eyes flick downward, catching sight of stripes across my lower belly.

I'm a mother– I breastfed my young.

There are more of us filling the Livas Oikos, at least I pray they still breathe, unlike my brothers and sisters and mothers and father. Is Cyrus still with me?

Fingers tweaking my nipple, I yip at the sharp bite, eyes locked in the mirror, staring at the ghost's right breasts. The skin is different, not quite the same shade, a fraction lighter. Tighter. No give. The breast sits higher, not sagging even though it ought to with how it is slightly larger.

Fingers moving on their own accord, that tweak elicits no noise from the reflection in the mirror. Those lips pull taut with distress, because no matter how hard we tug and pull and tweak, dig our nails in deep until we bleed, the sensation is naught.

Smoothing to cup the breast, it feels foreign, not part of us, never on our body until recently. We liked the breast we had, the mirrored twin to the one still on our left side. The ghost in the mirror is releasing silent sobs, tortured peridot gaze watering her cheeks.

A patchwork of scars litter our torso, wrapping around our side to reach up to our armpit. Not just the breast inside our skin, but the skin itself has never belonged to us. This is not our breast, and we don't want it– we want the old one back.

Eyes flicking between the shorn locks and the reconstruction that overwrote the mastectomy, the dreaded C word whispers through my mind.

"No," the ghost replies with insistence, the raging fire all consuming. "You were not sick. You were punished."

No one punishes us, for we are Kyrios.

Peridot blinking out, eyelids slammed shut, fists gripping the sink basin, I fight off the agony rampaging through the front of my skull. The migraine battering me from the inside out, eyeballs feeling as if they will pop from their sockets due to the force.

Vision returning, beneath the stripes across my flattened womb, I gaze farther downward to a place I instinctively know is not the same. The sensation is different, no need to overhear a grotesque doctor speak of fat bitch mounds and slutty bubblegum pussies.

More scars, not as faint, still in the last process of healing. The skin is a darker shade than my thighs, but that is par for the course with a vulva. Hair-free, which worries me, as I fear it will be similar to the breast that bleeds but has no sensation.

Sucking in a deep breath, the voice in my head reminds me that Miranda Livas suffers no fear. "I'm Mira now," I remind myself, embracing the fear. "Maybe they waxed it, so the hair wasn't in the way of operating and watching the healing process."

Sure. Sure.

Fear is the poor liar.

My labia minora was once visible from the safety of the labia majora, this I know to be true. Just as I know that the length of the inner folds is not indicative to promiscuous behavior, as my grotesque doctor believes.

My childhood nurse, Laverna, she called it a lady's clamshell, the dangling ribbons parted to reveal the pearl. Only the most trusted of men where worthy enough to shine the pearl. When asked, Laverna said I'd know who was trustworthy because my body would produce the oil used to shine the pearl, leaving it glistening with beauty.

Clamshell perfectly cupped, no more ribbons, I fear for my pearl after enduring a nonconsensual labiaplasty. There are telltale healing scars running in rivulets from the crease between my thigh and groin, which means the skin of my vulva has always belonged to me. The left side of my labia is missing a small chunk, a wide scar running inward.

With splayed fingertips, I part myself to see what damage was inflicted. Knees buckling, I hit the floor, not having the presence of mind to catch my fall to soften the blow.

Palms hook under my armpits, numb heels dragged across cool tile. Ramsey's rapid speech just a rumble in my ear, not taking root inside my mind. "Don't sedate me," ejects on a body-wracking sob. "Please, don't sedate me."

"Mira," is nothing but a guttural grunt, hands placing me on the bed. "You've had enough for today. You've gone farther than before. You'll go farther next time."

"No!" Hands batting, I try to order Ramsey to obey. "I am your Kyrios. Do not sedate me again. They were talking about me!" is a hysterical outburst, hand flailing to knock all the beauty products off the rolling tray table by my bed, brush clattering across the floor.

"Who was talking about you?" gives Ramsey pause as he shoves the table across the room, rollers smoothly flowing across the tile.

"The perverse doctor– he was talking about me! Implant! Labiaplasty. Vaginoplasty. Metoidioplasty. You made them release my clitoris– I have a lady cock!"

Rage and terror converges into a fight for my life, because the doctor said the patient underwent a metoidioplasty so that the man could rape her while the light dies out in her eyes.

"We had no choice." Ramsey growls down into my face, struggling to contain me. Months ago, he wouldn't have taken me. He would have relented. There wouldn't have been a fight. In my weakened state, he easily overpowers me.

"Mira," is wrenched from his throat, followed by a suffocating sob. So focused on the tears cascading down those usually happy cheeks, I fail to see the syringe coming in to pierce my skin.

"You were partially castrated," is the last thing I hear as darkness surrounds me, drags me down, rolls me back to begin the cycle of discovery again and again and again, because I wasn't ready to resurface yet.

# COMPASSION

Fingertips parted to hold me open, I stare down at the protrusion splitting my clamshell. I no longer have a pearl. More drawers open in my mind, files instantly revealing their contents.

Metoidioplasty.

As I lie in bed, what's between my legs feels foreign, even though everything that was there before still exists, just rearranged. Standing here before the bathroom mirror, my ghostly reflection begging me to keep my shit together…

The ligament attaching my clitoris has been severed, releasing the bundle of nerves that was once imbedded beneath skin. A hoodectomy preformed, where it was all cut away, leaving no trace behind. The ribbons of my inner lips were wrapped around the detached part of my clitoris, creating a penis-like protuberance from my body, the pearl now the head.

There is a two-inch penis hidden between the curve of my clamshell. Pulling myself farther apart, I discover a nonconsensual urethroplasty was also performed on me, where my urethra was extended and relocated inside my new penis, a slit opened in the head that used to be my clitoris.

Three fingers diving deep into my vagina, I discover everything as it ought to be.

Kyrios means head of the family, which is a male position since the dawn of time. Just because I hold the seat of power didn't mean I actually wanted to be male. My femininity was carved from me, butchered and rearranged, but at least my labia majora wasn't turned into a scrotum– at least they kept my remaining breast and replaced the one I lost. My womb better be in its natural state, or every head in this facility will roll.

Stalking out of the bathroom, more lucid than the last time, because I'm now remembering fragments of the recent times before, the sedatives not taking root as they once did. Ramsey promises these events have happened in the same order of business, the same information released, the same realizations dawning, only each time I go a step further.

The ghost in the reflection made me promise this was the last time, and as long as I promised, she would let me keep my short-term memories. The long-term memories she would dole out as she saw fit.

"Are my reproductive organs still intact?" Glaring down at the small head peaking out from between my nether lips, I snarl at the fact that it suddenly seems larger. "Am I still a woman? Never once did I question my gender, now I have all the wrong parts!"

"Mira." Ochre gaze laser focused on the floor by my toes, hands drawn behind his back, Ramsey won't look at my nakedness or the fact that I'm brandishing a tiny cock. "If you'd prefer, I can stay or go, but we best get your doctor in here to answer the questions."

Shifting onto the mattress, instinctively knowing I'm not one to submit, but I realize I must in order to get the information I seek. Once my head is positioned against the pillows, I tuck what shouldn't be enlarged back where it goes in its clamshell, then I cross my legs at my ankles, keeping everything safely hidden.

Releasing a shuddery sigh, a hand whips the sheet up to cover me. "Stay or go, Mira?" Ramsey tries to sound authoritative. To others, he might just be, but to me, he seems easily bent.

"Have we had sex together?" I have nary a clue if this is a new question I've posed or not.

Used to being asked the most insane of questions, "Yes," is said so quietly it barely registers. Fingertips nervously tuck the blanket beneath my armpits. "Twice."

I file that information in a drawer and don't allow it to be locked away from me. No more blocking out what I discover. "Recently?"

"Not during your recovery, but yes." More nervous fidgeting.

"Did I want to have sex with you?" is stressed heavily because Ramsey is acting off. The man has emoted guilt since I've retained memories, maybe because he forced himself on me.

The sharp bark of bitter laughter is answer enough, the man suddenly flushed. Lavender dress shirt pulled taut across his chest, buttons sustaining the stretch, nipples budding tightly, visible because the man seems to have an aversion to undershirts.

"Did you want to have sex with me?" The answer I receive is much the same, only he has to grab onto the side of the bed to keep himself on his feet. Dipped down to hide his reaction, I still catch sight of the bulge of an erection straining the front of his trousers.

That newly shaped part of me is suddenly difficult to ignore. "I don't understand the context, but I'll take your reaction as affirmation, correct?"

"Correct. Agonizingly correct." Reaching next to the bed, Ramsey presses the Call button. "Stay or go?"

"Stay, unless it's the fact that my clit doesn't look as it used to that is bothering you." Speaking of that body part makes it peek out of the clamshell, refusing to stay hidden.

"Your attitude is vastly different—"

"Than the other times?"

"No. Different from *you*," is heavily stressed, while Ramsey's fingertips act as if they wish to be holding my hand but is unsure of the reception.

"You're rolling with the punches, but not like you would have *before*. You would have slaughtered your way out of here by now. You don't ask, you require total authority. We're not allowed to know anything you don't know. It's strange for me to witness your vast knowledge over everything but yourself. I fear it."

"Why?" The door cracking open to admit a white-coat doctor has my arm raising unbiddenly, demanding a moment, in a commanding act as natural as breathing for me.

"I fear insulting you if I expressed an affection for this softer creature you've become." Ramsey distances himself from the bed, fear warbling his voice.

There's an air of sociopathy around me, as I try to resurface from detachment and disassociation, where I actually feel what human nature dictates, other than be observant from outside myself and reveal how others feel.

If this is me being emotional…

"This is me soft?" Now it's me who releases a bark of laughter, so sharp I fear I cut both Ramsey and the doctor. "No wonder I want to keep the ghost captive in the mirror— she sounds like a nightmare."

"Regardless." Ramsey's retreat is reversed, coming up to lean against the handrail on the bed. "Both incarnations of you, the before and the now, they are mirror images of one another. One just feels more strongly than the other. I am loyal to both, would lie my life down in a heartbeat, have always loved you, been *in* love with you... one is just less painful to love than the other."

"You may stay." Dropping my arm, I curl my fingertip at the fortysomething doctor hiding by the cracked door. Exhausted and haggard, with mousy brown hair and pasty skin, I have the feeling I've run her ragged these past few months. "Dr. Sabrina, I presume? You were intelligent enough to not allow Dr. Elian in my presence."

"Miranda has been retaining short-term memories," Ramsey explains for me, fingertips plucking at my sheet. "She was cognizant during later episodes of sedation."

Slumping against the door, knees giving out, the doctor is a few breaths from fainting out of pure fear. At least she doesn't piss herself.

Who is the monster ghosting in my reflection to elicit such terror? The real question begs to be answered, why am I proud of her for it? Why am I so pleased to understand that she is me, those action were mine, the doctor is terrified of my wrath, even if I feel as if we're separate identities.

"I was partially castrated." Just saying that has the dark smoke lurking in my psyche swirling up to pound the inside of my skull. My promise to the ghost in the mirror resurfaces. I must behave. Must not get emotional. Keep my shit together so I won't be sedated again.

"I am fully aware I'm not to ask questions that would affect my recovery. But I think I have every right to know how I am medically and why those interventions were necessary."

Witnessing the doctor recover her pride is a thing of rare beauty. Standing upright from the door, sweaty palm straightening her lab coat, shoulders squared, Dr. Sabrina walks toward me, tablet clutched against her chest.

"Dr. Livas," is forced between quivering lips.

Doctor?

That's something I did not know but not surprising. It feels right. Just. In the time it takes for me to glance at Ramsey in question, my doctor has recovered her composure, her confidence, and her voice.

The expression on her face is easy to read, how disturbing it is to introduce yourself to someone who undoubtedly already knows you. "I'm Dr. Sabrina Runyon." A palm jerks out, asking to be shaken. Feeling charitable, I return the gesture. "I was your surgeon, specializing in reconstruction and gender reassignment."

"I was mutilated, correct?" Looking nowhere but at her intelligent blue eyes, I ignore the battering inside my skull. "The past me said we were punished. Ramsey let it slip that I was partially castrated. I kept my shit together long enough to truly examine your handiwork this time around."

"It was my best work, under the circumstances." When they spoke together, I assumed they were terrified of Ramsey, as did Dr. Elian. Now I realize it's me Dr. Runyon is terrified to let down.

"Scars aside, which I can assume was part of the mutilation, you do exemplary work." Hands folded over my belly, only the sheet covering my vulnerability, I continue to hold my doctor's gaze. "Even if I do believe you'd benefit from a session a week from a licensed therapist."

A gasping laugh is barely covered by a cough, and I get the distinct impression I'm the brunt of the joke. Ramsey prevails in his silence, but his laughter rattles the bedrail.

"Instead of asking if I know you, because that is against the rules– rules I have a sneaking suspicion I was the one who created –I will ask if you know me."

"You personally hired me, Dr. Livas." Sabrina comes closer, settling the tablet on the rolling table. Then she walks the table and herself to my bedside. "I won't say you've worked with me for three years– I'll say I've worked for you for three years."

"This is my facility?" I hazard as a guess, thinking it something the original me would strive to obtain. "You're my employee? Do we know each other on a deeper level?"

"You know me on a deeper level," is muttered in a way to both explain yet hedge around the truth. "However, no one knows you on a deeper level." Her words have my gaze flicking in Ramsey's direction, his amusement relaxing my tense muscles.

"No need for formality, just rip the bandage off, please."

"Definitely enjoying this new softer you, Mira." Ramsey mutters wryly, attempting to smother his laughter. A palm lightly lands on the crown of my skull, a brief affectionate touch. "You are the epitome of formality. You would never say please to anyone save a select few."

Turning to gaze up at him, I have no fear our interaction will leave this room, as Sabrina is properly terrified of me. "One being you?"

"Sometimes, when you're feeling particularly amenable. Mostly, we all just do as we're told, subject to your whims."

"Everyone must be beside themselves with grief over my amnesia," is muttered sarcastically.

A rough, "They are," is torn from the man ghosting near my bedside. "They are, Miranda. We are hopeful you will return to your reign. Your ruthlessness keeps us safe, none of us able to mimic it accurately. But I won't be the only one who hopes this more emotional side of you stays."

If this numb detachment is me being emotional…

"Your right breast was removed down to the breastplate." Sabrina begins a no-nonsense rundown of my injuries, starting from the top down, which both the past me and the current me appreciate.

"It took seven surgeries to get us to where we are now." The table is pushed away, leaving me to believe that tablet is the entirety of my file, including images and video, something she fears I'll demand access.

"We used donated skin, attempting to match your coloring to the best we could– the difference is slight, but the results are beyond our expectations."

"Where did the skin come from?" My mind supplies information where skins graphs are generally transplanted from one location on the patient to another, due to a high probability of rejection. Remembering Dr. Elian's claims… "It wasn't taken, was it? You didn't kill and scavenge graphs to ensure your own longevity, correct?"

"Mira," Ramsey croons in a soothing tone, Palm settling on the top of my head again. Instinctively, I realize this isn't something the ghost of me would have ever been concerned over. "It was donated from someone who truly wished for you to have it. A selfless act of love, where they are healed back to normal, scar aside."

"You were covered in contusions, scratches, and cuts, most allowed to heal on their own, as the damage to your chest and groin region was the most critical. You had forty-nine stitches from your fingertips to your elbow–"

"Don't ask," Ramsey cautions, anticipating my next question. I only behave because I promised myself to not go where I'm not ready, as I will not be subjected to another round of sedation.

"They were delicate stitches, as it was both a body part that moves constantly, but also one that is visible to everyone outside of wearing a glove." Sabrina seems terrified that I will find my hand unsightly.

"Of little consequence," is muttered dismissively, raising the arm in question, "I appreciate your concern and thank you for minimizing the damage. Function over appearance, as long as I can regain all the strength it once had."

"Good." Sabrina swallows so heavily that not only can I see her throat work but I can hear it as well. "You had seven hairline fractures, three in your ribs. I vac-sealed the wound on your chest to prevent infection, then concentrated on your groin. You were partially castrated. Female castration–"

"Someone tried to take my ability to seek pleasure," is a whispered admission, mind ready to allow me to know at least that much. "The breast. My vulva. Judging by the damage to my arm, I stopped them from finishing their task."

Sabrina's cool blue, intelligent gaze holds me back as Ramsey stalks off to the bathroom, unable to hear more. The sound of retching tears me in half, both wanting to comfort and support Ramsey, while also fighting the craving to demand my subordinate answer anything I ask now that he's not here to stop me.

"When you were brought in here, you commanded me to not answer your demands now." Yes. Yes, Sabrina and I know one another well. "In such distress, you issued a protocol we've been following to a T. If you don't like how we've done it, you can punish us after the fact."

"That seems unfair," is mulled over, yet again deciding I don't like parts of who I used to be. Maybe that's why I have amnesia, perhaps because I can't handle who I am.

"You're fair, Miranda. You're just. You're balanced. You're emotionless, but never cruel."

"So expressing any emotion, showing concern for Ramsey right now, that is out of the norm?"

A slight shift in her posture, and that's all the answer I need. "Calculating that now was the best time to demand answers, that is classically Miranda Livas. The concern... I should give you the rest before Mr. Elezi returns. He is one of the softest people you know."

## ML

"Remember, you agreed to do whatever was necessary, my sweets." Father takes my hand, escorting me from the grapevines where I spend most of my time, expecting Cyrus to dutifully follow.

With immense pride, I take comfort in the cradle of our Oikos. This is one of the rare moments where I wished my mother were still with us. There are questions, and it frustrates me to be denied answers.

Did Mother feel as if she too were a part of the land, or did she feel as if she were Father's guest?

Not only do I feel as if I'm a part of the land, I feel as if it's rooted deeply inside of me, vines wrapping around my heart, giving life as much as taking. For without me the land would die. Nothing matters more than the cradle of our Oikos, for without it, the living embodiment of our Oikos has no home.

An Oikos is the balance between family, the roof that houses it, and the wealth that sustains it— if one fails, all parts fail.

With the rolling waves cresting along the cliffy shoreline, the wind wiping my waist-length hair to slap me in the cheeks, the deep-seated righteousness of my convictions settles like a crown to wear upon my head.

"I will do anything that is necessary to protect our Oikos, Father. Be it the cradle, the lifeblood, or the livelihood feeding both. Anything," I vow, an honor I will take to the grave, since I've placed many in theirs during acts of protection.

"It's a relief to hear you say that." Father is breathless, struggling to make his way along the rocky path to the back portico, even aided by Cyrus. He patiently pats the steady arm beneath his. "Both my sweets, yes?" is Father's way of asking for Cyrus's agreement.

"Yes, Uncle," is a forlorn rasp, Cyrus's pain a tangible thing of tragic beauty. If only I could understand it, experience it with him, perhaps I could alleviate it. "Whatever my Kyrios requires, my Kyrios shall receive."

"Come along now, your surprise awaits." Father draws us through the rear entrance to the grand walk, the white stone gleaming a mirrored shine beneath our feet, the sharp flap of curtains in the artificial breeze.

Father used to only take a handful of steps from planter to planter, where non-native trees thrive in the artificial heat. From olive to fig, what used to take a minute no more, now suddenly feels as if a lifetime passes.

The rasp of struggling breath has my feet slowing farther, has Cyrus offering to sustain more of Father's weight. I feel blessed to have shared Father for sixteen years— his wisdom shaping me, strengthening me, forging me into the next Kyrios. With his passing, I will mourn all that lost knowledge, while missing the comforting connection of a father and daughter with a similar spirit.

"You both have been my greatest joy," Father gasps the words, attempting to draw in more oxygen. "Every loss made me appreciate the gift I was given. Never lose sight of family in your task to protect the Oikos as a whole. The family is the reason we protect the hearth and wealth so fiercely."

Father knows. Father understands. Father is cautioning me, because this will be the tallest order for me, the hardest to overcome, because the ability to love escapes me. I am fiercely loyal, utterly devoted, faultlessly caring, but incapable of expressing the feminine emotions.

Father turns to enter the great room. More of a hall in actuality, not to be confused with a hallway. A grand hall, as in the seat of power within our Oikos. A gathering place. If we were true royalty, it would be a throne room where we commune with our people.

More than seventy people from all walks of life bow with the tilt of their necks, gazes fused to the stone floor in supplication.

Hands cupping one another in front of themselves, bowed heads, a pious display of loyalty earned through fear created, asking for protection in return.

"Miranda Livas," a deeply accented voice announces from across the span of the great room, body aligned with a stone pillar. "I've brought you a wedding gift from my son. Please find it a worthy offering."

Head tilted fractionally, I refuse to bow when I have no equal within this Oikos. Visitors bow to me, even those baring gifts. "I shall thank you once I determine the worthiness of said offering."

A rumble of masculine chuckles filter around the room, the females bred better than to do such a display, heads still bowed because I never gave the cue to rise. No matter how old I age, the men will never respect me as their equal, nevertheless their leader, always seeing me as a pretty little thing. Clingy. Emotional. Irrational. Prone to hormonal displays of insufferable incompetence, all because I wasn't born with a cock.

They don't understand me. They underestimate me. They devalue me, just as they do every female they encounter. They find me an amusement instead of a source of intimidation.

"The gift?" is said as an impatient reminder, hating how the man before me smirks as if I just pulled off a nifty trick. Filled with sharp teeth glowing in the distance, that smirk says it all, how he is arrogant enough to believe he can come into my Oikos, baring gifts, and expect to gain the seat of power through the son he will force to become my king.

Stolen power is no power at all. It must be earned, gained, respected, and feared, because true power is seated in the people following their leader. Wealth on the other hand, that can be taken. The wealth we've amassed over dozens of generations, an attempt of theft will be dealt with swiftly and ruthlessly, as it has been done in the past and in the present.

Breaking away from the shadows of the pillar, I learn two things at once. First, the virile man with the taunting laughter and arrogant smirk is Zamir Elezi of Albania, ridiculously young for the power he's amassed and notorious for unparalleled cruelty. Second, my father being a man who is unconditionally devoted to his only surviving offspring, his daughter the love of his life, Father denied this man the request to be my king.

A mortally wounding insult to have had his son found more worthy than he, Zamir Elezi is enraged, biding his time, as he *penetrates the Livas Oikos by placing his son of the same name as our king.*

*Leaving father to rest upon a padded ottoman, I walk across half the distance of the great room, with Cyrus's shadow two steps behind. Gazes fall upon me, only to return to the floor as I pass.*

*"Welcome, Zamir Elezi." Hands outstretched, I playact the role of an uneducated, boy-crazy teenage girl pretending to be the lady of the house. The false seductive tone in my voice is meant to sound false, as I shouldn't know how to project such an air at my age.*

*As a sociopath, I've been a student of emotion since I was three. A vital switch clicked off within me from the moment my hand sliced a femoral artery open, the arch of blood a thing of terrible beauty. Perhaps it was moments before, the sharp crack of my mother's neck being snapped, her soft breast catching air, no longer offering me substance but used as a method of control and terror. The blood tinting her thighs, womb used for a man's pleasure and a woman's constant threat of violation.*

*I am one semester away from entering medical school for psychiatry. At age sixteen. To be the strength of the Oikos, I must understand what makes the heart bleed and the soul weep. This is war, and all men are subject to the human condition, so I've made it my lifework to not only understand it but to master it.*

*Hands connecting with Zamir Elezi, smile broad and filled with vapid delight. "It's a pleasure to finally meet you, sir. My father has spoken of you so fondly." Fond, as fond as Adam and Eve were of the serpent slithering in their garden, tainting Eden with a bite of the forbidden fruit.*

*"Oh, how beautiful you are, sweet Miranda. No doubt the embodiment of your name." Warm skin, warmer eyes, luscious hair, and an arrogant smirk, Zamir is a charmer– a snake charmer.*

*"How you flatter me," is whispered in a silly ninny tone, because men love it when you praise them for their empty, unwanted platitudes. As first impressions go, this one is my favorite of them all. "Did you say something about a gift, sir?"*

*Amenable as my name suggests, emptyheaded as my age and sex, and solely focused on shiny things. Smile empty of intelligent life, eyes glistening with false pleasure, I hold onto Zamir's hands.*

*Just a sociopath toying with prey captured within her territory.*

*"Come, beautiful." Yes, because the only part of me that matters is my appearance. Zamir tows me several feet to the side, where a man is kneeling on the stone floor. "Here is your present— I brought you a plaything. But knowing how females think, you'll probably let him go."*

*Zamir knows nothing of how females think.*

*Before me is a man of fifty, cheap suit a wound within the great room filled with colorful dresses, modern styles, and designer suits. Zamir is dressed as a billboard for businessmen to aspire toward, tailored and dripping with excess expense. My gift appears to be a flunky, all of him brown, save for his pasty skin. Expendable fodder in the Elezi stable.*

*This gift is a trap. A false gift placed within our Oikos, extracted to make a showing of good faith. I do not fall into traps. I am the one who places bait. Underestimated and undervalued, I will make an example out of this man to put Zamir firmly in his place.*

*Chin down, peridot eyes rolled upward to peer through the thick lace of my lashes, my expression clearly expresses,* **"Make it do something. Why are you giving me such a cheap gift?"** *While my mind calculates exactly why this gift was given.*

*"A spy in your midst, Miranda." That arrogant curl of lips is directed toward me, hands gesturing helplessly to the sobbing man kneeling before us. "Whatever shall we do with him?"*

*Eyes flicking to the side, I ignore everyone in the room, because they're of little consequence to me. Just bodies with beating hearts, all wanting something from me. The map in my mind knows exactly where the people of importance are located, keeping track of their wellbeing.*

*Cyrus immediately comes to my unspoken call, bowed to press his ear to my lips. "Recording device," is barely a rasp of sound that will not travel past the shell of his ear. To add a flare of dramatics, I cup his throat in my palm, then place a soft kiss beneath his ear.*

*Stepping away with a nod, Cyrus acts unaffected by my display of affection, understanding it for what it was worth.*

*Bait.*

*Bait in a trap for Zamir.*

*Cyrus, with his bleached hair, is not a Livas, because why would a boy-crazy teenage girl crush on her distant relation? It's an insult levied at the Elezi family for me to show such affection to a person of little means, as if they are far beneath this underling. In actuality, Cyrus is a Livas, and with complete shameless disregard of sin, those luscious lips feel amazing pressed between my damp thighs.*

*We've only ever had each other. From childhood playmates participating in hide-and-seek in the grapevines, to pubescent explorers discovering orgasms in the apple orchard– a neat trick we engaged in earlier today.*

*Head cocked coyishly, flirty smirk in place, I engage a livid Zamir in a battle of wills and wit. "Was the spy armed?" Just enough emphasis is added, a slight quiver to make Zamir think that I'm both terrified yet turned on by the terror and promise of carnage.*

*"He was," Zamir stresses as if he's speaking to a child, because women and children are of the same ilk. Ignorant and ruled by hormones and emotions. "Would you like to see it?"*

*Hesitantly stepping forward, I curl in on myself, causing my already petite frame to seem fragile. Once I get within arm's reach of the spy, I squeak as if frightened, then jump backward from danger.*

*The sociopath always toys with her prey, thankful when she has the time to enjoy the experience.*

*A deep masculine chuckle of supremacy is smothered, an expression of safety covering the taunt. "Don't fear, Miranda– I'd never allow any harm to befall you." Except at your own hand, or the hand of your son, and not until you've locked down your base of power.*

*Speaking of how that will never happen. "Kyrios," Cyrus calls me by my official title, making sure it carries through every corner of the room, as he presses a small recording device into my palm, which is hidden in the folds of my skirt.*

*The laughter is no longer just a taunt, but the swirling, bullying kind that coaxes others to join in. Around the great room, many voices converse into a battle cry of mockery, with me as their target, because only a fool would call a teenage girl Kyrios, when her father still breathes, her future father-in-law is releasing the* battle cry, and her future king is hiding behind a pillar in the shadows like the coward he undoubtedly is.

Smiling serenely, as if I believe they're laughing because they think me cute and charming and pretty, and not because they doubt my worth as a female. "You said he had a knife? May I see it, please."

"Be careful, Miranda." Zamir turns the blade in his palm, presenting me the handle, voicing genuine concern in the patronizing tone of an elder to a witless child.

"Oh, I will," is said in a tone that causes Zamir to jerk upright. My real voice. The commanding one of a Kyrios within the great room at the heart of her Oikos. I stop toying and get down to business.

"Name?" With the tip of his own blade digging into the soft spot beneath his chin, I lift his muddy gaze to mine. "Atone by cooperating."

"David York," is hissed between clenched teeth, fear slithering like a snake. Such a brown name to match the brown clothes and muddy eyes and drab hair. I almost feel badly for ending his existence, but that's the relief of being a sociopath...

I feel nothing. Not shame, nor regret, nor guilt, specially not hesitation. He is a spy, which means he was instrumental in a plot for our downfall. David York is expendable to Zamir, which means he has done something egregious. As such, he deserves whatever punishment is met.

Kneeling before David York, I get eye to eye with him, making sure my voice won't carry.

"Miranda," Zamir protests, hand reaching to pull me to my feet. "That is not safe."

"But you said I was safe, sir," is whispered in a quivery tone meant to harden cocks, because men love nothing but helpless females. Makes them feel big and strong and capable as they fight their way into tight bodies that attempt to deny them entrance– the force part of the beauty. "You promised. You gave me a gift, please let me play with it."

Chuckling a song of pure sex, Zamir hitches his pant leg, attempting to disguise the growing bulge in his trousers. Oh, how envious he will be of his son. Oh, how he will attempt to sneak into my room at night. A thirtysomething cruel master slipping into a sixteen-year-old child's bed.

Anticipation curling in my belly, the pure pleasure of future prey to toy with.

Leaning forward, making sure to take the ear farthest away from Zamir, I keep the blade notched beneath David York's chin. "You will die in the next minute. It's only a matter of whether or not you wish to die with honor. Your choice– atone for your sins and be welcomed into the arms of your God or force me to commit the sin of taking a life."

Rising to my feet, skirts swirling around my legs, blade tip poised to press deeply in a killing blow. "Your choice, David York. Honor or taint my soul?"

Those muddy eyes roll heavenward to connect with mine. The decision has been made. Flipping the blade around in a lightning quick movement, David has the hilt in his palm before Zamir can react. The device is already recording, transferred into the palm which previously held the blade.

"Atone for the sin of disloyalty. Honor your people by dying with courage, David York." Kneeling at my feet, the man never takes his eyes off his queen, bladed edge sliced cleanly across his throat.

A heartbeat later, when the spatter arcs in a violent tide of crimson, my smile is no longer empty of emotion. Pure bliss radiates off me as I absorb the offering's sacrifice.

Recording device transferred to Cyrus, stowed safely in his huge, capable hands, I turn to an enraged Zamir. "Why did you do that?"

"A true Kyrios would never have to ask why. A true Kyrios would know why. But since you will never be Kyrios, I shall tell you." Advancing forward, Zamir retreats to get away from my blood-soaked skirts dripping all over the stone floor.

All I was trying to do was thank Zamir for the offering. Honest. How dare he reject the thanks given.

"An eye for an eye." Voice pitched to carry. "A life for a life. If we were to take David York's life, honor would require his people take one of ours. Then we in turn would take one of theirs. Over and over the cycle flows. He owed us a debt, a debt he paid with great courage to honor his own people. To protect the Oikos, we must outthink our selfish need for vengeance. The debt has been paid. The balance has been met. The cycle has been closed until it begins anew. The video is proof to be sent to his people."

David York's people stand before me, but I'd rather have Zamir continue to underestimate me than to reveal my hand.

In the distance, hidden in the shadows of a pillar, a boy steps forward with no need for an introduction. He's the spirit and image of the man who underestimated the girl, only he is a coward. One look and I can accurately predict our lives together will be nothing but misery, because he is only good for one thing and one thing only.

Bait.

My future king is nothing but bait to draw in those who wish to end my reign.

Arrogance and fear are a toxic mix that cause men to act outside of the dictates of the human condition. Which means this ochre-eyed doughy boy will be unpredictable, more irrational than man believe a hormonal woman to be.

Eyes sliding to the side, I spot a boy to his right. One not hidden in the shadows. Those same ochre eyes, that same inky hair, that same luscious skin, but the expressions they wear are vastly different. This one is exhilarated by my display. Aroused. An erection tenting the front of his trousers.

Pupils dilated, weeping from my clamshell in the way my nursemaid Laverna warned, never before have I experienced such a visceral reaction to another human being. Skin flashing with fire, muscles tightening, gooseflesh beading along the base of my neck. I experience lust for the first time.

"Sorry to disappoint, sweetheart," the unpredictable cowardly brother calls across the great room. "But I would appreciate it if you'd stop eye-fucking my brother, seeing as how I am your future king."

Eyes sliding back to the one who dared to interrupt my sick fascination with the pretty boy that is quite literally panting as he gazes in my direction. "You're right, you will be my king," is stressed heavily, a double-entendre that he will soon come to discover.

Zamir Elezi, son of Zamir Elezi, wholeheartedly believes he will rule me as my king. While I know only one truth, where Zamir will be my king, owned by me, ruled by me, and used as bait to protect the Livas Oikos.

The chess pieces on our Oikos board.
Miranda Livas
Cyrus Livas
Zamir Elezi
Ramsey Elezi
Jasper Elezi Livas
Oscar & Oona Livas

Panting roughly, eyes unfocused, the pounding behind my brow threatens to darken my vision and slide me back into a sedated state. The sound of Ramsey flushing the toilet and the feel of Sabrina's cool hand squeezing mine, I fight back the threat of reality destroying everything I've learned and retained.

"Mira," Sabrina breathes, voice filled with agonized compassion, thumb sliding against the top of my hand in soothing circles. "The one who assaulted you—"

"Is he dead?" is a demand that will be answered, because I need to know that person isn't walking free, able to harm my Oikos— not only my family, my properties, my household, but the ideal in which it represents.

"Yes," Sabrina whispers back.

"Did I right the balance?"

"Yes." Those three letters drain the fight out of me, slumping me back to the mattress. "He wasn't educated in anatomy, nor was he well versed in genital mutilation. He was acting on rage and envy and pure emotion."

"Just explain why I have parts as I do now." The pounding in my skull demands no more information outside of the facts. I can't handle more truths, not without being subjected to another round of sedation.

"In an attempt to carve your clitoris from your body, he ended up severing the ligament, but the nerve bundle remained attached. He made ribbons out of your inner lips, ruthless bloody strips of flesh. He bisected your left outer lip, clear to your pelvis– I believe that was the cut that nicked your urethra. He gutted you from vaginal opening to anus."

And then he raped me.

Raped me in the singular hole he had created out of two. A penetrating violation to my body cavity. A mix of blood and piss and shit and searing pain, my severed breast stuffed into my mouth as a fleshy gag to smother my screams for Cyrus.

For the first time in my life, I broke. I lost it. Emotions never experienced surfaced, and I've been repeating the endless cycle ever since.

Eyes squeezed shut against the sensation of my arm being shredded by jagged bone, this is only partially why the ghost of myself is hiding my memories, as the pain is too much to bear.

"The repairs," is a demand through clenched teeth, loathing how tears are burning my eyes and stinging my cheeks as they make their path of betrayal. This is new to me, I know this. Feeling emotion. I hate it already. "Just tell me about the reconstruction."

"As I said, I placed a wound vac on your chest, ignoring the less severe injuries. I worked tirelessly on your hand, because I feared leaving your artery exposed, while my team assessed the damage to your groin. It took twelve surgeries between your breast and groin until we were satisfied. It took almost four months for the wounds to heal enough that the threat of infection passed."

"My vulva?"

"Internal and external sutures, leaving a thin scar that mimics an episiotomy scar, which you already had. Sutures to your bisected labia majora, but there was no salvaging your minora. None. Shredded to thin ribbons. A perverse version of a female bris, your clitoris was hanging by a thread, hood entirely gone–"

"They didn't find the missing flesh, did they?"

"No." Shuddering in revulsion, Sabrina's eyes slip shut, as if as long as she doesn't see me, none of this is reality. I know the feeling, but I'm not fashioned to play pretend. "I feared a loss of sensation, so I did what I felt was best."

"Better to ask for forgiveness than permission, they say," is muttered wryly, instinctively knowing no one would apply that tenet to me. The old me was not the forgiving sort, evidentially, from what I've relentlessly gathered on my fact-finding journey.

"As the strongest person I've ever met." Sabrina gazes at me, revealing a rare burst of courage. "The coldest, most ruthless, you of all people deserve whatever joy and pleasure you can access. At that point, it didn't matter what the consequences were, it was my goal to save whatever sensation I could. Your urethra was severed, the strips of your minora were dangling right there, your clit was already released. From asshole to bellybutton, it was like he took a meat grinder to your genitals. The world fucked you, I thought you deserved to have the ability to fuck it back."

The rough rasp of breath escaping my lungs is eclipsed by the bathroom door opening. Head bowed, ochre gaze hidden beneath a fall of inky hair, those curled shoulders and the sluggish way he lifts his feet, Ramsey is feeling an immense wealth of guilt.

"Why?" is a demand, when I don't wish to put more pressure on the man.

Unable to look at me, Ramsey stares down at my arm in silent horror, lips drawn in a taut line. "That's not an answer you're ready to hear, Mira."

Everything I've retained has ignited the hottest of fiery rages within me, but hearing that hopeless quality in Ramsey's voice, that evokes an emotion I've never felt in my entire life.

As a diagnosed sociopath, I've always understood the value of each emotion and what it represented, even if I never felt it. Did I have a capacity to love? I don't know, but I understood the power in taking care of those who were mine, and the loss of worth when I failed them.

As my short-term memory turned to long-term memories, I've realized those diagnoses repeating in a slideshow are ones I've received over the years, my natural state of being since I witnessed my mother's slaughter and I avenged her death.

Without empathy, logic must prevail, or life would be untenable. In its place, I was able to learn what emotions *should* feel like, sometimes mimicking them to appear normal.

Reaching up, fingertips sliding against the wiry hair covering Ramsey's wrist, I tug his arm down to me from where it rests against my pillow. With catlike movements, I caress the top of his hand with the underside of my jaw, tears dampening his skin.

For the first time in my existence, I experience true compassion. Not the mimicked emotion that makes me seem normal. I *feel* it. Experience it deep within the soul I didn't realize I possessed.

Ramsey hurts, and knowing he hurts is hurting me on a level deeper than devalued pride. I loathe his pain, and not because I wish I weren't experiencing it, but because I wish he wasn't. I can handle it– swallow it, digest it, and shit it out to fertilize the rage building deep within me.

"Mira," is a harsh whisper of pure shock, palm flipping around to cup my cheek, but gone as swiftly as it made contact. Righting himself, Ramsey's demeanor shifts to that of a professional in charge. "What more does Miranda need to do before she can convalesce at home?"

The same air overtakes Sabrina, shifting her back into Dr. Runyan. "Dr. Brigand cautioned that once we hit this final stage, Dr. Livas should remain here for another forty-eight hours to be sure there is no mental relapse. She will need to meet with her psychiatrist before she is released, as is her own protocol."

My protocol– the protocol of the nightmarish apparition from months ago, the ruthless monster incapable of feeling. I am that monster, but I can at least admit that I don't want to take responsibilities for those actions just yet.

I'm not ready.

"Medically?" Ramsey prompts, my outburst of affection causing him to become more brazen, outwardly holding my hand for what feels like probably the first time.

"I examined Dr. Livas while she was sedated last. Everything is healed nicely. The only matter left to be resolved is sensation, which is a private matter." Pale skin flashing a ruddy red in an instant, Sabrina begins stepping backward toward the door, fetching her tablet on her way by the table.

"Dr. Livas should remain here in her room, and I suggest you accompany her, with little alone time." Sabrina backs into the door, hand latching on the knob from behind. "I'll send Dr. Brigand down in the morning for an assessment."

"Sensation?" tumbles from my numb lips, all the doctor-speak completely understandable, but not this. Why is Sabrina embarrassed?

"I'll give you privacy." Sabrina's eyes are fused with Ramsey's as the door closes, silently conveying something I don't have the capacity to understand.

# ℰERECTION

"Mira, I'm going to bar the door for this next part." Striding across the room, lavender shirt pulled taut across his back, trousers fitted to reveal the curve at the bottom of his buttocks, Ramsey flips the bolt to lock the door. "This is a private matter. If you would rather I step into the bathroom, all you have to do is ask."

"I don't understand," is murmured in confusion, eyebrows cinching in the center of my forehead. A queer look passes Ramsey's expression, amused shock, as if he's not used to seeing me in such a state. Perhaps that is true.

"Your libido rivals that of any male in his prime." Predatory steps perfectly placed, drawing Ramsey back to my bedside before I can thoroughly examine the meaning of his words. "When tested, your hormone levels have always been off the charts. High levels of testosterone, but it didn't affect your menses. Dr. Runyan believes it might have affected the shape of your body, the size of your breasts, the increased size of your clit, and the level of aggression you display, as well as your lack of mothering instinct. More hunter than gatherer."

"I am female," comes choked from a throat raw with aggravation. "I accept the rearrangement of my parts, but inside my head, I have always known I was female. This deep-seated need to protect doesn't make me male."

"No, it doesn't." Busying himself so he doesn't have to hold my gaze, Ramsey rolls the tray table around the end of the bed, placing it on his side at my left. "As a doctor, you of all people understand how hormones in the womb and after shape our personalities. You are a female, just as I am a male, even if I am the childminder once I return home from work."

Fingers turned to talons, nails twisting in the sheet, rough gasp-like pants are torn from my throat, because I'm not prepared to venture there just yet.

"You were a woman who had sex at least twice per day since you were sixteen and reached orgasm several times per day prior to that. Your libido is directly tied to the balance of hormones in your system and your personality. The fact that you're going on nearly six months–"

"Six months?" is nothing but a sound of pure panic. "I thought it was four."

Palm settling on the crown of my skull, Ramsey tries to soothe my emotions. I'd promised the ghost in the mirror that this time was the last. "Two more months have evidentially passed since that partial snippet of conversation was secured as a long-term memory. But with the sedation, you're confusing it with a short-term memory."

"I don't like this– I'm not used to feeling this off."

"It will pass, Mira." That soothing palm travels from the top of my head to curl around my jawline, fingertips brushing my cheek. "Your mind is the strongest part of your body. Your will in unparalleled. Your fierce form was shaped by the excess testosterone flowing in your system, affecting your desire for satisfaction and need to protect and conquer. Just because it is labeled as a male hormone, doesn't make you any less of a female, when it runs in all humans' veins."

"I've been getting erections, haven't I?" is muttered in disbelief. Not shock because I can't believe it's happening, but disbelief because I wish it wasn't. That stirring sensation, the oddness between my legs at off times, a body part that merely swelled when touched, now becomes a full-fledged erection.

"I don't see myself as the promiscuous type," is a grave whisper, eyes open yet seeing nothing. "You said you and I only laid together twice."

"Twice for sex, once for affection, which was our first touch after we met at sixteen." Suddenly sheepish, Ramsey's voice fades. "I was the forbidden fruit, as you were for me. Picked but not allowed to bite. Your self-control was forged from your need to protect me, but you gave in twice because I manipulated you into giving in."

"Somehow I doubt that." A funny little chuckle echoes around the hospital room, because the ghost in the reflection doesn't seem like the type to ever give in.

"For me, you couldn't help yourself." A palm lands to rest on top of my fidgeting fingers. "I lost control twice, which is… your strength was tied to mine. Your resolve was tied to my longevity. It was forbidden, Mira. It was forbidden."

"Did we have many lovers?" The person from weeks or months ago, that *we* would encompass the past me and the present me. This time it references Ramsey and me. "I may not remember, but that doesn't ring true for my personality."

"No. Neither of us are built that way." Ramsey opens a tiny drawer in the cosmetic case resting on the table, nimble fingers making a selection. "Loyalty and trust. You especially cannot reach climax unless you feel the person is loyal to you unto death, because you have to trust them to trust you in order to properly let go."

That heavy pressure is building behind my forehead, threatening to pop my eyeballs from their sockets. The darkening smoke in my psyche billows up, threatening to eclipse all that I've finally uncovered. Self-preservation has me backing off.

"We experience lust like any other person does, Mira. You just have the self-control not to act on it. The loyalty not to destroy that which we've built over a few seconds of stolen pleasure. That's something that many can't seem to grasp. The payout never fits the dire consequence, something we've both learned. You and I had one lover over the years, and we'll leave it at that."

As long as I make it about everyone else, the pressure subsides. Focusing on Ramsey, I can ferret out details of importance. "Are you in love with your lover?"

Four months ago… no, it was six months ago, I remind myself. I struggled with the concept of romantic love. The love of family is more about duty, their absence painful. Romantic love is unquantifiable, but the agony causing the pressure behind my forehead, I begin to wonder if fear is causing it, fear that I lost someone vital to my happiness.

"Love? Yes." Ramsey continues to play with the contents of the cosmetic case, opening and closing drawers, organizing their contents. "Intimacy. Connection. Lust. Family. Yes. Romantic love, I'm not entirely sure. It doesn't feel as I do for you. We're more brothers than anything."

"Brothers?" mulling that over with a flare of surprise. "Are you gay? Bisexual?"

Chuckling a deep rumble of pure amusement, Ramsey turns to me, those ochre eyes glistening with surprise. "These questions are amazing." Another rash of chuckles has me smiling along too.

"Try self-preservation, Miranda. Forbidden fruit or not, you would have slaughtered any woman I touched. You would have lost respect and affection for me. You would have treated me as you treated... let's not go there. It was no hardship for me. As I said, it was lust and pleasure and safety and trust and loyalty, and I wouldn't change it for the world."

"I'm a monster," is whispered in abject horror, seeing the ghost in the mirror reflected back at me. I am she. She is me. "Controlling and abusive."

"No." Palm reaching up to cup my cheek, Ramsey holds my gaze, thumb swiping a tear away. "My choices. My decisions. My consequences. Why would I disrespect you and myself by being with a woman who was a pale comparison to you, when if I were patient, the fruit would eventually ripen to become edible."

"Is it edible?" Understanding the allegories but not the context, my mind is fighting me every step of the way.

"You're the only one who can answer that, Miranda."

*"You can't catch me!" giggling like the servant girls my age, I run through the grapevines, ducking to dive beneath the trellises, knees dirty from our fun.*

*"The hell I can't!" Ramsey shouts from a few yards away, rolling gait surefooted along the soft soil. "Just watch me."*

*Fiendishly giggling, I roll out from beneath a vine and just lie in the middle of the path, allowing myself to be captured. This is play but not playacting. The giggles are real, not just what I assume a girl should be expressing as a boy chases her through the grapes.*

*Exhilarated, chest pumping up and down as I try to catch my breath, hair whipping to lash my cheeks and stick to my lashes, I allow myself to become the prey.*

*"Oomph!" all the air is expelled from my lungs as the boy lands lightly on top of me. Elbows taking the brunt of most of his weight, palms cup my cheeks, holding the hair back from whipping me.*

*"Caught you," is a whispered breath, Ramsey endlessly amused how I always allow him to catch me. I'm sure he realizes how thrilling I find the chase, the play the highlight of my existence.*

*In the handful of months since the Elezi family has joined our Oikos, I've split my time between medical school and being a dutiful Kyrios apparent. Father's health is waning, the last memories he'll ever make. Zamir the father is a serpent in men's designer clothing. Zamir the son is five years my senior, just as cruel and calculating and cold and power-hungry as his sire, already taking up the mantel at one of the Oikos's most important business ventures.*

*Ramsey and Cyrus are still tutored here at the cradle of our Oikos. Ramsey finishing up his high school career, while Cyrus studies for an undergraduate business degree. The Elezi children went to proper schools, not affording the best of tutors, so it's unsurprising that Ramsey is on par with our regular peers, instead of advanced due to a comprehensive, one-on-one education.*

*"Stop thinking– shut that big brain down." Then there is Ramsey, my joy and happiness. The reason I smile. The reason our Oikos now has a heart. But a shadow has descended above us, the clock ticking down to the final moments of my father's life, because my first act as Kyrios is to immediately wed Ramsey's elder brother.*

*Rolling around in the dirt, Ramsey forces me to forget all the stressful things, allows me to feel like the living embodiment of a woman, not just the blade of our family. The protection. The threat. The head.*

*Breathlessly giggling and laughing, grappling as we roll from one path, beneath a row of vines, to tumble back out onto another* path. Amused lips press against mine, the pressure shocking and enlivening. The slick prod of a damp tongue requesting entrance that I immediately welcome.

Never having been kissed on this pair of lips before, I'm unsure how, but nature takes over, Ramsey a good teacher. My hands offer another form of instruction, rucking up the back of his shirt, immediately tugging at the button on his trousers. My skirt is bunched up, panties missing from when Cyrus shined my pearl with his tongue this morning.

A struggle ensues, one warring within me, as I try to grind my clamshell against the very part that I wish to free from the confines of cloth. Panting roughing in my ear, these hiccuplike gasps of shock and pleasure, Ramsey aids me in the struggle, reaching down to tug his trousers off his hips.

That scorching length prods my clamshell, fully opening it, seeking out all the oil I made just for him, just as my nursemaid guaranteed it would. A squeak of surprise slips from my mouth into his, the head cresting to nudge at my pearl, the sensation unparallel to anything I've experienced before.

"Miranda and Ramsey," Cyrus calls from a few inches above us, having taken us both unawares as the lust rode us hard. A bare foot nudges Ramsey's hip, causing him to flop off me and onto the dirt path with a loud grunt of frustration.

As scolded children, Ramsey and I stare up at that disappointed peridot gaze, awaiting a lecture six months in the making. Where I expect to witness jealousy shining down at me, all I see is fear and worry.

Crouched on the balls of his bare feet, tapered fingertips dangling between his knees, Cyrus is long and lean, with broadening shoulders as he matures. The loathsome blond hair flutters in the breeze, covering the telltale peridot that marks us as blood.

"As the Kyrios, you must respect the hierarchy, Miranda." Cyrus begins, drinking in our vulnerable parts exposed to the air. "I am your second. No one can control me save you. I am your blade. Your protection. Your insurance. You are to love me or abuse me as you see fit, because I am also your greatest weakness. Even Uncle holds no authority over me. Now let your mind calculate what this means in relation to Ramsey."

Sucking in a sharp gasp, it took less than a second to understand the deeper meaning. The sociopath in me cannot *rationalize why suddenly tears spring to my eyes and panic flutters within my chest.*

*"I see you understand while you must remain nothing more than playmates. Sister and brother, comfort and entertainment, but never lust."*

*Ramsey struggles to right himself, elbows sliding on the dirt path. "I don't–"*

*"Miranda will have to educate you and your elder brother on the hierarchy within our Oikos at a later time." Cyrus raises an eyebrow, gaze riveted to the hard, damp length airing out from the gap in those trousers.*

*"Everything I am to Mira, you are to your brother. You are Zamir's to reward or punish… to destroy. You are his only weakness. Miranda holds no dominion over you, unable to protect you."*

*Reaching forward as if he can't help himself, Cyrus draws a line down Ramsey's length, panting roughly as fluid spurts out the slit at the top. "The only way you pose a threat to your brother is if you don't keep your pretty cock inside your trousers and out of his wife. A man wishes for his seed to be the one to grow his children. The only protection Mira can offer you is to maintain her self-control around you."*

*Uncharacteristically out of sorts, "I–"*

*"Shh… Mira." A warm palm lands on my bare thigh, calming me in an instant. "We can't have you both running around on adrenaline and hormones, posing a threat to yourselves. Feels nice, doesn't it?"*

*Hips jackknifed off the ground, the crown of Ramsey's head digs into the dirt, a guttural groan flowing from his lips. "Such a pretty cock, look how lovely it erupts all over my hand. Pretty. Pretty."*

*Not once in my existence have I experienced a moment where I was so thoroughly entranced that I forget my surroundings. I've witnessed torture. I've slaughtered dozens. I've come upon servants fornicating in the tunnels and gardens and orchards. Once I fell upon a man taking his pleasure in the barn… from a goat. I've witnessed a man raped before a tribunal, punishment for taking a woman that wasn't his. All acts of perversion befitting the human condition.*

Never did I expect such a display of debauchery to affect me so strongly. Blood-engorged cock nearly purple, retreating and emerging through the fisted ring of Cyrus's fingers, over and over, leaving stringy spendings to slick the path. The wet sound sinfully decadent combined with our labored breathing. Thighs quivering, clench after clench as my muscles pump oil out, preparing me for invasion.

On the ground by my side, Ramsey's chest is rapidly rising and falling as he draws in lungful after lungful of oxygen. Body writhing in jerky stops and starts on the soft dirt, cock erupting a milky fluid to drip along the side of Cyrus's hand.

"If your father caught you both as Mira's had caught she and I, you'd be snipped as I was." Cyrus issues a warning as he pulls his hand away, leaving a stunned Ramsey to stare sightlessly up at the clouds.

"Clean my hand off, Mira." One palm skirts up the inside of my thigh while the milk-covered hand is pressed to my lips. "Lick and suck it clean so I may satisfy you with it. Unlike mine, it's far too potent to have near your clam, there's seed thriving within the milk."

Yet again, uncharacteristically amenable, I do as Cyrus asked. Tongue peeking out for a taste before I fully commit to licking him clean. Tasting of warm skin, briny like the sea lapping at the cliffs below, bitter yet sweet as the finest of tapenades, I fiendishly devour my offering, body reacting to the wicked flavor.

"I bet it tastes better than mine, doesn't it?" No jealousy, no pain, no voice of violation expressed.

Cyrus made the choice– a vasectomy at fifteen or we had to stop playing in the orchard. We debated for weeks, because this wasn't a choice I would have made. To be unmanned. They say I am devoid of empathy, but all I could keep thinking about is how I would feel to have my womanhood taken from me.

The sacrifice was too great, even if it meant loyalty to me. Father finally understood my hesitation, explaining how what was to be done to Cyrus could be undone later on in life, so he could have children of his own. Clamped, not snipped. There were procedures that could be done, where the seed was extracted, even if the clamps weren't removed.

Cyrus protected me, and because of that, while I explore psychiatry to understand those I battle, I've gravitated toward human sexuality and the reproduction systems in medical school.

"Mira?" Cyrus displays a rare burst of vulnerability around me, always sure of my devotion to him.

"Not better nor worse, just different, Cyrus." Leaning forward, I attempt to press a kiss to his lips like Ramsey taught me earlier, but he rejects me before I make landfall.

"Potent, Miranda. Highly potent." With the grace of a surefooted cat, Cyrus rises to his impressive height, humor and lust boring down at me. "If your cum-covered lips touch mine, my lips cannot devour your nether set."

Tugged with purpose until I'm upright on my feet, my hands are slammed to the top rail of the trellis, insistent palms pressing my fingers to latch on. "Hold on– don't let go." Cyrus crouches to the balls of his feet, palms parting my thighs, then he buries his face against my clamshell, rutting until he opens me.

The heady moan crawling from my throat takes me by surprise, eyes flicking down to spot not just Cyrus crouched before me, mouth working my pearl as fingers dive deep for more oil– Ramsey has righted his clothing, the awed expression evolving from the one of pure lust he's displayed since we met.

Detonating within seconds, my call echoes through the vines, bounding past the cliffs and out to sea.

"I always figured you for a whore, but this far-exceeded my expectations," flows a cruel voice in my direction, taken unawares because of the false sense of safety both Cyrus and the land offered me.

"This will change once we're married." Zamir steps from between two rows of vines, coming to a stop less than an inch from where his brother is seated. "Cyrus will no longer be dining at your table… breakfast, brunch, lunch, supper, and midnight snacks. Because as your husband, as your king, your cunt will belong to me."

A wave of relief washes through me– Zamir sees what we're showing him. The deviant display of my distant relation slurping at my groin while my intended's baby brother watches on. At least Zamir didn't see what happened moments ago.

Hands dropped from the rails, with a singular step my skirts right themselves, swirling around my calves to cover my vulnerability. As calculating as I am, a smug smirk tugs at my lips, taunting Zamir into hanging himself with his arrogant delusions of what our future holds.

"You will obey, as is in your nature." Zamir begins to berate me, similar to the lecture his father has offered several times, always when he believes he's culled me from the herd, taking away my safety and security, when it's just another leg in my patient hunt.

The snake believes himself to be hunting the rat, because he doesn't realize she has wings and fangs.

"It's laughable how you prance around here, believing this Oikos yours, believing anyone would ever follow you." Head hitched back, false laughter rings from his throat.

This grown man calls me a phony on a daily basis, yet he looks like a doughy boy, no strength in those malnourished muscles because his body is fueled by fat. He calls me stupid because I'm female, yet he knows nothing about anything, barely skating through college.

Zamir the son is bait who believes himself the trap.

Leaning on the post, arms crossed in a purposeful defensive posture meant to a make Zamir believe I'm upset over how he's speaking to me, hurt feelings, bent pride, when all I do is see him as a joke.

"You will know your place at my side, raising our children and maintaining the household staff." Zamir steps forward, gazing down at Ramsey, and in a rush, I realize I underestimated him— he saw. Zamir saw it all.

"Will you continue to host orgies in your rooms?" flows out with deliberate calculation. "While I am to stay chaste, in the off chance that you wish to breed me, will you continue to host orgies?"

"Of course," this is said as if I've lost my mind for thinking differently. "It is a man's right to seek pleasure. A woman's orgasm is a myth— they act, put on a performance, but it doesn't exist."

"Science not your strong suit?" Stepping forward, I purposefully place myself between the brothers, allowing Cyrus to take my cue. Cyrus pulls a stunned scared Ramsey from the ground, then tows him over an entire row of vines for safety sake, knowing I can handle this myself.

"If a woman's orgasm is a myth, why were you screwing four women just outside my quarters in the hallway last evening?"

*Stepping around Zamir, my skirts swirl around his legs.* "Why bother? What is the sense in it if you're not trying to seed their wombs? If only a man can feel pleasure, why don't you all just fuck each other instead?"

"You are crass." *Dark skin flaming in a rush, bloated from too much drink. Fists curled at his side, Zamir swallows down the urge to punch me for saying such a thing.* "That is an abomination. A sin. Disgusting."

"Hmm... says the man of twenty-two who was mouth-raping a fourteen-year-old child last night." *High on rage, I located the girl's father who had sold her to Zamir, then gutted him in front of the entire Oikos, leaving his entrails to cool on the stone floor. No true leader would ever monetize those he was born to protect.*

"Says the woman whose cousin was just lapping at her cunt–"

"Fifth cousin," *I remind Zamir, enraged that Father revealed Cyrus's bloodline to the Elezi family.* "You and I are probably closer genetically, but then again, science and you are not on the best of terms."

"Your father is closer to death by the day," *is more than just an idle threat, as we all wait for Zamir the father to slither his way into Father's chamber and assassinate him for the Elezi family's gain.*

"You and I need to come to an understanding," *is not said in a seductive tone by a woman meaning to coax her future husband. It is said by a human being who will do anything to protect their people.*

*Walking forward, I herd Zamir down the dirt path, each step, along with each word, draws us closer and closer to the back portico.* "If I perish after our union, you still will not become the Livas Kyrios."

*Another step and another, the arrogant, ignorant bully is herded to where his father is lurking in the shadows of a pillar.* "If I bear you a child, and I perish, you still will not become the Livas Kyrios. Even if the child is too young to rule, you will be unable to gain power through him or her."

*Coming to a stop, Zamir's feet land at the base of the steps leading up to the back portico– his father less than a dozen steps away, thinking himself cleverly hidden in the shadows.*

"Even if you slaughter me, Cyrus, any children born from my womb, you will still not become the Livas Kyrios. There is literally no way possible on this earth that you would ever replace me, cock be damned."

"You can't hide behind Cyrus forever, never fighting your own battles, playing queen when you are nothing but a womb with a stretched-out cunt." That insult has no impact, because thus far I haven't given anyone my virginity. "Nothing will ever make you a man— you will forever be beneath me."

"You honestly believe what you speak, so blind to the world around you." Scoffing at with all his vast connections, Father managed to find the one person who isn't subject to the human condition. Completely insane. Illogical. Actions and reactions not befitting human nature.

A cruel sadist who gains power from the torture of others. The sex I've seen over the months, Zamir always makes them bleed, and not because he's hung.

"You are powerless against me—" swept off his feet in a maneuver I learned when I was just a toddler, I prove his statement false. Zamir finds himself ass-first on the stone, tailbone landing with bruising force, with my heel pressed directly over his groin with the promise of damage.

"King. King. King," rolls in a ringing tone off my moist tongue. "That word is meaningless. Powerless. Weak. The coward hiding behind the power of the queen." Grinding my foot into his groin, the monster in me brightens at the glorious bleat of pain released from his bloated throat.

"The queen does all the work. She is the blade. The protection. The power. As the king just sits on a square, allowing all of his followers to be used as cannon fodder. A true leader understands their role is to protect the weak, not use them as a barrier between themselves and their goal. The queen is the most important piece on the board, protecting, strengthening their forces, while the opposition only has focus on the cowardly, worthless, useless king and doesn't see the attack coming."

Whipping my skirts up, I hitch up my leg, keeping one heel firmly gouged into Zamir's groin. "Fuck whomever you want, as long as they are willing. I am incapable of jealousy. Because you will only have me once, and that is to seal the covenant of our union. I will not carry your seed. I will not stay chaste. You have *zero authority in what I do, because you will forever be beneath my rule."*

*Releasing the muscles in my pelvis, a hot stream of piss arcs to splash across Zamir's chest. "I'm better than you, because I can piss standing up without the aid of a penis. I'm better than you, because I have power and I didn't need a few extra inches of limp flesh to prove it. I am better than you, because I am Kyrios of the Livas Oikos, and you never will be."*

# ML

"Mira?" Ramsey gains my attention, a bottle of lotion clasped in his grip. "Do you need to rest? Are you okay? Can I get you anything? Are you hungry?"

"Just another…" Panting roughly, I drag a palm across my forehead, wicking the sweat away. "Another memory resurfaced, and I swear there is a method to the madness."

"What do you mean?" The lotion bottle is squeezed, a dollop poured into his palm, then warmed up by rubbing his hands together. "You haven't shared what memories you've regained. I know this must be difficult for you. Private. But know you're never alone."

In the silence, I try to organize my thoughts into a cohesive argument, one which Ramsey will understand. We all have strengths and weaknesses, and what I instinctively know of him, he is highly intelligent but the polar opposite of me.

"Where she–" pausing, I refuse to play that displaced blame game any longer. Mildly distracted by the fact that Ramsey begins massaging my thigh, the pleasure soothing. "I've come to realize the memories may have been withheld with a purpose differing than what one would expect."

Heated, I whip the sheet off my body, allowing it to tumble to the floor. There is nothing of me Ramsey hasn't seen, and I am far from being demure or insecure or embarrassed or modest.

"I have no conscious memory of the attack, and I fully support the withholding of information from me. Because when I ask the wrong questions, my brain literally feels as if it tries to blow out the front of my skull, taking my eyes with it. I had thought the issue was hiding a specific event, but I logically know what happened and with whom, details not mattering at this point. Another guess was that perhaps something more tragic befell me, something I cannot even voice, because fear and I are not bedfellows. But now I think it's something else, and that something else means I am ready to go home."

Always knowing his place, Ramsey says nothing. Digesting my words, attempting to understand them, his thumbs draw upward from my knees, path slick from the lotion, fingertips biting in to loosen muscles.

"The ghost in the reflection is cold, calculating, and I honestly saw her as a monster. Uncaring. Detached. Unemotional. A sociopath. But something has been unlocked within me, evoking emotions I have never felt. Father chose me as the one to keep our Oikos strong, all three parts."

"Mira—"

"No, Ramsey. You never want me to accept my own faults. I can always fall back on the fact that I was diagnosed as a sociopath with a detachment disorder for my failure. But Father warned me it would be the most difficult of my reign, but also the most important. I have protected our people, maintained their health, and care for their happiness. Our wealth flourishes. Our home is a place of safety and security. But we've talked around the three souls who I have not nourished. While not cruel, I was not soft either."

"A father is allowed to act as you have, Mira. I thought we discussed how the fact that you are female doesn't mean you should be treated any differently than the head of a family. Emotions do make some weak, and we needed you to be strong. Now that we are strong, you can afford to be weak."

"A father shouldn't use that as an excuse, nor should a mother." A slideshow of memories resurfaces, ones that have now returned to my vault. "I can imagine worse memories will arise, ones that will solidify my hypothesis. What happened could have been prevented from the beginning, if I had fostered the love of the people, instead of demanded loyalty through fear. A few see that as a challenge and revolt, actions outside the norm of the human condition when they feel up against the wall. Perhaps if I'd shown him love–"

"No!" A palm smelling of almonds slams down over my mouth, pressing the inside of my lips into my teeth, a coppery tang floods my tongue. "No, goddamn you! No. Absolutely not. I have no need to know which of the memories you've uncovered, but I can guarantee others will make you rethink this charitable mindset you've adopted. Any humiliation he endured was well deserved, and then some."

"A benevolent leader–"

"We would not exist had we been led by a benevolent leader." Ramsey turns uncharacteristically forceful, tossing the lotion bottle back into the cosmetics caddy. "You were exactly who we needed you to be, at the expense of yourself. He deserves not a single thought not centered around rage. With Cyrus taking up the mantle your father employed on you, that of a patient, *benevolent* mentor, and with me being the pushover caretaker, every need has been met inside our Oikos. You cannot be everything to everyone, Mira. It's impossible."

"Father–"

"No!" Ramsey has had enough, and even I realize how irrational I sound.

The victim overthinking things until they shame themselves. If only had I done this instead. The curse of the would have, should have, could haves.

"He was born rotten– you were not. Your professors, your colleagues, your fellow doctors, even back as far as twenty years ago, they all agreed what happened to you at three altered who you needed to become in order to survive. You are not a sociopath, even though the detachment kept you safe and secure from experiencing another devastating loss. You were not born a monster. You are not a monster. There isn't a single person in our Oikos who doesn't understand the sacrifices you've made in your quest to protect us from those who wish to destroy everything we represent."

"Ask Jasper, Oscar, and Oona if they appreciate my sacrifices," escapes before the words fully form inside my mind.

"Ask 'em yourself, Mira."

The level of disrespect, the asshole tone in his voice, not once in the twenty-one years we've known each other has Ramsey spoken to me in such a manner. The laughter is instantaneous and delighted. Other than adversaries and figureheads, everyone surrounding me acts as if they have no autonomy. It's impossible to figure out if someone is consenting because they want you, because they need you, because they love you, or because they fear you.

Continuing on in the same maddening fashion, simply to get a rise out of Ramsey, because it is entertaining me to no end. "If I hadn't tortured–"

"Tortured?" Scoffing, Ramsey jams his hand into the cosmetic caddy, retrieving something. "You repaid the torture, only a small fraction my father and brother dished out. We all saw it as little victories, while we were held hostage by them both for far too long. You did all you could do to protect us. Survived."

Another tube squeezed, the filthy sound laughable as the goop lands in Ramsey's awaiting palm. Frustrated and flustered, he keeps bitching and snarling at me.

"I think I'd rather have sociopath Miranda back at this rate. Life was easier. Less to explain. No hoops to jump through. No games to play. No feelings to soothe." Three fingers spear me between my thighs, diving deep with artificial oil.

"Are you?" Shocked beyond measure, I can barely get the words out as my body stills as well. "Are you rage-finger-fucking me?"

"Yeah, I am." Another jab, another snarl, another lip curl, causing me to burst out laughing.

Neck arched, head hitched high, bellowed laughter flows from my throat. Body quaking, I even help Ramsey out by parting my legs, for the first time recognizing that I have an erection.

"Tell me how you really feel, Ram." Fighting with Ramsey makes me just as hot as being chased by him, playing with him, yet almost as annoying as avoiding taking a taste of his forbidden fruit.

"Imagine being the only sane person on a six-month journey of madness. At least you were unconscious, while I had to suffer every insane minute of it with complete lucidity and no psychotropic drugs. I swear I wasn't sure how much longer I could survive it."

Palms rising to slap over my eyes, emotions battering at me almost as hard as the pressure building inside my cranium. I can't ask. I need to know but am terrified of the answer. The one question that has plagued me from the first time I woke from an artificial sleep. The one person who was there waiting for me when I crawled screaming from my mother's womb.

Cyrus hasn't been here. He hasn't visited. Instinctively, I know the children are safe, but Ramsey hasn't said a single word of Cyrus. Why hasn't he visited unless he can't? Unless he's no longer on this earth.

Wracking sobs jerking my body, too terrified to ask. One of the most agonizing emotions is torn free, forcing me to experience it for the first time since I suckled at my mother's breast. Not even nursing my own children elicited the emotion within me.

Love.

I've always understood loyalty and duty and devotion and care but never love. Father's loss was an intellectual one, where I grieved the wisdom lost, as well as the familial connection.

This is different.

Ramsey was there– I protected him by sacrificing myself, but where is Cyrus?

Reaching up, fingertips searching beneath the inky fall of Ramsey's hair, a raised scar has the breath hitching in my throat. It's real. The scar exists. The scar I created, laid Ramsey unconscious so he wouldn't have to witness what came next.

"Don't," is a surly slur, head jerking to the side to dislodge my touch. A heartbeat later, Ramsey crawls into bed with me, shoving me over so he can wedge himself onto the small mattress. "Welcome to the wonderful, torturous world of emotion, Mira. Guilt. Shame. Worthlessness. Powerlessness. Those are all the things I've felt since I woke in a hospital bed in this same facility."

"My entire existence is to ensure *your* safety." Hand reaching up, I try to pull Ramsey to face me. "I knocked you out for a reason."

"Have you…" Rolling to his side, Ramsey faces me, our noses almost touching. It's intimate, but I don't feel suffocated like I would with someone else. Breastfeeding my children was difficult, because they needed intimacy I was incapable of giving. "Have you remembered it yet?"

"No," is whispered softly, a shudder working its way through my body. Palm splayed across Ramsey's chest, right over his heart, my fingertips fiddle with a button on his shirt. "The details are a blur, but I do know what happened now. I think I've known for a while, actually."

"I hope the memory never resurfaces." Palm settling at the small of my back, fingertips skate up my spine. Up and down, both soothing and arousing. "If I was too weak to experience it without being blacked out, you shouldn't have to relive it a second time, after being tortured and maimed. Once was traumatic enough– it placed you here for the past six months."

Leaning toward him, I decide my self-control means nothing. Ramsey is no longer the forbidden fruit, ripe and ready to eat.

"Wait." The rejection stings, causing me to jerk backward. Strong hands cup my hips, yanking me back onto the mattress. Ochre eyes filled with nothing but a mix of pain and love. "No sex. I will not taint it with the aftermath of our last time, because it will force the worst memory you'll ever experience to resurface. Intimacy, no sex."

"Just hold me, please." Snuggling as close as possible, I align the front of my body along his. "I don't like feeling things."

A chuckle rumbles up from Ramsey's chest, the sound tickling my ears. "She said please." Nuzzling the tip of his nose along my jawline, a palm makes a path from my hip, along my side, and flutters the air across the breast that is not mine, not making contact.

Sob lodged deep in my throat, closing off my ability to breathe, the mattress is trembling beneath us, as if an earthquake is radiating from the center of my chest. There is only one person who would selflessly donate a large portion of their flesh to rebuild my breast. Only one person of age whose skin is nearly the identical shade of dark olive as mine... and I just hope they didn't harvest the skin at the morgue.

Moving swiftly, a hank of hair is twisted in my claw-like fingers, smashing Ramsey's mouth down onto mine. Kissing him with the same passion and lust and desire to escape as I did that first time, I sink into the warmth of someone who is loved by all who know him.

Rolling my body in a wave, breathy moans escaping between our fused lips, hands yanking and pulling because I can't get close enough to him. I need him– I need Ramsey's warmth and laughter and heart and joy.

Muscles taut, writhing on the mattress, blunt teeth are latched against the side of my throat, a hand working feverishly between my thighs. No need for artificial oil, I make all Ramsey requires. There has never been another man I've come across that sparks the fire in my veins like the man skillfully fingering me in two places.

Crawling moans spill from my throat, vibrating against the teeth latched to keep me in place. Two digits work tirelessly inside me, the dizzying rhythm mind-blowing, as two others stroke a part of my body that was never capable of that feat before. My engorged clit is being jacked by slick fingers in a rapid pace, glistening with the oil that pours from between my thighs.

The release is detonating, the sounds I release as foreign as the spurt firing from the tip of my clit. Body unable to keep the muscle taut when all the others relax, a dribble of urine making an embarrassing escape.

"I'm going to soil your pants," is a breathless gasp of mortification, body still suffering the results of my orgasm as I make a mad dash to the bathroom. Vagina clenching rhythmically to milk a cock that isn't there, oil seeping in a wash, urine spurting out every time my clit jerks.

Ass landing on the toilet seat, with Ramsey's laughter quick at my heels. "Let me show you a trick, or you're in for a nasty surprise." Grinning down at me, he makes a motion with his palm that I don't understand.

Seated at the toilet, it's different than before. Everything was neat and tidy and seated beneath me, able to empty my bladder without making a mess. Sure, after having a few babies, my pelvic floor muscles weren't as strong, so I ended up dribbling a little with every orgasm, but this is ridiculous.

"Mira, you're still erect." Brows hitching downward in the direction of the three or four-inch protuberance sticking straight up from between my legs. It's twice as large erect as it is just dangling inside my clamshell, narrow like a finger.

Unbuttoning his trousers, zipper flowing down next, Ramsey fishes out his cock, all the while I just sit here, allowing urine to dribble down my flesh with every aftershock clench, not daring to fully relax my muscles to urinate thoroughly.

"Watch." Cock semi hard, Ramsey holds it differently than how Cyrus taught Jasper and Oscar. "I can't piss with a full hard-on," is murmured wryly. "Unlike you. Physically impossible. But I can do it with a semi. Only problem with your dick grinning at the ceiling, the piss flows upward and makes a mess. Accuracy is key."

A hot stream of piss flows in rush to land in the small space between my thighs, directly into the toilet bowl. Stunned immobile, I just sit on the toilet while Ramsey pisses between my thighs.

"Take your fingers and push it downward– go on now," is a nonchalant order, as if he weren't doing one of the most intimate acts with me.

"Maybe I want to pee standing up?" If I wouldn't risk a golden shower on my way to my feet, I would be tempted to try it. After all, what good is a tiny dick if you can't piss standing up with it.

"Remember how we taught the boys to go potty seated first, how the little toilet had a pee-pee guard. Use your fingers as your own pee-pee guard. You must learn to piss with that thing before you enter the mastery class."

A long-suffering sigh rumbles up my throat as I use two fingers to point my clit downward. Blood retreating, it's not as engorged as it was, but not back to its rested state. While Ramsey dribbles and shakes himself dry, I concentrate hard on releasing muscles that are in a different location than before, and I can't do it.

"Is this the first time?" I don't elaborate, fearing I'll backslide.

"You got as far as noticing your clit about six or seven times, then had to be sedated. A catheter was used so you didn't soil yourself in bed while you were out." Zipping up, Ramsey steps away to give me space. "This is the first time– gotta say, never thought I'd have to teach you to piss, not in this lifetime anyway."

"The muscles are in a different spot." Concentrating on doing something that was second nature for thirty-seven years, but I'm no longer wired that way. Flexing my pelvic muscles, I keep doing it over and over again, accidentally employing kegals as well, anus clenching too.

"Runyan was terrified the nerves were severed, taking your ability to climax away." Ramsey has always skirted a fine line between appearing smug and glowing with pride. His beauty removes the smarminess.

"You came hard before, but…" Trailing off, Ramsey plans on torturing me until I literally piss or get off the pot. "Gotta say, you came harder than a goddamn freight train in there, and it's only bound to get better."

"How do you figure?" is murmured absentmindedly as I keep trying to locate which muscle is wrapped around my urethra, everything rearranged so I would regain function after being mutilated down there.

"Just let go," Ramsey coaxes, just as I figure it out. Urine splashes into the bowl, causing a gasp of shock to bubble past my lips. The sensation foreign but pure relief. "Just let it flow, Mira. Just let it all go next time, experience a true release."

# ⸜LOVE IS...

"May I ask you more questions?" Seated in the back of a limousine, the privacy shield raised to wall off the driver, the windows are tinted to the point I can barely see out. It's obvious the luxury car is bulletproof.

This is Ramsey at rest. The Ramsey who arrived a handful of hours ago was stressed, fully clad in businessman armor. Once he realized I agreed with my doctors that I was safe to go home, he turned into the boy who chased me through the grapevines.

Draped across the seat opposite from me, button undone leading to the divot at the base of his throat, satisfied grin tugging at his lips, Ramsey's erection is pulling the fabric of his trousers taut.

"As long as the questions are about me," is muttered with a shrug. A shift in his hips, the erection is now pointed downward toward his thigh. I have a case of penis envy, both because I crave the flesh displayed before me, and because mine is nothing as spectacular. "You know the rules– you wrote them. We're merely following them."

"I don't actually remember writing them," is murmured wryly, eyes flicking toward the ceiling.

Memories have been slowly whispering in. Not a confusing bombardment, but the sensation of remembering something small, which is a normal occurrence throughout everyone's day. Only what I remember is more important, because it fits the puzzle pieces of my bisected life back together.

There are shadowy blanks for major events. No matter how hard I try to remember, I get nothing but a punishing migraine for my efforts. I took the cue, I'm simply supposed to allow them to be whispered or punched into me– I can't force it.

"I know things on an instinctive level. When I need to know something, it presents itself. If I ask the right question, as soon as someone gives the smallest detail, it's a prompt for all of it to be remembered. It's like, as you sit there, do you remember every single thing that ever happened to you? Every name of an acquaintance? Or does your mind supply it when you ask it to? *Do you remember the woman who brought the honey cakes? Who? Oh, you mean Sally?"* Then a bunch of information is dumped inside your head. It's how the mind functions."

"I see what you're saying, I truly do."

"What do you do for a living?" Ramsey chuckles in reply to my question, finding me suddenly hilarious. "You said to make it about you."

"Ah, as boring as my job entails, I can see why you'd block it out." Little bubbles of laughter burst as that ochre gaze stares at my scrolling facial expressions. "Director of Development at a small media company that you own. My job description is even more inane than my title. I spend my evenings with the family."

"So you're a legit businessman–"

"Until otherwise indicted, yes." That tone is even more wry than the eyebrow waggle. "But I'm sure there will be some flunky who will take my fall."

Now it's my turn to laugh, because our criminal activities are not something I've blocked out, too ingrained in the fabric of my personality. The constant need to protect my Oikos is directly tied to the fact that it's a criminal empire, spanning to several continents. Random assassins do not break into sprawling estates of average everyday Americans.

"Do you wish things had been different for you? Marry the love of your life, have kids with her, live a simple life?"

"No," Ramsey says without hesitation. "I'd trade nothing about my life. This is the way it was supposed to be. If you asked me this a few months ago, even last week, I might have said I struggle with what occurred between us, where I wouldn't have manipulated you into allowing me to touch you again, but not now. You've changed, and I think you were supposed to change."

The fact that I'm sniffling and wiping at my eyes is proof positive as to what Ramsey means. "I hate feeling things. It's foreign and absolutely tragic, almost as annoying as getting random erections. None of it is rational or logical and it's driving me to the brink of madness."

"Pretty sure you just left a six-month stay in madness land, my sweet." Hearing that term of endearment from Ramsey's lips causes another round of weeping that can't be contained.

Cyrus.

"To steal Jasper's favorite phrase, Jesus fucking Christ, Batman! Make the waterworks stop." Laughing through the tears, I dry my eyes with a pocket square stolen from Ramsey's jacket.

"They won't greet your arrival," Ramsey warns, answering an unspoken question I couldn't muster the courage to ask. "We retrieved the nursemaid, now that it's safe. They're sequestered in Laverna's quarters. We felt it better for you to acclimate to your surroundings until morning, before you meet your children for the first time."

"It won't be the first time," comes in jerky stops and starts as I blow my nose. "I birthed them, Ramsey."

"The you as you are now will be a complete stranger to them, no differently than they will feel to you after six months of memory lapses. You've raised Jasper as your father raised you, so you can guess how agreeable he is as a person."

"Thanks a fucking lot, Ram!" is sputtered in rage. "I'm a monster, I know this."

"Ah, you prove my point." Flipping around to sit his behind in the seat as it was meant to be used, Ramsey's feet settle on the floor, that shit-eating grin impossible to find other than intoxicating. "Your reunion with Jasper will be an absolute delight."

"Good thinking on waiting until I was settled first." I can admit when I'm wrong, which is something I doubt the ghost in the reflection would ever do. I'm striving to only pick the best qualities of her to emulate.

"Jasper has attempted to be the Kyrios Pro Tempore in your absence– hasn't gone well. Our people are too loyal to you. It's been twenty years since a teenager attempted to rule things. Jasper didn't cut his teeth as an assassin. He wasn't arranged in marriage to join with another empire. The political climate has changed– society has changed. They see Jasper as a little shit, so be prepared to experience his wrath because your dainty shoes were far too big for him to fill."

I can't ask. I can't say his name aloud. If Jasper was attempting to rule, when it would have been Cyrus's position as long as I drew breath, at least from an advisory standpoint.

"Our son is not pleased his mother is coming home, I take it?" An evil giggle escapes my lips. "Boys. Boys. Boys. Always thinking their cocks make them bigger, badder, smarter… all it does is get them into trouble, because their growth is slower than their ballless counterparts."

"Guess who has a cock now, though." Ramsey is never going to let me live that down. Shifting to the edge of his seat, he grins at me. "Best of both worlds."

As the tires slow, I feel the change beneath the car. The anticipation builds, because Ramsey knew where we were before I realized it. Breathlessly panting, I can hardly wait for the car to be shifted into park before I'm attacking the door handle.

Wide-leg trousers swirling around my calves, spiked heels sinking into the cracks of the stone walk, I can't even gaze ahead to the villa looming three stories to the clouds. Darting to the side of the property, jogging along a stone pathway that shifts into dirt, my trajectory is the dormant grapevine trellises, representing both my mother and my father.

Falling to my knees, palms catching my weight. Fingernails digging deep, deeper still, gathering soil in the palms of my hands. Breath catching on jagged sobs, forehead pressed to the earth. The wind whipping my shorn hair. The waves crashing into the cliffside.

The roots are woven deep into the marrow of my bones, tendrils wrapping tightly around my sluggishly beating heart. It draws life from me to nourish the land, in return it feeds my soul.

The cradle of the Livas Oikos.

The foundation of my identity.

Home.

Prostrate as in prayer, my gaze rolls upward to a spot in the distance, down the dirt path between two rows of grapevine trellises, catching the glint of peridot. With a strangled breath, I'm on my feet, charging forward as fast as my weakened body will carry me.

With an oomph of shock from the force of my body colliding with his, Cyrus catches me. Face pressed against the side of his neck, homey scent seeping down into my soul. Chest pressed against mine, heart to heart, arms tightly wound around one another.

Love is…

This is what love is.

In total hysterics, the nonsensical maddening sounds bubbling from my throat. Hands seeing by touch, reaching everywhere.

"What's wrong with her?" is said above my head in a rough voice filled with tears. "Should we take her back to the clinic?"

"Cyrus Livas, meet an emotional Mira." Ramsey's hand settles on the crown of my skull, quivering with his own pent-up emotions. "The trauma seems to have evoked Mira back into a time when she could feel things. You'd remember her if you weren't a small boy yourself at the time, no doubt. Trust me, she's one helluva trip now."

"An acid trip?" Cyrus bends down to support my knees with his forearm, picking me up while I cling to his chest. "Shh… my sweet– I've got you." blindly walking, lips press to mine and hold. "I've got you."

It must be winter now, November by my calculation. The brisk air, the dormant vegetation, the frost-packed earth, but I feel no chill. The banked heat in the center of my chest keeps me toasty warm as Cyrus settles us onto a padded settee, just outside the main rear doors.

In the silence, Ramsey lights the outdoor burners, the flame igniting to warm the patio. Continuing the nursemaid routine– a facet of his personality shown far before the past six months –he drapes a wool blanket over my lap.

"I have arrangements to attend," is directed at Cyrus, the meaning pointed but not for me to understand. "I'll give you two privacy for your reunion."

Ochre gaze held wide in question, Ramsey cups my cheek. Seeing whatever he was looking for within my expression, he presses a fleeting kiss to my lips. To my total shock, he repeats the same with Cyrus.

"That's new," is muttered in wide-eyed mystification.

"And you'd know that how, since you remember nothing?" Tone playful, Cyrus is toying with me.

"I remember." Turning in his lap, I stare up at Cyrus. "Not once in two decades have either one of you been affectionate in public or in my presence. I assumed what was happening behind closed doors—"

"Not much, since we were either at work or with the kids, and I warmed your bed every night since the Elezi family encroached upon our Oikos."

"Don't deny you've fed your lusts on his." Snorting at how Cyrus can mask his emotions, I realize we both were proficient in that feat.

"These past six months, I've slept so well." Again, the words are playful, the cat toying with its prey. "You are the most insatiable creature I've ever encountered, while Ramsey is the most affectionate. I struggled to give you both what you needed, when you needed each other but couldn't feed the hunger."

"So you haven't..." is trailed off, causing Cyrus's eyebrows to dip low in surprise.

"You are different." Arms tighten around my torso, palms cupping my hips. "No offense meant, but you actually sound like a jealous woman attempting to trap her man with no-win questioning."

"I was actually just curious, but okay then." Mouth flattened into a taut line, so much for our happy reunion. The rage returns. Deeper, more important questions demanding answers. "Why didn't you visit me?"

"After what happened between the three of us and the dire consequences paid, no one has had a hunger to be fed." Suddenly, the usually silent Cyrus become chatty. "As long as it feels good, Ramsey has no stopping point. I will admit to finding that quality intoxicating. While you're the total opposite, where you rarely allow me to take charge. It's the best of both worlds, and I wouldn't change it for anything."

Tucking the blanket around my shoulders, Cyrus palms my ass, pressing me closer to him. "The kiss? My guess is that Ramsey finally feels safe and secure enough to express himself without fear of harming you or I."

Shuddering at the revelation, Cyrus attempts to warm me, knowing that it's not the crisp air that forced a chill down my spine.

"You were the one who said I wasn't to visit, Miranda." Squeezing me tightly, Cyrus lets his growing frustration show. "It was your protocol set into place, where you said, no matter what, you'd recognize me. Ramsey was worried, because over time, you always recognized him."

"I don't understand– this is something that hasn't been revealed by my mind. I get that the facility is mine. The sedation protocol is mine. The staff was hand-picked by me. But how did this come about? It's a total blank in my mind, but I get no migraine when I try to uncover it."

"What happened to your mother shaped you– I do remember you prior, your three to my five." Drawing in a deep breath, as if Cyrus is dragging my scent into his lungs. "You were a sweet and silly and happy child, so very much like Oscar."

Our son's name causes my heart to clench and my mind to reach outward, seeking and seeking, looking for my children, instinctively knowing they are close by, but not close enough to touch.

"The way women have been treated, especially in a male-dominated society, it's never sat well with you. You believe the personality dictates the position of power, the deeds dictate the level of respect. As soon as the sadistic father and son duo, Zamir Elezi elder and younger, began their torture games, it spurred you to help everyone."

"I've blocked most of that out, but on an intellectual level, I can accurately predict some of what their reign of terror included."

"I highly doubt your mind has conjured up the truth without the memories to sharpen the horrific details," is gritted out between clenched teeth, a rage to rival my own revealing itself.

"You were studying psychiatry to understand human emotions to gauge how your enemies ticked, also reproductive anatomy and sexuality to understand how their victims felt. You created the facility and the sedation protocol to help the victims used in our war.

"Women have never been treated as equals in our society. Gay males were seen as women, many not surviving the toxic environment within their families. Lesbians were raped into compliance, married off and turned into broodmares. Your father's wives and children are a perfect example of what happens when enemies get their hands on loved ones, anything to weaken their competition."

"The facility is a rehabilitation center?" Why I question this, I don't know, because deep down I know this is just and right. This is who I would have been, wish to still be.

Just like that, the answers are revealed, like picking ripened fruit from the vine. As Cyrus speaks, the memories don't assault me. The truth just whispers itself through my mind, the pieces rejoining the fabric of what makes me who I am.

Dr. Sabrina Runyon was playing a game with Dr. Elian when I overheard them, she told me this very morning. She is my second-in-command at the facility, where the doctors and nurses are told it's human trafficking to keep the real identities of the patients a secret, so their abusers can't locate them. It keeps the staff loyal through fear and keeps them honest through the crimes they believe themselves to be committing. Many of the patients are victims of human trafficking in the first place, the atrocities they experienced firsthand, with the people there to help them, heal them, and give them a proper safe home.

"Some of your patients were able to return to their families, memories intact after they healed enough to handle them. Some were completely erased, new lives given. You stormed into compounds, stealing their women. You rescued gay teens and gave them positions in our Oikos. You weakened our egocentric competition by strengthening their abused."

"The irony is that the very protocols I put in place to help others, eventually were used on me. Now I can accurately assess the process through both perspectives. I remember how cruel family members thought me to be when I refused to allow them access to my patients, and then I did the same to you, honestly believing you dead."

"Deep down, I believe that was your biggest fear, with both Zamirs holding us hostage." Sighing heavily, eyes slipping shut, Cyrus rests his forehead to mine. "Ramsey wondered if you thought that about me, curious as to why you never once spoke my name, when he knew you fully remembered me."

"I think…" palm running up his chest, over his shoulder, my fingertips seek an indented scar at the back of his neck. "On a subconscious level, I believe I was mourning you."

Hand plucked away, Cyrus presses his lips to my wrist, then tucks my palm between us, directly over his heart. Just as Ramsey did with the scar on his forehead, Cyrus doesn't want me to touch him in a location that will spark the memory that I couldn't handle the first time around.

"I missed you terribly," words washed across my cheeks, breath tickling me. "The only thing that helped was that I knew you were okay, with Ramsey giving me constant updates and pictures of you sleeping soundly in bed."

"I was enraged that you abandoned me," is muttered underneath my breath. "But it's me who needs the punishment for keeping you away in the first place."

"We've been punished enough, Mira." Face buried against the side of my throat, Cyrus shows a rare burst of emotion, groomed just as I was to reveal no vulnerabilities. "This new you will fight me over what Ramsey is preparing now. The old you would have immediately calculated the reasons as to why it was necessary."

"Cyrus?" it takes all of my self-control not to shriek, keeping my voice even and calm. This is a moment where I miss the old me as well, because calm and calculated was my constant state of being.

"We are vulnerable right now, especially since I had to inform everyone of your return. The servants here at the villa were given instructions, most loyal enough to remain quiet, but there are still Elezi holdouts that pass information to our enemies. Your son is in the public eye. He won't be able to stay quiet for long."

"This is our life– it's always been our life," is muttered with a shrug, truly incapable of calculating where this conversation is headed, which puts me at a disadvantage I don't appreciate. "The constant state of awareness, always looking over our shoulders, knowing there is a target on our backs. We took the hits so others could feel safe and secure beneath the umbrella of our protection."

"As a vulnerable widow, they will have a reason to request visits to the villa, where they say they are presenting you with options for a new king, but it's only so they may assess your physical strength and mental capacity, then attack accordingly."

"Par for the course." Mind spitting out a list of priorities, already catching on to where Cyrus is headed, already figuring out what Ramsey is doing inside the villa. "That was our entire childhoods."

"I know you know what's happening," Cyrus calls me out. "I also know you would rather I rule by your side, but that is not what can happen. You will marry Ramsey this evening. He will become your king. I'm already respected and feared by both our allies and enemies, seen as the obstacle between them and you. Ramsey is seen no differently than a wife."

"I understand that none of Father's wives were his queen, not even my mother. They were simply wives, mothers of the Kyrios's children. But that was not how Zamir was seen. He was king."

"Ramsey is not Zamir, loathed and feared for his cruelty. Ramsey is respected for his compassion and shrewd financial capabilities, but he is not feared. He will not have a target on his back. He will not be used to harm you. He will be seen as your husband, the paternal figure for your children. I cannot be your righthand and your king and your husband. With your marriage, it stops the encroachers, and it will be seen as apropos for a man to marry his brother's widow– that's how it's done."

This new emotional side wants to feel the bitter sting of rejection, but the calculating, unemotional creature who gazes out of my reflection immediately orders the logical and rational aspects to this plan and presents them inside my head, immediately soothing the emotions.

Worried I'm yet again stepping on their toes by taking their autonomy away and ordering them to live against their own wills, I get to the root of the issue. When you have absolute authority, it's difficult to discern whether someone wants you because they desire you or because they fear you.

"Are you in love with Ramsey?"

Eyebrow raised, a queer chuckle rumbling up his throat, "Another no-win man trap again, Miranda?"

"No. This isn't silly ninny games played by an overemotional woman," is snarled with loathing, disgusted that Cyrus would see me that way. Disgusted that he would see any woman that way, even if some do exhibit similar behavior. "I need the answer before I give my answer."

"Total awe, Ramsey has been in love with you since he saw the joy on your face as you toyed with your prey, covered in lifeblood. He's the heart of our Oikos, but he is also highly manipulative in getting his way, especially if he knows you want to do it in the first place. He's loved by all."

"That doesn't answer my question." The woman who interrogated encroachers, who tortured evildoers, who cut the heads from snakes... I am she. She is me.

"Without you voicing a word to me, I've always known it was my heart that you feared harming. It wasn't your king's reaction that upset you when his brother begged and pleaded for your attention. You feared I would suffer from jealousy and rejection, as if you were cheating on me with Ramsey. In two decades, you slipped three times. You never feared either of the Zamir's reactions, because both only loved Ramsey. It was me."

"Psychoanalyzing me doesn't answer the question," is muttered with increasing frustration, the rage swirling, hoping to be welcomed home. "If I had been capable of feeling love, we both know I would have been in love with you."

"You were capable, and not a single soul who knew you doubted your utter devotion, loyalty, and love for me, Miranda." Palm cupping the back of my skull, Cyrus turns my head to face him.

"My intimacy with Ramsey started because I sensed your struggle. The intense hunger, the strong desire to love him, and how it made you feel guilt because of how you felt so strongly for me. You knew I saw what you had to endure with Zamir as a necessary evil, but you feared my reaction to you feeling true emotions with Ramsey. I took Ramsey off your hands so he would stop being a little tease, because he knew no one would harm him. He was harming you."

"Even if I thought that you were giving me permission to enjoy Ramsey in my bed, simply by you becoming his lover too, we both know Zamir would have punished me for it."

"That's why I kept Ramsey's attention–"

"Such a hard task, that, right?" Scoffing, I scuff Cyrus up against the head. Gods, why won't he answer me. "Such a chore to have those luscious lips wrapped around your cock."

That smug smirk is a thing of terrible beauty, causing my lips to slide into a smile in return.

"I believe our love, devotion, loyalty is so beyond measure, that we cannot decide if we are merely in lust with each other or in love. We love each other as companions, brothers of sorts, enjoy our time spent together, both in and out of bed. Experience joy as we play with the children. But to be in love with you, to be loved by you, means all other forms of love pale in comparison."

"You stole my line," Ramsey whispers sheepishly as he magically appears from behind a pillar. Shoulders bowed, head ducked, hair hiding the emotions reflected in his eyes, it's beyond obvious that he was eavesdropping like a small child.

"I'm having flashbacks from the past seventeen years," Cyrus mutters wryly, smiling from ear to ear at Ramsey. "There's no privacy from Jasper. The boy's hunger for knowledge is only comparable to his thirst for gossip."

"I have no idea what you're implying." Totally shameless, Ramsey winks at me. "The boy takes entirely after his mother."

Head hitched back, true laughter rings out from my throat. The sound echoing off the cliffside, causing birds to take flight. Our son is entirely a product of his mother's rearing, that I do know as fact, foggy memories or not.

"Miranda." Knees thudding to the stone, Ramsey kneels before the settee. Warm palm cradling my hand. "I'm spoiled yet relentless. Moody yet happy. Thoroughly naughty. Utterly shameless. Please, I beg of you, manipulate you, coerce you, emotionally blackmail you," all is said in a playful tone, listing his own personality flaws.

"I ask this of you, not because I wish to keep us safe, nor because I don't want anyone to come sniffing around you, nor because I will now be considered protected by my legal tie to you. I ask this of you because I want nothing but to be yours. All I've ever wanted is to belong to you."

A ring is wiggled down my finger, the metal cool and smooth, when Zamir never gave me such an offering. Zamir Elezi only wanted to take from me. The band is intricately designed, featuring peridot and ochre. Instead of dripping with expensive diamonds, instead of being a billboard to display power and wealth, the ring is dainty and creative and sentimental, evoking emotions within me that have lain as dormant as the grapes in winter.

"This is not a political maneuver– this is out of love." The ring is wiggled downward until it is seated in its rightful place. "Please accept me as yours, Miranda."

"Since the moment our eyes connected across the great room, you've always been mine, Ramsey Elezi." Smiling down at my husband-to-be, tears pooling in my eyes, I watch on in wonder as he kisses the ring he placed up on my finger.

A palm cupping the side of my head, Cyrus makes it appear as if he's kissing my hair. "My sweet, thank you for making Ramsey beyond happy."

…and with that simple comment, Cyrus finally answers my question, whether he realizes it or not. I have no doubt Cyrus loves me, nor do I doubt Ramsey's love. I've always known Ramsey was in love with me.

This wasn't a political maneuver either on Cyrus's part, no matter the logical reasons he presented. Yes, I've always feared Cyrus feeling rejected, all the way back as far as I could retain memories. First, because he was the hidden Livas, meant only as a substitute, and I never wanted him to feel as if he were merely a replacement. Then as he watched me marry a man out of duty. Then as he learned of my slips with Ramsey. I feared Cyrus would feel rejected if I married Ramsey for love, because deep in my soul, Cyrus has been my partner since birth.

Ramsey is mine, but he also belongs to Cyrus, because Cyrus and I belong to one another.

Cyrus unintentionally answered my question. Wrapped in the warmth of Ramsey's kisses, I come to realize Cyrus wasn't rejecting me by never placing himself in the running…

Cyrus is in love with Ramsey, and selflessly gifted Ramsey his heart's desire.

# TORTUROUS WEDDINGS

White nightgown swirling around my calves, pacing around my chamber as if I hadn't been gone for the past six months, things remembered just where I left them. The book on psychological torture techniques is still on my side table, as if I just placed it there last night.

No amount of amnesia could make me forget how it's six paces from the bedpost to the door to my bathing chamber, nor which drawer held my unmentionables. Not that any of this comes as a shock, since this has been my private quarters since birth, my mother's before me.

Emoting is such bullshit.

The wedding night is important, this much I know is true. Expectations apparently don't poof into thin air when purposefully giving yourself amnesia. It's supposed to be a big deal, correct? The wedding is too.

This new emotional side of me is doubting itself. Being a sociopath was both a blessing and a curse, never doubting myself, even when I was wrong.

We signed the wedding license in front of a lawyer acting as both the officiant and a witness, with Cyrus acting as the other witness. No vows exchanged. No promises made. No words of love shared. Not even a Kiss the Bride.

Straining my psyche, I attempt to unlock memories of my first union, and I experience hell to pay for it. The pounding behind my forehead intensifies, eyeballs feeling as if the pressure will force them from their sockets, sight fuzzy around the periphery, ears ringing.

Does the groom not wish to consummate our union?

Perhaps our escapade in my hospital bed a few days past was traumatic enough.

"Stop acting like a silly ninny girl, Miranda!" I shout at myself, fists punching my thighs. "You're the Kyrios for fuck's sake."

"Spiraling into madness again, I see," is spoken in a teasing voice, Cyrus stepping into the room via our adjoining door. "Ramsey warned this was par for the course, even gave me your notes from previous patients."

A glare. An intense glare as powerful as a thousand suns.

"Your groom is currently brandishing the wedding license to your children, acting as a child himself," is murmured with amused affection. "Seems you've made a proper man out of Ramsey. A husband, as it were."

With a flourish to draw my attention, Cyrus unties his robe, then lands his rear on my sofa, feet automatically pushing the coffee table away, in a gesture so familiar is sparks dozens of déjà vu sensations.

"There are things we could just tell you, but it would neither help nor heal you, Miranda," is said not unkindly, tone filled with a plethora of emotion, sympathy and compassion. "We're doing this the same as before for a reason."

"When Zamir and I were joined, this is how we did it?" voice soft, the confusion is replaced with understanding. These are my rules, which have slowly been filtering back to me over the days since my short-term memory returned.

If you don't believe the patient is ready to relive a memory, then you do everything to avoid the spark. If you wish them to regain knowledge, you purposefully trigger the memories.

"Ramsey would very much enjoy a late spring wedding, inviting as many people who will fit on the property. This isn't a contractual agreement, Mira. Not for him nor you. It's a union for life built on love."

Sniffling into the back of my hand, "Gods! I loathe feeling things. My eyes perpetually leak. It's worse than the random erections or climax incontinence."

"Speaking of..." Cyrus trails off, unfolding a bath towel to drape across a cushion. Then he stands, removes his robe, lying it across the back of the sofa, then sits his ass on the towel. Hand reaching to remove his erection from his pajama pants. "If you would please seat yourself on me."

Peridot rolled to connect with peridot, a litany of curses scrolls through my mind, and I almost say, *"How romantic,"* but stop myself a heartbeat before it flees my lips.

"Do you really want to have sex with me, or is this some type of therapy I devised? Because I have to say, even I'm getting sick of my own goddamn rules at this point." Salivating between both sets of lips, "I want you to want me, not feel forced or obligated to touch me."

"May I please have my Miranda back?" Those eyebrows hitch high into loosely tousled inky strands, and it's the first time I realize Cyrus stopped bleaching his hair. That, more than anything, announces how safe he feels we are.

"This insecure creature is driving me to the brink of madness. I miss how sure of yourself you used to be. I find the emotions exhilarating and new, arousing even, but stop questioning yourself."

"You want me," I say with slightly more confidence.

"There's never been a time that I didn't want you, Miranda." Expression serious, tears glistening in his eyes, Cyrus reveals emotions always masked. "There will never be a time when I won't want you. These past six months have nearly broken my spirit."

Stalking into my bathroom, I snare a washcloth to dry off my face. Voice rough and slurred as I re-enter my room, "Why do you have to say such romantic things?!"

A string of naughty chuckles flutters past Cyrus's lips. "As opposed to when we gave each other our innocence. *I give myself to you, Cyrus."* Then you sat on my cock."

*Stalking down the hallway toward my quarters, I struggle to swallowing down the rage, wanting nothing more than to slaughter anyone in this household that is an encroacher. Vengeance is a luxury I cannot afford, especially on my wedding night.*

*Self-control, mind over matter, I refuse to experience the panic building deep within my belly. Papers signed within three minutes of Father's last breath, right at his bedside, body cooling into a corpse, something so momentous taking no more than three heartbeats.*

*My father-in-law's words keep ringing in my head.* **"Little Miranda, shall I break you in for my son?"**

*Sociopath that I am, even I cannot wrap my mind around how men are born with an inherent ability to turn every interaction into a sexual assault, using rape as their ultimate weapon. In reverse, these same types laugh in a woman's face for pointing out how they would not like to be treated as a sexual object.* **"The hell I wouldn't, Little Miranda,"** *is how Zamir the elder responded to me moments ago.*

*Father deserved better than to be assassinated by the snake that slithered into our Oikos, the snake he purposefully invited in, allowing me to be at the snake's mercy, when snakes have no mercy.*

*The rage builds with every footstep. Father's corpse laid out for the servants to say their final goodbyes. The disrespect leveled, most of it directed toward me from Father inviting the Elezi family into our Oikos.*

*Deep dread, intuition firing how this was the biggest mistake the Livas family made in centuries.*

*Zamir Elezi the elder is not the Livas Kyrios, nor is Zamir Elezi the younger. Do not bow down, do not bend, do not negotiate. Miranda Livas, you are the Kyrios of the Livas Oikos– never give up control, no matter what.*

*Charging into my chamber, door slamming shut at my back, I stalk across my sitting room, then waltz right into Cyrus's quarters through our adjoined door. "I will do my duty, but I will not give myself to that doughy sadist. Once. Zamir gets once, and only once."*

*"Marriage suits you," Cyrus mutters drolly from his seat on the sofa, peridot glowing in the shadowy darkness. Wine dangling from his fingertips, those eyebrows inch higher. "I swear there are sparks flying in your hair."*

*"Gods! My blood is boiling." Slamming the door between our rooms, I lock us in nice and tight, then lean on it for good measure. "That cruel bastard assassinates my father, forces me to sign a*

document over Father's corpse, then propositions me less than a minute later."

"If only I could figure out how to kill the bastard and make it look like an accident." In the darkened room, the glint of the wine glass raising to his lips catches my full attention. "The snake is too smart for that, though. An entire battalion of guards surrounding him at all times. They even check the whore's mouth before she's allowed to swallow the snake's cock. How did your new husband react to his father harassing you?"

A bark of bitter laughter floods my mouth. "The coward got back at me for the pissing incident—"

"In Zamir's defense, you couldn't have emasculated him more unless you quite literally castrated him. But it was certainly effective for putting him in his place."

"Gods! I just wanted Zamir to feel for a few seconds how dehumanized a woman feels over an entire lifetime. Besides the point." Hand raised, I clear that away. "Zamir said that if I were the Kyrios now, then I didn't need my new king running to my rescue because his daddy hurt my feelings."

"Puke." Another sip taken, those predatory eyes glowing at me from across the sitting room. "You can negotiate with Zamir as long as you don't emasculate him further. Stay out of Ramsey's bed, and Zamir will leave you alone. It's the father that you need to fear."

"I am incapable of fear," warbles as the words are gritted out between my teeth, calling me out as a liar. "Zamir I can handle easy enough, aside from consummating our union—"

"I already have a physician on call, because your new husband is going to destroy you from the inside out, and not just because of the pissing incident. I had to put down a woman last month, after he nearly gutted her via her womb canal."

Stalking forward, skirts swirling around my calves, I stop in front of his feet. "No need to inject terror into my veins, Cyrus. I had to snap a girl's neck to put her out of her misery. Zamir and I reached an agreement when I threatened to snap off his cock like I did the girl's neck."

"That explains why Zamir's behaved as an angel the past few nights," flows deadpan, followed by another swallow, and another and another, until his glass is empty of wine because his belly is full. "I don't believe you wish to hear my perspective right now, Mira. I'm trying to keep a cool head, because you will need me in the aftermath."

Skirts shifted until they're hooked around my hips, I straddle Cyrus's thighs. Hands wrenching his pajama bottoms out of the way, I release the cock that has been in my mouth and in my hands multiple times daily since I was fourteen.

"I will never give Zamir anything," is a vow I plan to keep. "Not my virginity, nor a child, nor my consent." Moving my skirts out of the way again, I hitch up higher, positioning the cock at my core. "I give myself to you, Cyrus," is punctuated by a searing sting of penetrated flesh and a sharp gasp of pain.

The mating is fast and hard and lasting no more than thirty seconds. There is no pleasure for either us to take, as this is the first march into battle.

Leaving Cyrus to take care of himself, I stalk from the main door of his quarters, down the hallways, and enter the King's quarters, knowing Father's things had already been evicted within a heartbeat of his last breath.

There is no fear, only knowledge, immense courage and unwavering pride and unrelenting rage powering my ability to put one foot in front of the other. Skirts hiding what is running in rivulets down my inner thighs to wrap around the back of my knees.

"I will never give you anything," is how I announce my arrival, door swung wide open at my back.

Blindly entering, my new king is already in the act of shredding a woman's vagina, judging by the agonizing whimpers flowing from the rear of the sofa– Zamir enjoys dragging his prey into hiding spots, like a predatory cat or juvenile serpent, where he consumes them by digesting their fear.

Without looking back at Zamir, I lean down over the edge of a low chest of drawers, elbows braced, hand gripping the edge of the top, fingernails sinking deep into the wood to anchor me. My skirts are flicked up to bare my ass and the backs of my legs.

"You did not get to steal my innocence, nor did I gift it to you." Cyrus's spending and my maiden blood trickles downward, lubricating the pathway, while preparing for the invasion. "You were not awarded my virginity in the marriage contract. I am not your property."

Sensing movement behind me, the sharp catch in Zamir's breathing draws an evil grin on my face, because he will destroy me, yet I will drag him down to hell with me.

"You get one chance, and one chance only, as this is the only time I am legally bound to do my duty. After that, I will only allow you to penetrate me if I touch your brother or if I desire your seed, but only on my terms with me taking from you."

"The Great Miranda, the Livas Kyrios, honors me by negotiating the terms of our consummation." Harsh laughter heats the back of my neck, not a single hair of his touching my body. "If the seed mingling with the carnage of your maidenhead belongs to my brother, I will end you."

As threats go, I've learned an Elezi only makes promises, their follow-through unparalleled.

"Only Cyrus deserved to have the gift of my innocence," is spoken in an emotionless voice filled with the power of my ancestors. "Cyrus is snipped. I honored my word, my husband, and your manhood by not coming to you with the seed of another inside me."

"You will regret coming to me soiled," is accompanied by a feral growl in my ear, breath searing my flesh, as a sweaty palm curls around the curve of my bare ass. "As agreement on our negotiation, I will honor you by not taking your ability to bear my sons."

The level of arrogance, thinking myself stronger than most because I am a sociopath who feels no emotion, thinking myself powerful enough to endure anything. Blood-curdling screams escape my clenched teeth, chipping several as I fail to endure the onslaught. Unable to hold my bladder or my bowels, the agony so intense my throat is burnt raw.

The torture is never-ending, my confidence left in bloodied ribbon inside my vagina. I had believed I could survive with the knowledge that I would only have to experience this once in my lifetime, but I was wrong.

In the end, I suffer the dehumanization of needing to have my vaginal canal rebuilt, multiple surgeries and over two months of bedrest... the torture never deep enough to reach the mouth of my womb, just as Zamir promised.

"That took longer than I expected," Cyrus murmurs to me as he carries my hysterical form from the sofa and lays me on my bed. "I honestly didn't think you'd get to the point where you'd straddle my lap before the memory broke through."

Lost in the torrent of emotions, as if this moment in the aftermath is what I should have felt when it first happened.

The agony of grief from losing Father, something I didn't experience the first time. The guilt of never avenging Father's death. The rage at Father for putting me into the hands of evil serpents. The powerlessness as I struggled to lead over a thousand souls, let alone survive.

The terror of having the man I legally bound destroy me from the inside out.

The agony and guilt and shame and worthlessness of feeling as if I betrayed the one I cherished, simply because another man entered my body, even if unwanted.

The powerlessness and shame and violation of being raped, even if I rationalized it by thinking it a choice I made when I signed on the dotted line. The way gaslighting was used by Father, where he groomed me to believe being tortured by the man he placed as our king was for the good of the Oikos.

The only way to survive was to render myself emotionless.

Wracking sobs quake the bed beneath me, inconsolable as waves of emotions thrash through me. "Do you need to sedate her again?" Cyrus's tormented voice filters through the panic, hands grappling to catch my wrists, as I cannot break my promise to the ghost of me in the mirrored reflection.

"No." Ramsey joins the madness party, sounding more confident than I've ever heard him before. "This is part of Miranda's protocol but altered by her psychiatrist. Miranda has it worse because she's still learning how to process emotions, something we learned as newborns."

A cool cloth is swiped across my face, dampening my hair until the strands stick to my forehead. "Miranda was not unfeeling as a girl." Strong hands cup my armpits, then drag me until the crown of my skull is resting on a pillow.

"Miranda's doctor believes more happened during her mother's murder, something fundamental is causing a memory blockage, outside of the bounds of the protocol. The forced sociopathy was a defense mechanism the attack destroyed, because she was emotional when brought to the facility before the protocol was administered."

"I didn't know that," Cyrus whispers, voice close and soothing as he scoots to curl around me on the bed. "How did I not know that?"

"Concussed or not, I was up and walking after being roused. On the other hand, you were down for nearly a week."

"Four days," Cyrus cuts in, amusement riding his tone, realizing their inane conversation is soothing me. The sobs quiet, the quakes still, and the sniffles slow. "Possibly three and a half."

"Okay, tough guy." Tone playful and light, Ramsey crawls on the bed to join us, arm immediately seeking my waist. "You win the worst patient award for checking your own ass out of the hospital, then needing to have a blood transfusion here at the villa, because you're a stubborn bastard who likes to terrify me over your health."

"Healthy as a horse." A hollow thud echoes round the room, alerting me to the fact that Cyrus just tapped his own chest with pride. Eyes swelled shut from crying, I can't see anything in the shadowy darkness.

"Mira, my sweets." Fingertips slowly push hair off my forehead, then lips press a gentle kiss, warming my skin. "I'm going to leave you and your husband for the evening. I've been advised a reunion between us would spark a memory too painful to bear." The last of what he says is barely audible, even when breathed into my ear. "So I'm going to carry the lurker in the doorway off to her bedroom."

Movement shifting the mattress before I can understand what he meant, Cyrus is charging across the room. A bellowed victory cry eclipses a deep oomph. "Who taught you manners? Seriously, your parents need a spanking. Off to bed with you." The carefree giggles fade in the distance, my daughter's trust endless.

"Does Cyrus plan on spanking himself?" My sarcastic question brings about a round of Ramsey's laughter. Catching, it's the world's best medicine.

# MANIPULATABLE

"A few more minutes should do it, now that I have you how I want you." Amusement overriding all other emotions, Ramsey's confidence in me has calmed me tremendously. "Storing the gel eye mask in the cooler did the trick."

Laid out across towel-covered sheets, completely vulnerable in my nakedness, I whimper nary a complaint, because Ramsey enjoys pampering me more than I enjoy the pampering. Honestly, I believe the root cause is that no one else is allowed to treat me with such familiarity, so it makes Ramsey feel special to treat me special.

A frigid mask is settled over my eyes, reducing the swelling. Strong palms are massaging lotion into my skin, the scent of almonds riding the air.

Ramsey tried to manipulate me into buying that the towels were to keep the lotion from staining the sheets... I may be mentally altered, but I am far from witless.

"I've never been on your bed before." Lifting up on his elbow, Ramsey bounces us a little. While it seems childish on the surface, it balances out the flaws in our personalities, so never once have I curtailed the behavior. I need the levity, as does Cyrus.

Jasper is almost as bad as I am, leashing his playful side. The twins act as children ought, experiencing the childhood Cyrus and I were denied, and in some ways, Jasper was as well– I was hardest on him as my firstborn, carrying the Elezi genes.

"It's best not to store forbidden fruit in one's bed," is deadpanned from nearly immobile lips, since some type of ointment is smeared across them. "One tends to take a bite with temptation so close."

"And I made it very, *very* difficult to resist the temptation." Tone crawlingly low, dripping with seduction, Ramsey uses a soft cloth to wipe the ointment off my lips. "Your bed isn't what I would have chosen for you. The mahogany posters are very masculine, but the carvings are quite sensual."

"More like erotic. Father commissioned the bedframe for my mother." The fondness in my voice is not something I'm used to hearing. "Instead of a nursery, I slept in the same bed with my mother. Laverna wasn't hired until after her death– she was my mother's childhood friend, did you know that?"

"That explains why you protected her so fiercely." The soft cloth is run over each of my nailbeds, cleaning off the gunky cuticle gel Ramsey applied.

"I found it loathsome how your brother took over my father's quarters, but I was surprised Zamir respected me enough not to harm the contents."

"I should have recorded Jasper stomping around the villa." The eye mask is lifted just in time to witness the look of pure pride on Ramsey's face. Ochre eyes glowing with joy. "I wish you could have seen it. He charged up to Cyrus and declared himself your king. He reminded me of you, actually."

"Naturally," is murmured with amusement, because Ramsey's moods are always catching. "Father never called his wives his queen. As his only surviving child, I was declared queen upon my birth. Jasper will never respect you as king, Ramsey. You know this."

"I'm Dad." None of that joy dims, because Ramsey has never been one to hoard or seek power, that is not his gift to the Oikos. "No one contradicted Jasper, and I think it shocked him. Nothing like a teenage temper tantrum, where we all just ignored it and went about our day."

"Aww... you took his fun away." Chuckling, I think of the hundreds of times Father would have rather tanned my hide than hug me, but he just carried on. "I think I know exactly how he felt."

"So imagine my surprise when I came home from work one evening, only to discover Jasper had moved into the king's quarters, declaring it his for all eternity. Slamming doors and stomping feet, saying whomever you married next could sleep out of doors or at the foot of your bed like a pet."

"And when you showed him the marriage license this evening?"

"He just grumped and stalked away, stating I already had my own quarters." Lips sliding into a smug grin, Ramsey rests his chin on my belly, eyes rolled to gaze up at me. "And then I caught him smiling like he just won a war."

"Teenagers," flows out on a tiny chuckle. "Father would be so proud of Jasper."

"He would." Voice feathery soft, Ramsey displays a rare burst of contemplation. "He truly would."

Shifting swiftly to his side, Ramsey reaches over to grab something else out of the cosmetics caddy. Somehow hearing the sigh I released, he darts back to glare at me. "Don't even begin to pretend you're not enjoying this, Miranda. You now have a built-in pleasure indicator."

Schooling my features, I toy with the prey who believes he's properly manipulating me. "Oh, yeah?"

"Like a pop-up turkey timer, that little nub nudging open your clamshell declares you a liar." Scooching down the mattress, Ramsey flashes me a filthy smirk, eyes filled with anticipation. "Don't even bother to pretend you don't enjoy the pampering."

A wet tongue lashes across the tiny crown, causing my back to arch off the mattress. "Gods!" As I come back down to earth, I spot the twisted moue on Ramsey's lips. "It might smell like almonds, but surely the lotion doesn't taste like that."

Sputtering, making a dramatic show of it, Ramsey keeps brushing his tongue off with his palm, only to end up ingesting more lotion. Eyes dancing, forever enchanted with the idea of entertaining me.

"A shower could fix this situation–"

*Lather swirling around the drain, steaming hot water raining upon my scalp, I rest my forehead on the cool tile, body conflicted by*

*two distinct temperature differences. I luxuriate in the conflict as my system tries to regulate itself.*

*Working directly under Dr. Witmer, I doubt I'll survive residency. In my little world, I am queen. Out in the real world, where normals don't understand the hierarchy of a criminal empire, my toes are gripping the bottom rung on the ladder, trying desperately to hang on as I struggle to reach two rungs above.*

*Meanwhile, I've got med students trying to crawl up my pant legs, doctors trying to nudge my fingertips off the rung, with my mentor tossing boulders and hot tar from the top of the ladder down upon my head. Administration and the insurance companies are wielding chainsaws to cut the rungs. Big Pharma is breaking the fire extinguishers. The nurses are firing rocket launchers from the ground, while our patients somehow got their mitts on nuclear launch codes, because the United States Government canceled their Medicaid.*

*Last night, I slit the throat of a worthless nobody who bought a small boy as his own personal sex slave. This afternoon, I had to pretend I didn't know how to slaughter my mentor in a billion and one different ways with the handful of inanimate objects surrounding us, all because he talked down to me.*

*Murder in my Oikos is easily cleansed. Bludgeoning a doctor in the middle of a hospital room, while the patient and three first-year residents look on...*

*With my issues of authority, I wouldn't do well in prison.*

*Somehow, I've got to bypass their ladder by erecting my own, for both my sanity and longevity's sake.*

*Insistent palms skate up along my spine, taking me unawares when I hadn't heard anyone approach. Fingertips bite into the fleshy muscles of my shoulders, deeply penetrating to relax the knots.*

*A crawling moan unfurls from my throat, the pleasure exquisite as a wet, hot, soapy male body aligns their front to my back. Arching my spine, I rub my ass against the hardness prodding my cheek.*

*Mind working sluggishly after two dozen eighteen-hour shifts in a row, the steam from the shower creating a fog, and the relaxation from the expert massage... "No, Ramsey!" Flipping around with a glare, I back my command with power.*

"I thought you were Cyrus." Enraged, the pressure behind my eyes building, harsh pants escaping taut lips. "You know better than to tempt me. This has gone too far!"

"The clock just struck midnight." Damp hair sticking to his forehead, those eyes hidden behind the darkened strands, only Ramsey's pouty lips in a downward cast are visible on his face. "It's my twentieth birthday, and I can't do another year as a virgin."

"If Cyrus hasn't popped your cork by now, I'm seriously doubting his skills." Unfathomable, strings of shocked laughter spill from my throat. "We can both agree that the man is hung and insatiable, so I call foul on your virginity status."

"With a woman," Ramsey stresses, managing to pout even more. "There is no one I want more than you, Mira. Never! Just this once, as a birthday gift to me. You'll never have to give me anything for as long as I live."

"You are unbelievable–"

"You want me." Slinking closer, hands cupping my hips. Just the feel of him so close has my eyes slipping shut, has me leaning toward him like budded leaves on a vine facing the sun.

"My desire for you has never been up for debate." Jerking backward, I realize how close I was to taking Ramsey's bait. He knows how difficult it is to deny him anything.

Palms cupping across his face, slicking his hair back to reveal his expression, Ramsey looks me dead on. "How about I just bathe you?" While confident, there's a jittery quality in his voice. "That's not breaking your negotiation with my brother, is it?"

The issue is the potent seed threatening to spurt out the tip of that gorgeous cock. While it took my mind a few extra seconds to catch on, there is a noticeable difference between Cyrus and Ramsey.

Long and broad, Cyrus is hung like a quarter horse. Then there is Ramsey, who Cyrus dubbed Pretty Cock. Average length and girth, with a ripe plum head and a wicked curve.

"I'll behave." Maintaining a straight face, Ramsey reaches for the sponge and bar of soap. "Washing you will be present enough for me this year."

Bitter laughter flows, all of it directed inward, I turn to face the tile. "Kill me," is strangled from my throat the instant contact is made, because the little shit does not use the sponge or the soap, suddenly finding inspiration as a feline.

Nails clawing at the tile, teeth sinking deep into my bottom lip until the coppery tang of blood fills my mouth, the moans rolling through me are disturbingly erotic. A hot tongue carves a path down my spine, "bathing" me, and it does not stop once it reaches my ass crack.

Curling over my tailbone, its natural slick unaided by the rain from the showerhead, that sinful tongue keeps going lower and lower. Strong palms lash out to grip my hips, keeping me on my feet as my knees give out on me, muscles liquifying.

The fact that Ramsey expertly tongues the bud of my ass is not lost on me, before venturing to a more southern locale. Palms shifting from my hips to grip my ass cheeks, Ramsey opens me, hot mouth latching on with hard suction, the force propelling me against the slippery tile, where it's impossible to gain leverage.

Blood igniting in a fiery rush, it takes a patter of heartbeats before the first wave crashes over me. The cold sweat, the contractions in my womb, the insistent clenches in my groin, begging to latch onto something. Not that any of it has to wait long, because Ramsey gives it exactly what it demands, slamming into me without hesitation.

Pounding in long thrusts, the wet slap punctuating the nonsensical guttural groans escaping my lips. Ramsey shifts his hold, palm cupping the front of my throat to keep me on my feet, as he fucks me up against the shower wall as if carnal pleasures is the newest Olympic sport and he's gold-medaling in it.

"Virgin, my ass..." is a raspy accusation, eyeballs fluttering inside my head as another orgasm crests, a hot wash filling me from the inside.

Fingers tightening on my throat, "I can take that next if you like– Cyrus surely can't get enough of it." Cock jerked out of me, Ramsey flips me around. Back sliding down the slick tile, he catches me before my rear makes contact with the bottom of the shower.

Once I'm propped up against the wall again, fingertips grasp the back of my knee, notching it over his hip, and then Ramsey is plunging himself back between my legs, facing me. The shower raining down upon us, hair slicked back until there is nothing hidden between us.

Ramsey is a grown man who plays a boy.

*"You knew the instant I came in here that I wasn't going to leave until I got what I wanted." ...and then he's rolling back into me, as hard as ever. Smooth waves, dragging the curve over and over something sensitive deep inside me.*

*"There's only ever been you for me, and now Cyrus." There's an unspoken vow riding beneath the surface of his words. "A virgin when it came to women? Yes. Innocent? Never with a father and brother named Zamir Elezi."*

*Stunned is the only way to explain it. I'm stunned. As someone who studies emotions like they're a foreign language, where I can read and write the words but I cannot fluently speak it, stunned is the only state of being I can use to accurately describe how I react to the fact that I turn pliant, amenable, submissive, as a usually playful and subservient Ramsey fucks me over and over again, dominating and using me.*

*Lips swollen from insistent kisses. Groin sore from a constant barrage of thrusts. Muscles lax and body sated from innumerable climaxes. Womb contracting to swallow load after load of potent seed.*

*"I help you study," Ramsey explains as he finally pulls free of my body, water long ago gone cold, but the chill is chasing the sleepies away. It took a long time to drain him– I hadn't realized the differing amounts of semen men create, especially when sperm is added to the mix.*

*Leaning into me, a flash of guilt is masked by pressing his forehead to mine. "I tracked your cycle for months." Stark terror slams into me. "I couldn't be your second. I couldn't be your husband. I couldn't be your king... the only thing I've ever wanted in life was to plant the seed for your firstborn."*

*"You... Gods!" Beyond flabbergasted, I fling my hands up and stalk out of the shower stall, leaving the water running. "You manipulated me."*

*Grabbing the soap, Ramsey has the audacity to soap up his well-used cock, lathering the pubic hair decorating his balls. "You're easily manipulatable, Mira."*

*"Do you get the gravity of what you've just done?" Yanking my nightgown off the back of the door, I slip it over my damp body, the fabric sticking to me in a perverse fashion. "Not to mention the*

*fact that I'm not ready to be a mother– I'm still trying to get my footing in residency."*

As if he doesn't have a care in the world, completely delusional, Ramsey continues to bathe himself as I simmer and stew before him. *"Your nursemaid still lives here, Mira. You are far too powerful to put up with bullshit doctors, when you could be the top doctor at your own facility."*

Turning his back to me, those ripe buttocks flexing with every movement, somehow managing to make me drool from both sets of lips, even after the sexual marathon we just battled.

*"As for my brother, you have a bargain. He will not harm you again in any way unless you emasculate him. Zamir doesn't need to know it's mine."*

Sucking in a deep draw of breath, every ounce of blood ready to burst out of the top of my skull. *"Firstly, I'd know, and I do have something called honor."*

*"You also have something called self-preservation, intelligence, and cunning. Zamir doesn't have to know. Your honor can take a flying leap to the sea. Our happiness means more than your honor."*

*"Secondly,"* I continue on as if the madman hadn't just interrupted me. *"You get that I now have to go fuck him, right? The man who put me in the hospital? Because as dumb as a box of rocks as your brother may be when it comes to science and biology, everyone knows you don't carry a child in your womb for over four years."*

Gazing at me over his shoulder, those ochre eyes seem to suggest, *"Really?"*

*"Zamir's dick is small, else he wouldn't be so easily bent about being emasculated. His doughy body suggests he has low testosterone. He's probably shooting blanks, so I have no fear his dribble of seed will overpower the nine loads I just pumped into you. It will take all of three minutes tops, because he's going to be just as stunned stupid as you were when I came in here. He'll probably just sit there the whole time anyway."*

*"You manipulate your brother too, don't you?"* Stunned. That's the only way to explain why I'm not snapping Ramsey's neck.

*"Everyone has their talents– you're all easily manipulatable."* Turning away from me with a scoff, he continues

to wash and rinse. *"Be careful, Mira. If Zamir harms you in any way, Cyrus will exterminate me."*

The noise of complete frustration I release is like nothing I've ever heard before, damp feet stomping from the bathroom. *"Mira!"* Ramsey stops me dead in my tracks. *"You sounded like a real girl just now."*

Unable to contain myself, that noise flows again. *"Hey, Mira?"* flows closer, as if Ramsey stepped out of the shower. *"I'm sure our love child will be a perfectly well-adjusted human being with a sweet disposition. Not at all bullheaded or frustrating or cunning or manipulative."*

Gods help me, I make that noise again, only this time I don't stop to listen to Ramsey's taunting commentary.

Panting roughly the entire time I march down to the king's quarters, still too stunned to form a proper plan, when I am the last person to fly by the seat of my pants. The only advantage I have is that my white nightgown has shrink-wrapped itself to every single curve on my body, fabric translucent, which was no doubt part of Ramsey's insane plan all along.

As Kyrios, I don't bother knocking. I just stalk right in, as I have since my birth. Only Zamir is usually up to things I would have never caught my father doing. But in Zamir's defense, he has behaved himself exceptionally well since he took a meatgrinder to my vagina.

With his father slithering around the villa, creating havoc and torturing the servants, leaving a trail of dead bodies littered in his wake, it would take a serial killer rampage through a small village to make Zamir look bad in comparison.

If there was a way to break through my father-in-law's defenses, we would have found it by now. We've even resorted to ditching the accidental death schemes, poisonings that mimic natural causes, not having a care if we bring a scourge down on the Livas Oikos for outright murdering him, but we cannot break through the army of bodyguards perpetually circling him.

If my king has been up to no good, he's doing it discretely elsewhere, happy when I toss him a female in need of punishment. By punishment, I mean to be put down. Permanently. That's when Zamir's sadism truly shines, and there is a small kernel in my blackened soul that feels slightly sympathetic for the poor female, dependent on the crime she committed against me and mine.

Working like a good boy at a cushioned armchair near his desk, Zamir isn't playacting a businessman. At twenty-five, he's been spearheading our largest source of income for nearly half a decade, while exceling at it too. Science may not be in his wheelhouse, but thieving money, growing money, and keeping money safe and secure surely is.

"My queen?" Eyebrows hitched high in a look of total shock, it reminds me of someone and that someone isn't Ramsey. "Your state of undress is rather questioning."

"I need your seed." Sighing heavily, I stalk toward Zamir, skirting around the coffee table before him. "We had a bargain. You got to get your rocks off on turning my vagina into a blender. Now you have to behave while I extract your seed."

"I–" a sadist rendered speechless is a thing of terrible beauty.

I've witnessed Zamir be confrontational, taunting, bullying, abusive, the lashings of an insecure animal, and downright cruel, even to my standards, but I've never seen him caught off guard before.

"No sleeve," is a warning as I round a stack of files before him, then stop shy of an inch from his knees. "While that might help you get off, it's not just your seed that is important tonight. My vagina has to stay in good repair."

"Uh... um... why tonight?" Flustered, yet intelligent enough to know this is not love-making or lust-feeding or bloodletting, Zamir only unbuttons his trousers.

"I'm ovulating," is all the information he needs to know evidently, seeing as how Zamir hitches up his ass so that he can shove his pants down his thighs, leaving his boxers to cover his groin. "It's a seventy-two-hour window. But sperm tend to stick around for a while in a nice warm womb, awaiting an egg to fertilize, so once should be enough with how potent you are."

That last part earns me a narrow-eyed stare, because it was too close to flattery, or perhaps sarcasm.

"Look, Zamir... I'm a goddamn doctor." Snorting at how ridiculous all of this is, I hitch my nightgown up over my hips, making sure it doesn't slip down my ass. "Psychology was my passion, my hobby of sorts, but I made reproduction my career, can you at least trust me on this?"

"Straddle my thighs and close your eyes." Zamir reveals his vulnerable side, and I realize Ramsey's estimation of his brother was most certainly correct.

Passive while still in a position of power, I hitch my nightgown up higher, then settle myself over his lap, doing my best to not touch him elsewhere. "Are you capable of ejaculation without the aid of torturing your bedpartner?" This is said in a cool, calm voice devoid of any judgment or insult, because I do have a strong sense of self-preservation.

"You're willingly fucking me, Miranda." Those ochre eyes roll to the heavens, that double chin shakes left and right, and a suffering sigh bubbles up past those lips. "Now close your eyes."

"Forewarning, I'm super wet." Leaning on years of playacting a normal person, I allow a bit of sheepishness to seep into my voice. Embarrassment. "I tend to get leaky when I ovulate, my body's way of paving the way, so to speak. I also added a bunch of artificial oil, because I didn't want it to hurt."

"I've seen Cyrus taking a leak," Zamir rumbles in crystal clear annoyance. "You could take a fist to the cunt without issue. If Cyrus is a grower, I'm fucking envious."

"He's just a show-er," I lie through my teeth.

"Good. Now close your eyes– I won't ask you again." Doing as Zamir bid, I hear a rustling sound as he pulls himself out the fly of his boxers, heavily panting as he does so. "I don't expect you to act the part of a whore. No phony orgasm sounds, as we both know that's a myth. It's insulting to hear."

Gods, give me strength!

There is no need to reply to that, so I just flow without hesitation as Zamir moves me, only a single fingertip on my hip to guide me. Even when he was destroying me on our wedding night, nothing but his cock inside the sleeve touched me, his pungent breath burning the back of my neck.

Barely feeling anything but a slight prodding, as if the tip of a thumb is pressed inside me, I come to realize thrusting is not an option. Loathing how I have to grind on top of Zamir, because that involves engaging my over-simulated clit, self-preservation engages. It's either risk getting off on him, which I will hate myself if it happens, or attempt to thrust up and down and embarrass

Zamir, and risk getting my neck snapped in a fit of emasculated rage.

Palms coming to a rest on either side of Zamir's shoulders on the backrest of the chair, I leverage myself back and forth, back and forth, faster and faster, friction building along with my momentum.

Beneath me, a roughly panting Zamir behaves, almost as if he fears touching me will snap me out of it and I'll stop. Eyes slip shut, I drift off after a few minutes, my breathless rasps picking up speed. He's not so much inside me as tucked along my clamshell, engorged head notched along my clit, which presents a serious conundrum for me, because after the shower, anything could spark the fuse.

Unable to help myself, my harsh breaths manifest into audible sounds, fingers biting deep into the upholstery. The slow grind against my clit, the depravity as Zamir slides in his own brother's spendings. I detonate, body spasming over top of him.

Without the aid of pain, I believe even Zamir is shocked he reached completion, probably only because a myth so ingrained was debunked, and it fed the hunger deep inside his depleted ego.

Breaking my word, my eyes automatically open as I crawl off Zamir's lap, catching only a half-second snapshot of what is beneath me. Leaving without another word, I don't open my eyes until I reach the door.

Someone as homophobic as Zamir, he would never see another engorged cock, even though he knows his soft cock in comparison to theirs at the urinal is vastly different. What he'll never discover, which is my saving grace, is how very little ejaculate he releases compared to other men, nary a few drops, most likely all seminal fluid.

Sociopath that I am, even I feel guilt and shame over what I've done, along with the cold wash of pity. The only reason I don't flagellate myself is that I think I just blew Zamir's mind, leaving him sprawled in his chair, sticky cock airing out, along with a transference of semen that belonged to his brother, which will have Zamir believe he just emptied the largest load into my womb. All of which will nourish his ego.

Blindly fleeing the king's quarters, loathing myself for innumerable reasons, my capacity to protect myself is seriously compromised. Something in which I don't realize until I end up plastering my face against the chest of my snake of a father-in-law.

*Fingertips snaring my chin, "Little Miranda," the serpent purrs in a lilting voice, forked tongue both venomous and poisonous. There's always been something about his voice that makes my skin crawl and causes bile to rise in my throat.*

*"You've been a busy, busy girl this evening, haven't you? Fucking both of my sons back-to-back. I must admit, I'm impressed you managed to climax for my namesake."*

*"What do you want?" Wrenching my head to the side, I dislodge his disgusting fingers from my flesh. "If you're here to blackmail me, you ought to reevaluate." Stepping around the human-shaped obstacle filled with nothing but evil, I stalk back down the hallway, suddenly realizing it's too far of a trek back to my quarters.*

*"One word from me and your entire world will implode, my dearest Miranda." Longer legs easily keeping stride with me, only slightly out of breath from most certainly spying on what happened with his son. "What shall you offer me for my silence?"*

*The hard press of an erection against my hip has me snapping. "You have one option, and one option only. I will not even attempt to barter, or bargain, or pay for your silence. I will not invoke my status as the Kyrios of this Oikos that you're currently holding hostage. But the fact remains, you only have one choice."*

*"Do I, now?" Face brightening, a sickening smirk tugs at lips far too familiar to me. "Color me intrigued, my dearest Miranda. Do explain."*

*"Your namesake only loves one person more than he loves himself." Gesturing, as if to say, "This goes without saying." I flip around to glare Zamir Elezi down, unrelenting.*

*"Your only choice is to walk away and stay silent. If it comes down to it, which do you think would be more of a blow to the ego? Me fucking his baby brother, when he has full knowledge of how badly we want one another? Or you and your predatory behavior, attempting to seduce then blackmail me into your bed?"*

*Expression twisted in deep thought, the snake is considering his options, still unsure if I've calculated his risks accurately.*

*"I'm your meal ticket, so you can't actually kill me. Torture me. Annoy me to hell and back, but not actually slaughter me. Zamir only loves Ramsey– his ego will heal from the blow, especially after the performance I just did back there. But if you're*

*the one who tries to overpower his seed, that is a blow that Zamir will not survive. He'll go postal, taking us all down."*

*"But that's only if he finds out." The serpent has the audacity and arrogance to cup his crotch, bulge disgustingly large with a widening damp spot on the front of his trousers.*

*Doing an about-face, I flip around to head back to the king's quarters. "I'll outright tell him the truth. How Ramsey manipulated me the same as he does everyone, then I tried to cover it up by having sex with Zamir. Then how his father tried to blackmail me into sex, because he of all people is so potent and masculine and hung, that his seed will take root."*

*Speaking over my shoulder at a coldblooded immobile snake, I state with total confidence. "The only one making it out of this situation alive is Ramsey." Before I can even blink, he vanishes, leaving me a half dozen paces from Zamir's open door.*

*"Cowards, the whole lot of you." But that's only a half-truth, because the snake is smart, biding its time until the next attack. "I'm a coward too," is muttered underneath my breath as I stalk back to my quarters.*

ML

Blinking out of the memory, Ramsey's horrorstruck face inches from my nose. "I take it the shower is off the table now, huh?"

"You manipulative prick!" Lunging to the side, I tackle Ramsey on the mattress, only to release a heady moan as my erect clit slides against smooth skin, the sensation so much more intense now that there's no hood protecting it. That part of me is continually accessible now, stimulated and needy.

Flesh overheated, moisture flooding between my sprawled thighs, all I can do is release a filthy string of chuckling over my ridiculous reaction to this shameless man. "I'm so beyond manipulatable."

The bastard disrobed while I was stuck in the past.

Giggling like a little kid, Ramsey alligator rolls me beneath him, groaning as our slick skin slides easily against one another, thanks to the almond-scented lotion. Notching us from toes to foreheads, groins snug, Ramsey nuzzles at my nose.

"Instead of a sociopath, I feel like a narcissist–"

"You are neither, Mira," Ramsey says with such conviction that I almost believe him. With a struggle, he unwraps his arms from beneath my back, then rests on his elbows near my ears, bracketing me in while leaning above me. "You're healing is all, no differently than if you had broken a bone. You of all people understand the delicacies of the human psyche."

"The servants have melded into the walls, more so than ever, to the point I have yet to sight one. I have not contacted any of our people, heard from our allies, or been made aware of any threats our enemies may pose."

"It's quiet right now, Miranda, because you are well-respected, even by those who wish to usurp you. You helped place many into power, even those as your competition. They are not ones to strike when someone is in a weakened state, because there is only honor in besting the strongest opponent. It's not sporting to kick someone when they're down, nor is it as challenging or thrilling. Cyrus and our son have kept everything running smoothly– Jasper can become surprisingly charming when it comes to negotiations."

"But what of you and the children and Laverna and her family? I haven't asked how you're dealing with your grief. I haven't seen our children, and it's discomforting to feel guilt over it, as well as a dose of incompetence and bent pride from failing to have a mothering instinct. As the important memories unfold, I am left feeling disquiet, unsettled, because I feel badly for the part I played with your brother."

Inky brows lowered to cover the expression his eyes reveal, Ramsey displays a stoic side I hadn't realized him capable. "You came into the villa through the rear veranda, then walked promptly to your quarters, of course you've seen no one on that short journey. As for the children, we prepared them for your reunion."

"And what of you?"

Lashes lowering, Ramsey shutters the ochre of his eyes, a few tears escaping. "It has been six months, two weeks, and three days since the tragedy, Mira," is barely a breath of a sound, tone infused with mourning and terror.

"I healed as you healed. Cyrus and our son taking care of the Oikos and our outside interests helped them work through their issues. The twins had all of us, Laverna thrilled to be welcomed back into a safe environment. Me helping you heal helped me heal along the way. I was beside myself with grief for at least half of that time. Suffering severe flashbacks, when you saved me from the worst of it. But I'm better than ever now, with a few hiccups every now and again."

"What changed?" While intrigued on the innerworkings of Ramsey's mind, this strong desire to comfort him is new to me. Before, the ghost in the reflection, she simply listened to understand, to educate herself and grow in her craft, while I simply listen to connect with the man cradling me.

The last few memories, whatever occurred has been evoking deeply buried emotions within me. The ghost in the reflection, her name was Miranda Livas, and she has been evoking Mira into becoming the empathetic woman our nature destined us to be before Mother's death nurtured us into an unfeeling sociopath.

"What changed?" Eyebrows hitched high, Ramsey drags me back out of my thoughts. Fingertips fiddle with my hair, and I calculate how long it will take to get it back to its original state. I instinctively know– and by instinctive, I mean the pounding behind my brows –that I'm not supposed to examine what happened to my hair just yet.

"You started to remember me." A queer quirk of Ramsey's lips has me smiling along, but not because it's a kneejerk reaction to hide my emotional shortcomings. I truly wish to smile because he smiles. "You intuitively remembered me, never scared when you woke from sedation, but you stopped asking my name and started calling for me when you awoke."

"Do you think me a monster for the maltreatment of your brother? For the good of humankind, I understand how it benefits us that Zamir is gone. But on an intellectual level, I was fashioned to understand why one behaves as they do. There was a good side to your brother, one he fought to reveal, and it was loathsome how that was lost. I never dared to ask how it came about. Your father was pure evil. Nature versus nurture, I do believe Zamir was nurtured to be the way he was, havocking evil. But none of this changes the fact that I treated Zamir poorly, without respect, emasculating him, and was an unsupportive wife. I lied to him, used him. Tricked him."

"Shh…" Soft whiskered cheek coming in to nuzzle at my chin, Ramsey attempts to comfort me, to wash away my guilt and shame by using a combination of our tears. "I see the protocol is working, as you've yet to remember–"

"Remember what?" Cold dread settles into my soul. I can guess what put me here. Cyrus came right out and said I would be wrong, without the important facts.

"The good will harm you far worse than the bad, I think." Drawing back, Ramsey reaches for my hand. "If I could, I'd permanently take that last memory from you, finally experience all of it for myself. But I was conscious for the part that will hurt you the most, because you will finally learn the devastating effects of grief."

"I don't understand," slurs in confusion, as I allow Ramsey to tug me from the bed.

"Jasper, and Oona and Oscar, there's a reason you're to not see them yet. You're not meant to understand yet either. Tomorrow will bring the last two memories you listed, the triggers thus far so accurate that my awe at your intelligence only grows. You've done revolutionary work that will be respected for decades, maybe even centuries after your death, with you as patient zero."

Ramsey towing me across the room, I stumble to keep up, my foot twisting in the bedsheet that had fallen to the rug. "Where are we going?"

"Tomorrow will be painful, let us play this evening." Drawing me into the bathroom, mischievous sparks firing in those ochre eyes, Ramsey reaches for the taps. "Let us shower– it's been nearly eighteen years. I think it past time for a do-over."

"Saying that makes me feel ancient." Blinking rapidly, I'm confused as to why I even said that, let alone thought that. Alike Father, gaining wisdom was an achievement I strived to gain. As I aged, the more respect I was offered. No longer a silly ninny teenage girl, I was seen as someone whose voice mattered, gender no longer a curse nor a gift.

Snickering at my ludicrousness, "Gods! I sounded like a girl just then, didn't I?"

Pouty lips curled into a naughty smirk, Ramsey knows better than to reply to that. Stepping into the stone enclosure, the shower heads rain down upon his body, glistening invitingly. Those lean muscles, firm beneath my fingertips. Rounded buttocks flexing with every movement. Dark skin taking on the smooth texture of velvet, where it becomes impossible to resist… to touch or kiss or lick or bite, leaving my brand behind.

After two decades of reining myself in, not allowing myself even the smallest of tastes. Ignoring the sparks of joy felt when I was the one who caused Ramsey to laugh or smile or smolder. Avoiding our connection, not because it was vital to his safety and longevity, but because it was vital for mine, knowing deep down in my soul it would have killed Ramsey to lose me.

None of that matters any longer. Not only can I taste the forbidden fruit, I can devour it, consume it, draw it deep inside me and keep it as mine forever. For it has ripened, safe without buzzards flocking overhead, no longer poisonous to ingest.

Stepping into the shower, the warmth of the cascading rain heating me from the outside in, when this man strokes the flames from the inside out. "Husband." Hands skating down velvety flanks, a quiver of anticipation crests throughout me. "You're all mine now."

"I was always yours, Mira." Lust slowing my reactions, Ramsey uses that to his advantage, flipping around to reverse our positions, until my back is to the cool stone, with his front pressing against mine.

"As much as I enjoyed our first time, I'm not as shameless as you believe me to be." Suddenly sober, serious, when that is not Ramsey's natural state of being. Those expressive eyes capture me in their gaze, begging me to understand.

"I was a spoiled boy who manipulated you into doing something you weren't ready to do." Chin jerking to the side in a violently rapid movement, Ramsey breaks our connection. "I won't apologize for the events that transpired because of my behavior, but I do owe you an apology for forcing you to get pregnant, which ended up causing you to be forced to become pregnant the next time. I won't do that to you again, that is my vow to you as someone who just recently grew up after learning many painful lessons."

Beseeching him, palms landing on his water-slick hips, "Ramsey–"

"No more dark and dourly conversations– that's not the mood I'm trying to set." Ducking his head to peer at me through the thick lace of his lashes, Ramsey grins, and with it sparks a chain reaction within me, where I can't help but join him.

"I dreamed of consummating on your bed, especially with all its erotic carvings," Ramsey trails off, dangling the reasoning for the shower before me. Embarrassment floods my cheeks, not something I'm accustomed to experiencing.

"You will let go for me this time, Mira," is a command, when Ramsey is anything but commanding. "You will let go, and it will be the ultimate release. Your bladder will be emptied, so you needn't fear embarrassment while we make love in bed."

"Or I could just piss in the toilet," flows deadpan. Just because I'm experiencing feelings, doesn't mean I won't choose the most logical choice.

"Where's the fun in that?" A string of naughty chuckles rumble up Ramsey's throat, a look of pure mischief that has me going on alert. "I want to try a few new things in here, things that I've always fantasized. Fantasies you created in more than just me," is loaded with inuendo that goes over my head.

"Generally, reality never lives up to the fantasy," I remind him, knowing this to be true.

"Trust me, reality will be even better." Manipulating me in the finest of ways, Ramsey's touch both soothes the nerves and ignites the desires. A peppering of kisses flutters along my jawline, fingertips ghosting across slick hips, running downward to open my nether lips.

Ramsey's brand of convincing is downright pleasurable, which is why he's a master manipulator.

"Curiosity." The rough raspy quality in Ramsey's tone has me looking down to where he's placed distance between us. Cock in hand, swollen head ruddy with need, just peeking out the opening of his foreskin, already covered in a layer of precum to smooth the path.

A single nudge almost lands me on my ass, lotion activated from the spray in the shower. Sliding and slipping and flailing about, I try to regain my footing, only to have my ass skate along the rock wall.

Giggling in delight, Ramsey catches me with his free hand. "Never thought I'd see the day the great Miranda Livas, Kyrios of the Livas Oikos, rendered senseless by the mere brush of my cockhead over hers."

"Sensitive," is all I can grit out, body slipping and sliding further from quivering with intense hunger. Ramsey is… beautiful. Inside and out, heart and soul, everything good in the world is cradled inside Ramsey Elezi.

"You're missing yours, so I want to share mine." Naughty. Naughty. Naughty. Ramsey reaches for the three inches peeking out of the protection of my clamshell, annoyingly indicating how devastatingly I desire the man in front of me.

"She'll be safe and snug in here with me," is a rolling purr as Ramsey snuggles the head of my clit next to his cockhead, then pulls down on his foreskin, connecting us together.

Pulling and releasing, Ramsey drags his extra skin up and down my clit, jacking me, allowing me to penetrate him in a way I never contemplated. Covering and uncovering, revealing how swollen with need it has become. Just a nudge, the lightest of contacts between our heads, and a warm spurt fills the protective skin surrounding us.

Overexcited, it may have been me, because I've yet to master those muscles. It may have been him, but all I discover is that it detonates Ramsey. In a violent quick lash of a snake striking out, Ramsey has me flipped against a slick stone wall, cheek, tits, and clit making contact first.

Just as the first time between us, Ramsey is shoved deep inside me from behind before I can react, our combined grunts of madness echoing through the shower chamber. Seeking leverage, a palm cups the front of my throat, fingers biting in with bruising force, and then the thrusting starts. Ramsey is skilled, able to conserve energy by moving his hips with only tightening and releasing the muscles in his buttocks. Smooth rolling movements, weaving through both our bodies, the curve of that stunning cock gliding over and over that sensitive spot deep inside my canal.

My remaining nipple and elongated clit rub constantly across the slick stone, the stimulation like nothing I've ever experienced before, combined with how my husband is owning me from behind, it's my turn to detonate.

It's impossible to climax while not allowing all of my muscles to let go. Going bowstring taut, the orgasm has crested, refusing to fall from the precipice. Muscles shaking with the need to relax, even with the warm rain showering down upon us, a cold sweat flashes throughout my body, beading my skin.

"Mira," Ramsey whispers in my ear, purposefully assaulting that spot deep inside me, a spot that also makes me feel as if I need to release my bladder. Erections are bad enough in the way my body has been fashioned, losing bladder control is not a welcome surprise.

Palm tightening on the front of my throat, fingers biting bruisingly deep, demanding I obey his command. "Let go, dammit!" is a fierce snarl in my ear. "You can't always be in control. Just let go."

Slumping against the slick wall, the litany of moans, groans, and curses echo around the shower chamber. Palms finding no purchase, I trust Ramsey to keep me on my feet, simply by tightening his palm against the front of my throat, trust he won't harm me.

Warmth cascading down my thighs to swirl around the drain, the release is unlike anything I've experienced before. A puppet with all but one string cut, I'm connected to the master by the cock lodged deep within my body, as he empties himself within me. First with his seed, then again with something more astringent, flushing his seed away.

Mind swirling to keep up, body confused as to what's happening as shocking warmth floods from the outside in, aftershocks continually quaking up and down my spine... my husband is behind me, no doubt experiencing the strongest orgasm of his entire existence, same as I am.

On and on, a kink fed I didn't realize he had, Ramsey is panting rough rasps against the shell of my ear, bursting laughter rumbling up his chest throughout all of it. Shaking tremors, those fingers release my throat, only for the arm to quickly catch me before I fall. Forearm braced across my belly from hip to hip, flopping forward like a ragdoll. Ramsey struggles to keep us both on your feet, slick from lotion, seed, and urine.

"Guess you know my kink now, huh?" Shocked laughter radiates around the shower chamber, but not nearly as shocked as I feel. Suddenly taking on the quality and traits my name encompasses, I turn amenable... pliable. Submissive.

Another hunger fed, Ramsey is delighted over how I don't balk as he takes care of me. Washing me thoroughly inside and out, making sure there is nothing of his left inside me.

"You only have one person to blame for it, Mira," is murmured wryly as a towel is wrapped around my torso. "Watching you piss on my brother, I'd never self-combusted before, but that did it. Gods!"

More delighted laughter echoes around us, Ramsey's ochre eyes blazing bright, taking on a light as if he's consumed intoxicants. "All I wanted to do in that moment was whip out my cum-covered cock and piss all over you. It wasn't to put you in your place, I just... I have no idea why, but it's all I wanted to do."

Utterly shameless, without a shred of embarrassment, Ramsey picks me up off my feet, then carries me back into the bedroom. "Now that I've done it, I want to do it again already."

"Ramsey," cautions from the bed, startling me senseless. Arms wedged behind his neck, Cyrus is tucked in on his side of the bed, just as he has been since Mother no longer slept in this bed. I've never slept alone until the facility. "Behave," is a chastisement that only has Ramsey releasing a string of filthy chuckles.

"You wouldn't let me do it to you, remember?" Ramsey has no shame, placing me in the middle of the bed, situating me until I'm facing a stoic Cyrus, then he crawls up onto the bed to snuggle in behind me.

In this moment, I discover where Ramsey practiced enough to become the Gold Medalist in Sex. That rolling thrust maneuver, where he glides the curve of his cock over and over and over the spot deep inside me, guaranteeing I'll ignite... Cyrus was Ramsey's willing penetration victim.

With their physical differences and personality traits, I assumed it would be the other way around. I've learned yet again to never assume, especially since Ramsey never fails to get what he wants.

"If I asked enough, you'd eventually say yes," Ramsey whispers from behind me, snuggling in deeper, leaving me and Cyrus to face each other while lying on our sides.

"Allowing you to spurt cum inside me is well enough," flows in a dry voice, hiding the amusement and affection lying beneath. "No clue why you're so obsessed with pissing on people in the shower. I indulge you enough already."

This insane warmth is blooming within me, radiating from the center of my chest to my extremities, consuming what was left of the ghost reflected in the mirror, or perhaps it is at long last releasing her from the reflection.

Wrapping myself tightly around Cyrus, with Ramsey snuggling to curl perfectly aligned down my spine, never have I experienced such a sensation before. The warmth. The safety. The security. The happiness.

With Ramsey's father holding our Oikos hostage, I could never indulge in my addiction to Ramsey. Cyrus was in my bed and heart, occupying Ramsey from pushing it too far until I would be harmed.

Shuddering in relief, our world is a different place than minutes before the tragedy took place. Reaching back, I grab Ramsey's wrist, drawing his arm to wrap around my waist, holding him as tightly to my back as I hold Cyrus to my front.

We needed this, the ghost in the reflection and me– we finally feel safe.

Palm cupping over Cyrus's shoulder, my fingertips seeking the scar at the side of his neck. "No, Mira," flows from a raw throat, the inflection in his voice is absolutely gutted. "No. Enjoy the rest of our night, please," dives down into a pleading tone.

After decades of sharing a bed with this man, most of them as grown adults, as if we were husband and wife, the past six months feel like days to me, days since I retained short-term memory and allowed it to be retained into long-term memories. There was no distance of time that made my mind murky, Cyrus's body as familiar to me as if I just touched it yesterday.

"Cyrus," croaks out, palm settling over his chest, feeling the scars and the odd texture beneath my palm. Leaning forward, I press his gift to me against the sacrifice he made for me. "No," is a delusional protest, as if I say it enough it won't be true. "No."

"Miranda." Palm cupping the side of my face, Cyrus pulls me forward until our foreheads rest against one another. Once he's positive I'm going nowhere, not that Ramsey would allow it from behind me, Cyrus cups my false breast.

"I know what you're going to say in defense of me, and I understand on an intellectual level that you're right." Palm squeezing, fingertips feathering over numb skin, all I feel is pressure and a slight temperature difference. No sensitivity in a body part that isn't mine, not the skin nor what lies beneath it.

Frozen silent behind me, Ramsey tries very hard to offer Cyrus and me privacy. "My entire existence is in protection of you, our Kyrios, the love and light of my life. I failed you, no matter how hard you try to defend me. The donation is nothing what anyone who cared for you wouldn't have done. The sacrifice returned my honor, allowing me to stop obsessing over my failure."

"I–"

"Let it go, Mira," is whispered against the nape of my neck, Ramsey snuggling in deeper, shameless enough that he wedges his erection between my buttocks. "You should know better than anyone not to argue with someone over how their mind functions. Cyrus needed to do this for you, and it comforted him to do so, so just let it go."

"Your breast should have never been taken from you. Now when I look at it, instead of seeing the travesty committed, experiencing nothing but rage, I feel a strong connection between us, because you share the same flesh as I."

"Since awakening– all my life, if I'm being honest –I'm struggled with the balance. Whether or not someone does things for me because they want to or because they feel obligated. I want everyone to be here because they trust me, respect me, no longer because they fear me."

"Don't act like a woman and overthink every single detail," is said in a cool tone, then a heartbeat later, Cyrus releases taunting laughter, both to insult and to spark humor into a dark conversation. "Gods! A girly acting Miranda Livas, my mind can't wrap around it."

"I love girly Mira, she lets me have anything I want," flutters against the back of my neck, lips curled into a smirk, which causes mine to rise upward as well.

"When didn't she?" Cyrus mutters wryly. In the dark of my quarters, I expect to see him both grinning and rolling his eyes heavenward. "Ramsey is the most indulged person in our world. At least he stopped asking for things we weren't willing to give."

"You said no dark conversation," Ramsey chastises Cyrus, reaching around me to tweak whatever body part was exposed, causing a meep of shock. "It's playtime," is punctuated by the rock of his hips, dragging his heated length down the crack between my buttocks, leaving a cooling trail of precum in its wake.

"Insatiable," is whispered about Ramsey, but it's breathed between my lips as Cyrus comes in for a kiss. Palm skating across my shoulder, down my arm, curving around my hip, going in a downward trajectory. His touch ignites tiny sparks, anticipatory bumps beaded on my flesh, but a cold wash of embarrassment.

"No." Braceleting his wrist, I halt Cyrus from touching between my thighs. It was different with Ramsey, as he was there when I awoke, there for my discovery, but also because he didn't know my body better than I know it myself.

"It's different, Cy." Unexpected insecurity leaks into my voice, leaving me feeling unsettled and disquiet, because it's not something I'm used to feeling, when I'm not used to feeling anything but the strongest of emotions. "I'm not how you remember me."

"Shh…" is breathed against my lips, Cyrus talking me down. Calming me with his touch and with his presence. "I will desire you when we're octogenarians. My cock will be a shriveled-up prune, sack swinging to my knees. Your nipple will be kissing your belly button, and your clamshell will resemble loose flaps billowing with a windsock flopping about from the cleft… and we still won't be unable to keep our mouths and hands off each other."

A sharp burst of chuckles vibrates against my neck, the body back there quaking to the point the mattress is shaking. "What a picture Cyrus paints…" Ramsey trails, endless amusement riding his tone. "Mira, Cyrus sucks my cock– he'll enjoy yours just as much."

"Uh! Ohhh…" drawn out on a moan, the pleasure is indescribable as Cyrus nudges my clit with the head of his cock, rubbing it back and forth, up and down, acquainting them with each other. Then he's sliding deeper, seeking the oil dripping from my clamshell, using it to push inside of me without any pain.

A visceral switch within me is flipped, because this is familiar to me, as familiar as my own face staring back in the mirror. I'll never not recognize Cyrus as the other half of me. Facing one another, his length joining us as one. Notching my knee against his hip, rocking and swirling, trying to get closer and closer, clit seeking friction in the thatch of his pubic hair…

A cock nudges me from behind, refusing to be forgotten nor ignored. The dampness spurting out is fiery hot, mixing with my own oil to pave the path. "Mira, please trust me– I'd never harm you."

In this, I will forever trust Ramsey. His father was nothing but the agony of delivering pain. His brother tried so desperately to clutch the softer side of himself. While Ramsey has never been about anything but the decadence of pleasure.

A nudge. That's all it takes. Just a gentle nudge asking for entrance, slipping slightly from the bud between my buttocks to where Cyrus is rooted… and the blood-curling screaming starts.

## ꮯM𝕃

*"Do you think the garnets are enough?" Someday, but that day is not today, Zamir will start sounding confident in himself instead of forever self-conscious. "I thought the blood-red jewel would be good symbolism."*

*"Yes." Turning my face to the side, I hide my smirk against his thigh. Resting on the rug by my husband's feet, palm draped over his knee, I fight back my amusement, for he would see it as chiding not affectionate teasing.*

*A tightrope balance Zamir and I walk. His ego is fragile, just the slightest thing will set him off, even for me that's a terrifying thing to experience. As long as our society sees him as our king, me as his loving wife, and our children as coming from his loins, Zamir is pleased.*

*It's natural in our society for Zamir to have a mistress and a dozen more. Whereas my having a lover would make Zamir a cuckhold, losing the respect of our allies and enemies. Since Zamir sees Cyrus as virile and masculine, he doesn't take it as offense, especially since those same allies and enemies respect Cyrus as my partner. By extension, Cyrus is Zamir's asset, a tool in his considerable stable, strengthening him because of the connection Cyrus has with his wife.*

*We've found a balance, and in that balance we've discovered a fondness for one another. I ignore Zamir's proclivities. He feeds his hungers outside of my knowledge. His ego is fed by the fact that my fondness is obvious to our allies and enemies. We share three children, which also lends to his overall virility.*

"I'd say a garnet encrusted collar is exactly what a sadist should gift his lifelong masochist." *Rolling my eyes upward, I make sure Zamir can see how genuine I'm being.*

*Zamir often calls me out on how he can't read if I'm lying or not. Instead of defensiveness, I always thank Zamir when he says that to me, as that is the highest compliment one can pay a sociopath, as we excel at acting like a normal human being.*

"The symbolism for bloodshed would be a good one." *To hide my smirk, I nip at his thigh, leaving a slight damp spot on his trousers from my saliva.*

"I've behaved– I haven't accidentally killed her yet, and we've been together for five years tomorrow night."

"Yes, but what about purposefully killed?"

"Well…" *is trailed off, an evil giggle punctuating the air.* "When I misbehave, I do it in a grand fashion, my queen. But it's been nearly two years since I fed that particular hunger. Sephira is surprisingly durable, and I've learned the limits the human body can sustain. I no longer use the sleeve. We've tried to touch your way, but neither are built for that when we're together. I respect that you only desire pleasurable touching."

"Intellectually, I understand your sadism and Sephira's masochism, but I do struggle to truly empathize, even after you've shown me a taste by allowing me to witness your connection to your mistress."

"You don't empathize well, my queen," *Zamir murmurs wryly, fingers sinking deep into my hair, nails scratching at my scalp. All affection must have a little bite of pain-dealing with it to truly entertain Zamir.*

*Over the years, Zamir has tried to embrace the softer part of himself, similar to how hard I fight to reclaim my emotions. Nature versus nurture. At one point, Zamir would have had a similar temperament as his brother, but as the eldest, their father shaped Zamir in his image. I've yet to discover what nurtured me to cut off my true nature, but that day is not today.*

"Definitely drape Sephira in bleeding garnets— the symbolism is perfect." Smiling up at Zamir, it genuinely reaches my eyes. His love for his mistress makes me feel hope, because two creatures of opposing temperaments found the perfect counterbalance in one another, their needs met without harming innocents.

"I believe you should ask Cyrus's permission to allow my guards to service you with their bodies, my queen. Last time in your bed, you begged and pleaded, but we all respected your earlier edict."

"Gods!" A filthy little chuckle bubbles up my throat, body igniting in a hot wash of remembrance. Zamir has a fondness for torture, managing to turn pleasure into a torturous event as well. "I lost count after twenty-seven climaxes."

"Imagine how much better it would be if you allowed Ayres and Jax to penetrate you with their flesh instead of blown-glass."

Gods! Those glass phalluses! After Zamir's body is drained of seed, he enjoys torturing me with two phalluses at once, until physically exhausting himself, then he sics his guards upon me. Tied to the posters on my bed, they twist me into unimaginable shapes, mimicking the carvings. By dawn, I can barely walk, yet I sleep the sleep of the dead, relaxed more than ever in life, mind entirely shut down.

"It's not..." Rolling my cheek along Zamir's thigh, I try to process my emotions. "I struggle, as I don't exactly understand what I feel. I would very much enjoy being tortured by your guards, but I don't wish to hurt Cyrus either."

"You enjoyed it when I invited Sephira to entertain my darker hungers while my guards continued to service you with orgasm torture. Perhaps Cyrus would like to join them. This play has brought us closer together, relaxed us so. Why does it have to be one or none?"

"Apologies," flows from the open doorway to the king's quarters, Cyrus attempting to back up before he truly interrupts us. His expression is shuttered, emotions hidden. "Ramsey was most insistent that I enter."

To this day, I always jump slightly, as if caught in the act. I always feel dishonorable when caught gazing at Ramsey when he makes me laugh or smile, as if I'm betraying Cyrus. But this is decidedly worse. Zamir might be my husband, but I still feel discomfort after we're intimate, as if I've betrayed Cyrus yet again.

It makes my heart ache. As Zamir turns more human, I've discovered parts of my sociopathology chipping away, where I feel things. I feel things strongly, and it's hard to handle it after nearly four decades of only feeling the most violent of emotions.

"That was my plan." Palms planted against Cyrus's back, Ramsey pushes him inside the king's quarters to join us. "Interrupt them. Join them."

No need to make accusations, I merely raise an eyebrow in question, knowing Ramsey's hand is in this.

"I did not plan that," Zamir goes on the defensive. Relaxed around me, those muscles in his thighs tighten up the instant he believes someone will doubt his word. "My brother may be pretty and sweet and blissful about taking care of others, but he is highly calculating, you know this, my queen."

"Most certainly has his signature written all of it." Smiling up at Ramsey, because I cannot, I wink at Cyrus. "But if anyone is uncomfortable, they're not being held hostage– they may leave."

Personal relations are vastly different than professional orders. It bothers me how if I asked, I would receive. When I wish they were here because they truly wanted to be.

We weren't being sexual with one another, merely seated while having an intimate conversation. Cyrus has always been uncomfortable around Zamir, and Zamir has always been uncomfortable around Cyrus. This tension is obvious when we host events and everyone in the villa can sense the vibe they exude.

Then there is Ramsey... who falls to land on the sofa, practically draping himself over his brother's body, reminding me of how Oona and Oscar are always seated as such. "You need a haircut," is whispered in a teasing breath, fingertips tugging at inky strands. At thirty-seven, Ramsey still has the tendency to behave as a baby brother.

My eldest has a long life ahead of him to be pestered, and he most certainly has the temperament of his parents. I have no idea how our twins ended up so silly and playful, when their parents are anything but.

Indulging Ramsey, all Zamir does is give him the side-eye, not even bothering to bat the hand that is fluttering in front of his face. Compartmentalized, Zamir seeks his affection through pain, *allows physical affection from Ramsey only, and seeks sexual release from me.*

*"When you asked if they allowed me to watch them..."* Ramsey trails off, righting himself on the sofa, eyes never leaving the open door to the king's quarters, where Cyrus is just standing inside the threshold. *"You were surprised that they don't allow me even that little taste."*

*"You're forbidden, Ramsey,"* thick and choking, this is said with an air of tragedy. *"I don't wish to know what you and Cyrus do in private, nor can I have you intrude on my time with Cyrus, because it makes the temptation far too great, and I'm not strong enough to resist."*

*"You know I don't care any longer,"* is spoken down at me. *"Jasper just turned seventeen. The twins are eight. Our people would feel joyous if we had another child."*

*Long ago, Zamir confided in me how after Jasper, he didn't care the paternity of our children, as long as our people believed the children to be his. Fearful he's impotent, Zamir would rather our children be fathered by Cyrus or Ramsey, than there be no children at all, as that would be a sign of his impotence.*

*"It's not you Miranda is fearful about,"* is a rough rasp as Cyrus steps farther into the room, feet coming to rest butted up against mine, seeking to comfort and support. *"You must know he's biding his time to end the plan he set forth into motion twenty years ago."*

*Heart beating a rapid tattoo inside my chest, I gaze up at Cyrus with terror in my eyes, unable to handle this conversation. I'm pragmatic in all arenas in life save one, because I am powerless to stop it.*

*Sensing my disquiet, Ramsey is a soothing balm on frayed nerves. "I was curious, you were curious, and you said something intriguingly filthy that sparked my interest. Tell them, brother."*

*Dark skin flushing darker, Zamir gazes down at his hands, unable to look any of us in the eye as he speaks. "I was seated in a chair, thoroughly entranced as Jax and Ayres tortured Miranda on her bed... and a thought popped into my mind, and I've yet to shake it."*

*"What?"* flows in a hoarse voice– part accusatory, part terrified. Cyrus crouches on the balls of his feet, hand possessively cupping the crown of my skull, drawing me to his chest and away

*from the brothers on the sofa. I allow it, simply because I do understand that Cyrus and I belong to one another.*

*"Is it a difficult procedure to reverse the vasectomy?" Zamir stuns Cyrus, body bladed against mine, and that is not something that occurs ever. "I can only imagine how rewarding it would be to seed Miranda so deeply, especially with how hung you are. Much more rewarding than a procedure in a clinic."*

*"What are you playing?" Voice tight with annoyance, Cyrus drags me a few feet away, then shifts to seat us both on the rug, facing the sofa. "You toy. You dangle the carrot as bait, and once we reach for it, you jerk it away."*

*"I'm not my father," Zamir breathes in a harsh tone, causing both Cyrus and me to shudder at the violence laced within. "After my queen and I made amends, I've been nothing but respectful of your union."*

*"Tell him." Ramsey smiles, attempting to put us at ease, but it's with great difficulty. Ramsey is beloved by his father and brother, never truly experiencing the depths of their evil. He loves them as much as they love him. "It sounds exhilarating."*

*Suddenly bashful, Zamir flashes a look at his brother, then goes back to gazing at his hands clasped in his lap. "Once Cyrus's vasectomy is reversed, I thought of an idea. As I said, my guards with Miranda sparked the idea. Ramsey tracks her cycle. We could spend an entire seventy-two hours in bed, taking turns seeding her, torturing orgasm after orgasm from her. Whoever's seed fertilizes her womb is the winner."*

*"The winner?" Cyrus mutters dryly for me.*

*"Not forever," Ramsey scoffs, smile flattened into a taut line. "Just for fun. A little manly play. Bragging rights just between us. Instead of simply feeling a paternal connection to our children, it would be more real, because we'd be there when they were conceived."*

*"I'll think about it," Cyrus states firmly. Then thinking the better of it, palms skate up and down my arms in a soothing rhythm. "This is wholly Miranda's decision. She was quite literally trapped into conceiving Jasper. Then forced into conceiving the twins. If she doesn't wish to have more children, that is her decision."*

*"I will think it through," is whispered softly, mind conflicted, body completely on board with the idea. The dampness between my thighs, the tightly budded nipples, the sparks radiating across my flesh. It's not entirely sexual though, as I never felt more feminine or connected to my children than when I was carrying them within my body and nursing them at my breast.*

*"Cyrus will need to decide for himself on the procedure." Autonomy has always been a luxury Cyrus and I could not afford. He was clamped when we were teens, even though he agreed, there was truly no decision on his part. Just as, even though I agreed, there never any decision to have children on my part.*

*"Zamir has a suggestion," Ramsey drags me kicking and screaming from my thoughts.*

*"I do?" is rumbled with amusement next to him. "News to me, brother."*

*"You wanted to see, as do I." With a nudge, Ramsey nonverbally reminds him of a conversation that took place in a private setting.*

*A string of embarrassed chuckles flees Zamir's lips, face flushing brightly. "A test of sorts." Jumping up from his seat, he gestures with his hand to the cushion he vacated. "If would you," is said to Cyrus. "Please sit here and allow Miranda to pleasure you. If we experience no envy or possession... it would be best to explore it now, versus in the middle of conceiving our child."*

*The logic is sound and so very Zamir-like.*

*Sensing Cyrus's unease, I glance over my shoulder to catch the hidden expression on his face. He silently asks me for guidance.*

*This is Zamir, my husband of over twenty years. This is Cyrus, my soul mate since our births. Zamir understands our dynamic better than Cyrus. Cyrus is already feeding the unending hunger in one brother, he is terrified he'll have to take on another, one he doesn't particularly enjoy in any capacity.*

*With a quick jerk of my chin, I cut off that line of thinking within Cyrus. Zamir has no attraction toward men. Jax and Ayres have been with him since they were boys together, never once touching.*

*Zamir lives vicariously, having been cursed with a small member and a sparse amount of semen. He lasts seconds once stimulated. Which is why he had used the sleeve while feeding his sadistic hungers. Now he uses a harness with blown-glass phallus on me, mimicking all the sex acts, and once he's tired, he lives vicariously through his guards.*

*We tease one another. I lack empathy because Zamir has my share. He is directly tied to whomever he is torturing, experiencing the strongest of emotions. He reacts as if he's the one committing the acts when his guards act as his proxy.*

*Leaning forward, palm resting lightly on Cyrus's chest, I whisper in his ear. Even though it is rude, I don't wish to upset Zamir with the truth, bruise his already fractured ego or have him believe to be teased.*

*"He doesn't covet your cock in the sense you are imagining." Shifting to rest on my shins, I press deeper against Cyrus, muscles shuddering from the blissful contact. "He will vicariously derive pleasure as if your cock is his. It's not voyeurism."*

*Nodding in understanding, Cyrus settles a hand over mine, firmly pressing my palm to his chest, then he rises to his considerable height. Escorting me to the sofa, he lowers himself to the cushion, helping me sink lower down to the rug.*

*Fingertips automatically going to his fly– "No, have Miranda do it. I want to watch." Zamir practically begs, voice warbling with need. "I want to pretend it's me."*

*"Me too," flows softly from Ramsey, shifting to the side to press up against Cyrus, going as far as to wrap his arm along the back of the cushion. "Go slow."*

*With a pair of quirked lips, Cyrus headbutts Ramsey in the shoulder, a trail of flirty laughter rumbling up his chest. "Behave."*

*"This is me behaving," sounds as if it's coming from an excitable child. "Gods! Mira, hurry. This is killing me."*

*Beyond keyed up, the three of them don't need me to put on an act, no seduction necessary. On an intellectual level, I understand the dynamics taking place, knowing this doesn't so much have to do with me as bonding them together, tightly weaving them in a socially acceptable manner as men.*

*No great seductress of otherworldly beauty, just the woman they all care for in varying degrees. My ego is based in the power of intelligence, so this understanding doesn't wreak havoc within me.*

Button popped, zipper slowly lowered to amp up their anticipation, fingertips slip into the slit of Cyrus's fly, wrapping loosely around hard flesh. Pulsating heat, the flutter of excitement pounds beneath my touch, slick dampness pumping out to pave the way.

The sharp exhalation of breath beside me has moisture pooling between my legs, skirts offering no protection as it trickles down the inside of my thighs. Womb clenching, begging to be filled.

The sound echoing isn't from Ramsey, even though he is bright-eyed with anticipation, licking at his pouty lips as if he wishes to take over for me. No, it was Zamir, impressed with the display of male virility plucked from inside those trousers.

To appease all three of them, I scoop out the heavy twin globes, potent enough to seed this entire Oikos and beyond.

Lips parted, tongue extended, I roll my eyes upward and to the side, gazing at my husband as my mouth engulfs my lover's cock. A purr of pleasure escapes me, the decadent taste always affecting my nether parts in the most delicious of ways.

With a whimper of pain, Zamir's palm lands heavily on my shoulder, catching himself before he fell to his behind on the rug. Knees weakened, the look of utter longing– not to taste the cock himself, but an unanswered wish to be as virile as Cyrus.

"Gods! Miranda, suck him to the root." Fingertips clench bruisingly so, nails digging in deep enough to break skin. "Please, my queen."

Acquiescing, mouth open wide, with two decades of experience, Cyrus fills my mouth to the root, head nestled snugly inside my throat. A spirt of semen adds a maddening flavor while paving the path, as Cyrus struggles not to jerk his hips forward to thrust deeply.

"Please, brother!" Ramsey's voice pitches high, visibly gyrating on the sofa cushion next to us. "Please, this is misery!"

Zamir's, "Yes!" is eclipsed by Cyrus's sharp bark of, "Gods! Do it before I die!"

Taking pride in my work, head rising and lowering, tongue dragging along the engorged vein on the underside, I have no idea what their communication is about until Ramsey is scuttling across the rug, my skirts flung over my buttock, then he is balls deep before I can even react. Body eagerly swallowing all he has to offer.

The song that ejects from my throat is a deep and crawling moan, going on and on, even after the initial wave of pleasure fades. Above me, Zamir sways, suspiciously sounding as if he too is close to climax.

"No more, brother." That palm moves, halting Ramsey as he curves over my back, producing a series of whimpers and a string of profanity from a man denied his fun after more than a seventeen-year wait. "Don't stretch her out fully yet. I want to know what she sounds like as she sinks down on Cyrus's horse cock."

Womb clenching, enough oil leaking from my shell to support a full-fledged orgy, I'm not one to take direction. But this time, this time it's exactly what I want. On the edge of climax, I can't wait to sink down onto Cyrus, flesh contracting to milk his cock, wishing for not the thousandth time that he could gift his seed to me.

Moving before neither Ramsey nor Zamir can react, I rise to straddle Cyrus's hips, hand grasping that slick shaft, then I drop down on it with all my weight, the wailing sound spilling from me unlike anything I've released before.

The climax rushes through me as if I careened off the cliffside and landed against a rock wall. Body jerking in stops and starts, nails barely able to find purchase on the sofa cushion, they're not faring any better than I am.

A gargling grunt is expelled beneath me, Cyrus using all the self-control he possesses to halt his climax, a wash of heat flooding my canal. Ramsey is whimpering and cursing, cock drooling against my buttocks. Then there is Zamir, shuddering as if just the thought of me sinking down onto that humungous cock, along with the song we all created, was too much to bear.

"May I please make use of her rear?" Ramsey begs in a guttural tone, sounding beyond unhinged. Not waiting for confirmation, he fists his cock and begins rooting around behind me, sparks of pleasure radiating outward with every brushing pass.

"Do you want me to take you within my mouth?" is said to Zamir, voice lowering in pitch. "They won't see."

Nodding sheepishly, Zamir reaches out to cup my breast. "This one is my favorite. You always latched the babies onto it first, and it fascinated me how warm and happy and healthy you made them feel."

*Heart bleeding, because Zamir had that feeling of safety tragically taken from him when he was a small boy, just as I lost my mother. I loosen the tie on my blouse, allowing his skin to come in contact with my breast.*

*Reaching out, fingers seeking Zamir's zipper, Cyrus is still beneath me, as Ramsey struggles to press into a location that had only previously been entered by a narrow glass phallus. Nudging me, slipping in my slick oil, Ramsey accidentally tries to slide inside my canal alongside Cyrus's shaft.*

*Fondling my breast, Zamir's murmur of pleasure is cut off as a crimson cast rains down over us, the arc of cascading lifeblood. Frozen in shock, a heartbeat later, the screaming starts and doesn't stop until it's too late.*

# LOVE IS UNIMAGINABLE GRIEF

"We're going to need to sedate her," demands a commanding voice as hands grapple to gain my wrists. "She's harming herself. The gouges are bleeding."

"Let me think," flows in a panic as he leans above me, trying to press my shoulders down onto the mattress. Lashing out as a wild animal, I need to get free, unable to handle the onslaught battering me from inside my head and heart and soul.

"Don't ponder it too long."

"Sarcasm is not appreciated at a time like this," is lashing bark of annoyance. "Mira will never forgive me if we sedate her and start this torture at the beginning again. I doubt I can survive it either."

"Fair enough. But you have thirty seconds to calm her before I sedate her for you," flows in a breathless rush as Cyrus is almost knocked from the bed.

"What triggered it?" Ramsey rests his entire body on top of mine, trying to restrain me as I buck and rear upward, feet aimlessly kicking. "What memory was it, Cyrus? This isn't what Miranda plotted out. The children were supposed to trigger these memories."

"This is worse, Ram. Much worse." Their speech soothes me some, Cyrus able to gain my wrists, tucking both into one of his fists. "I think the memories resurfaced out of order."

"What do you mean?" A cool damp cloth is pressed against my forehead, causing me to simmer down, muscles falling lax as the hysteria wages on inside my mind, battling my heart and soul because we don't understand. Don't understand any of it.

"I think when we tried to touch her at the same time, it triggered the memory of the last and only time we tried to do the same."

"Gods!" An entire bathing sheet is draped over my chest, cold dampness halting any struggle left within me. "You mean... Mira hadn't regained the memories of my brother yet, not the recent ones anyway. Imagine how confusing it must have been to be dropped in a time and place a decade later, where she was in love with the man she previously loathed."

"Nothing like learning you're in love with someone, only to have them die seconds later," more sarcasm at the worst possible time. "I can only assume the memory ended with Zamir's lifeblood raining down upon us, because she would be worse if the rest was revealed." Cyrus climbs on top of my body, palms pressing my wrists to the pillow beneath me, protecting me from myself.

Vision blurry, fading into shadowy darkness around the edges. Their voices and the vibes they release cue me into their location, since I cannot truly see. Part of the panic was having my vision taken from me, not that my mind chose to do that instead of helpful amnesia. No, the torrent of tears took my sight. The choking sobs stole my breath. The loss of someone I hadn't known I loved crushed my spirit and clouded my mind.

"I wish I knew what happened next so I could help her." Ramsey's voice sounds far off, yet I sense him directly next to me, hands patting the damp cloth across my neck. Tears. It's his tears cloaking his presence.

"I lasted about five seconds longer than you, and I wouldn't wish those seconds on anyone, let along the minutes longer Miranda lasted. If you thought you knew what stark terror was, you thought wrong."

Palms magically release my wrists, landing to cup my cheeks. "My sweets, you are the bravest human being I've ever encountered. The strongest, with the fortitude of the rocky cliffs outside our home. You will survive the loss of Zamir, I know you will."

"Cy, you don't get it," Ramsey whispers, body leaning into mine. "For us, it was over six months ago. For Mira, it happened seconds ago. Probably is still playing out inside her head. She must be terrified. Her body still in flight or fight mode."

"She's calming. The most intelligent, logical, rational person. She will fight the madness and come back to us. Because if not, we will have to sedate her and start all over again," is a threat meant to terrify me into good behavior. "Trust yourself, Miranda."

The battle wages on, mind unable to process such complex emotions. The part of me that resided locked inside the reflection of the mirror, I understand her now better. Focusing on that helps me handle the onslaught of grief. Unable to handle the pain, she closed a door inside her psyche, shutting her emotions within, allowing logic to reign and survival to rule.

This hurts– so loathsome to emote so deeply. Sociopathy was tranquil, simple. Restful. Yet it was also dark and drab and as lifeless as dormant vines in the winter.

Emotions are the spark of life, and I'm not sure I'm capable of living.

"I don't understand how Zamir and I became so close or why what happened next happened," slurs in a sluggish voice, adrenaline fleeing, the oncoming crash barreling in on me. "In the memory, I was thinking of how Zamir hosted orgies, with me tied to this bed, and I allowed it. I reveled in it. I wanted more. How? I remember every detail of what happened on this bed, but not how we got there."

"Let this be a comfort to you, Miranda." The strongest man I know has tears in his eyes, lips clenched as the bottom one fights off a warble. "The memory as to how you and Zamir came to an agreement, and from that agreement grew a friendship of sorts, it's a good memory, my sweets. I wish you hadn't received the memories out of order, because reliving it will hurt, but it might help in the long run, have you cherish the bittersweet, when before you were incapable."

"What of Sephira? The choker–" is cut off, swallowed by a heavy wail of mourning. Body shaking, the pain reignites. Mind unable to process the influx of emotions, body systems shorting out.

"Hey!" Palms repeatedly slap my cheeks, swishing my head left and right, as water is squeezed from a damp washcloth onto my forehead. "Stop, Miranda. You're stronger than this. Stop this hysteria and we will offer you knowledge instead."

"We'll let the children share the bed with you," Ramsey tries a softer approach, damp cloth hoisted above my head. "If you calm yourself, you'll be rewarded. If you keep diving back into madness, I will have no choice but to sedate you. You won't be any more ready to experience the grief next time around. Stop the cycle, or your entire life will become the cycle."

A logical Ramsey gets through to me faster than Cyrus's slaps, because logical is not Ramsey's natural state of being. "Tell of Sephira. What of Jax and Ayres?" Heart latched onto Zamir, I choose the people closest to him to focus on.

"Your son anticipated your needs, Miranda." Cyrus's palms fall lax against my bare chest, fingertips splayed across my torso, trailing down to the caesarian scars, because I could never naturally bear my children after enduring the sleeve, canal not strong enough to withstand the birthing process.

"Jasper took charge while we were all out of commission–"

Eyes cutting in Ramsey's direction, "It was only three days," Cyrus rumbles with agitation.

"Four," Ramsey volleys back with a grin. "Day six where you almost bled to death again because you were a stubborn fool. Day nine when you rejoined the land of the living."

"How you exaggerate," is a grumble of pure affection, palm lashing out to grab the back of his lover's head, drawing their foreheads together for just a brush of a touch. "While you toddled around the villa, hand seeking walls, suffering vertigo from your concussion for weeks on end."

"Jasper was in charge for four days," Ramsey stresses hard, eyes on Cyrus, waiting to be contradicted again. "Personally executing thirty-nine that betrayed us, in honor of his fallen father. To regain their honor, Jax and Ayres were allowed to end those who kept them from rendering aid."

"You're getting too close to triggering the rest of that memory," Cyrus warns in a deadly calm voice. "No one is as proud of Jasper as I, but let's hedge around that please."

"Fair enough." Ramsey slips off the mattress, seeking where his pajama pants are draped over the ottoman at the foot of the bed. "Sephira is heavy with child, staying at the villa until she can speak with you."

"She is?" is a burst of pure delighted shock. "Did anyone give her the choker Zamir commissioned for her?"

"Jasper collected all of his father's belongings," Cyrus interjects, because talking of Zamir is affecting Ramsey, causing his movements to falter and his hands to shake and his eyes to leak.

"Sentimental items were passed out among the children, then to Ramsey, a few pieces given to Jax and Ayres. He saved the most personal items for you to either keep or give to Sephira yourself. He didn't want to take away a task that is meant to bond women, since you both lost Zamir."

Arm outstretched, a silent Ramsey hands Cyrus a pair of pants. "You gather your children, I will fetch my son. We needn't allow Mira any privacy."

"Let's get Miranda settled into bed first." Cyrus steps to the floor to don his pants, then comes back to remove the cool damp bathing sheet from my torso and throat. "She needs a healing sleep for her mind and emotions to catch up to speed, and for that toxic stew of chemicals coursing through her body to dissipate– for her, a tragedy just struck. Once she is resting, we'll bring the children in, so they can greet her when she wakes."

"I have more questions–"

"In time, your mind will provide all the answers you seek." Ramsey says not unkindly, as he folds the bathing sheet and washcloth, before disappearing back into the bathroom.

"Is the grief always this close to the surface for him?" Compassion bleeding from my voice, my eyes gaze at the spot where Ramsey disappeared behind a closed door. I feel it too, the driving urge to be overcome and taken under, never to resurface again.

"No," is a soft breath. Cyrus helps me beneath the covers, rolling me to my favored side, then pushes a pillow beneath my cheek. "We both blocked out the good that happened prior, what I assume you remembered just now. Ramsey longed to share such an intimate moment with his brother, and now he grieves that we never got to join together in this bed."

"You mean... oh!" Realization dawning, tears instantly well in my eyes. They never fought over Jasper, equally sharing him, no matter whose seed created our son. Ramsey wished to be there with Zamir should we conceive another. "We lost so much."

"A noble sacrifice to pay for all the pain Zamir had inflicted against his victims, leaving us with safety and security." Settling his hip on the side of the bed, Cyrus touches me softly, in a manner in which Ramsey always does, fingers trailing along exposed skin.

"My sweets." Cyrus leans down, pressing his lips to mine, sensing the inevitable crash is on the horizon. "I had the clamps removed while I was recuperating at the facility, so that if ever you are ready, Ramsey could experience it with me. I do mourn the loss that Zamir can no longer join us, because it is something he would have cherished."

"Zamir died happy," is a whispered breath of truth, the rightness of it ringing in my soul. "He didn't see the strike coming. He felt no terror. He was safe, happy, connected with us, and then he was just gone. No more pain."

With great wailing sobs, Ramsey lunges into the bed to curl around my back, arms squeezing me as if to hold himself together. Damp face buried at the nape of my neck, we three grieve together, teaching me valuable lessons in empathy and the rainbow of emotions known as the human condition, far more than I learned in a lifetime of mastery.

Long after I settled, Ramsey weeps, where I'm still connected to him during partial sleep.

"Stay," Cyrus whispers, as if fearful he'll wake me, when I'm not truly asleep. Eyes at rest, I see nothing but feel everything. "I'll bring our impatient ones."

"I would not change anything," Ramsey breathes against the shell of my ear after Cyrus's footsteps fade in the distance. "Because I wouldn't give this up for anything in the world. I love you, Mira."

"Love you too," is a whispered breath, lips ghosting over the cheek resting next to mine.

"No, Oscar," comes a voice that has an electrical current lightning striking through me, only to realize the immense hope I felt was for naught. The voice is the same but spoken from a younger tongue. "You have to sleep at Mother's back."

"But Dad is in the way," flows a pouty voice that sounds far too much like Ramsey, when they have not a single drop of blood in common.

"Daddy's getting up," Ramsey rumbles a chuckle into my ear. "Good luck." Then he is leveraging himself off the mattress.

"I want to sleep at Mommy's front, like they let me at the facility." Demanding and forceful, the slight pressure of a little boy crawling onto the bed, now he reminds me of his father.

"Mommy's naked," Ramsey mumbles as he skirts the end of the bed. "Only Oona gets to touch Mommy's naked front."

"Here," flows that protective voice again, then a bouncing shift on the mattress, followed by a warm smaller body curling around my back. "You're a man. Men are the big spoon, always between the open door and the women."

Caught in the limbo of half-sleep, I reach to cradle my youngest son's hand between my breasts, directly over my beating heart. Peaceful bliss filling me as he snuggles up behind me with a sigh.

"The breast looks good. Real. Almost identical to the other." That voice says again, only closer this time. "Good. Mother could withstand its loss, but it would harm Oona."

"Why?" comes from a little boy, sparking a flare of memories to cascade across my mind, a kaleidoscope of why, when, where, and how, asked from a fellow knowledge-seeker always thirsting for the truth.

"Twins or not, Oona is still a girl." Curious fingers press on the top of my breast, dimpling it slightly, the numbness barely registering the touch. "Imagine if your father had his nuts cut off– you'd be upset too."

"Excuse me?" Cyrus says from far off, voice getting progressively closer. "My nuts, what?"

"Just trying to get Oscar to understand something is all," sounds exactly like a petulant teenage boy, causing my lips to spread into a smirk. A ghost of remembrance, back to a time when another sounded exactly the same.

"Hi, Mommy!" whispers an excitable voice from an inch in front of my face. If not emotionally exhausted to the point of immobility, I might have jumped out of my skin. "We get to sleep together in your bed this time. I hated it while you were gone. We had to sleep in our own rooms. The bed in the facility was too narrow, so Daddy made me go home."

As Oona snuggles in deep, her front to mine, tiny face pressed against my false breast, more memories descend, the emotions amazing. It flows as a whisper, easy to digest and restore.

Born in this bed, I shared it with my mother until her death. Then I shared it with Cyrus. From such a young age, Jasper was too independent to sleep with me, opting to sleep in his father's quarters.

Once the twins were born, they hadn't slept a night without me, until Oscar matured to independence, wishing to have his own room. Oona slept with Cyrus and me, cradled in the warmth of her parents' safety and security and love, up until that horrific night I just remembered.

In the back of my mind, I feared I was an abusive, neglectful, cold mother. Feared this because both Ramsey and Cyrus were keeping the children from me. But as the puzzle pieces of my life realign, I realize there was no sense in worrying. With the parents I had, Mother loving me with such deep maternal devotion, and Father regarding me as his queen, emotions locked safely away or not, my children would be loved and cherished.

"I want the old one back." Oona roots around, trying to get comfortable, palm cupping my breast like she did as a toddler seeking soothing milk in the middle of the night. "How will she nurse without a nipple?"

"She had two, Oona," Jasper lashes out, not quite a chastisement but still filled with impatience.

"If your mother decides to have another babe, and if she is incapable of nursing, I have no doubt that someone would be honored to donate milk to their Kyrios' newborn babe."

"You can go, I'll handle this," that voice is both painful and soothing to hear, sounding exactly like his father.

"Oh, I can, can I?" is nothing but pure sarcasm, Cyrus and Jasper in an era of time where they battle each other. It's the perils of two alpha males, both posturing for the same kingdom, determined to earn the favor of the females. "Kicking me out of my own bed, with my own children, are you? This isn't the king's quarters."

A smacking kiss brushes against the side of my breast, Cyrus leaning down to say goodnight to our daughter. Then a thick head of hair tickles at my spine, as he dips down to kiss the top of our son's head.

Sensing another kiss as a more mature arm brackets us all together, "Goodnight, Uncle," is said as an affectionate dismissal.

"Goodnight, son," is trailed by proud laughter, the song dimming with each passing footstep. "We'll be in the adjoining quarters with the door open, in case your mother experiences another memory."

"I can take it from here," Jasper declares, causing a burst of laughter to echo from the chamber beside us. Ramsey delighted in their war.

"Of that I have little doubt, son." The voice diminishes as Cyrus steps away, but the pride continues to ring loudly. "Little doubt."

Blindly reaching, I locate the man-sized palm, dragging it to clasp against the small of his sister's back, bracketing us all in the warmth of his safety, the door at his back.

Tears spring, because Zamir had his back to a door, and it was the end of his existence, something that must be bothering Jasper, else he would have never cautioned Oscar over such a thing.

"I missed you," is said in *his* voice, causing the grief-stricken weeping to begin anew.

*Lounging in the king's quarters, I experience a rare free moment where I can read a fiction novel. Both Ramsey and Jasper are drawn to Zamir, seeking him out, even when he's working. Lying across the foot of Zamir's bed, I am more entertained by watching my family than I am with the novel.*

*Quiet, self-contained awareness, those insecurities and that bruised ego mean nothing when Zamir is working, proficient and confident. Zamir is seated in his favored chair, forever more* productive there than being held captive at his desk, files spread across the low table before him and the rug at his feet.

Huddled up on the sofa, Ramsey is teaching Jasper how to sketch– at nine, it was time to learn a hobby that soothed the soul, rather than being hyper-focused on education while obsessed with what the future may bring.

Like my education, Jasper is taught weaponry, hand-to-hand combat, political negotiations, diplomacy, and how to rule. Unlike my education, Jasper won't take his first life by either protecting mine or avenging it, not if I can help it.

So sketching the likeness of a cat statuette, it is...

"Sons!" is spoken from the corridor, causing all heads to snap up at attention. "Grandson," is murmured with immense pride. "Little Miranda," lilts off my father-in-law's forked tongue in a purr of pure menace, disrespect the undercurrent, never failing to cause a quiver of fear to weave down my spine.

"Father," Zamir murmurs in annoyance, mind too focused on his work for whatever gameplay his father is about to deliver. "Are you here to visit or detonate a bomb you have hidden in my quarters?"

A peal of childish snickers, Ramsey and Jasper look to one another, then cover their mouths with the back of their hands, because what Zamir said was rather entertaining, in a dry, honest sort of way.

"The resemblance is astounding, isn't it?" Swarthy lips curled with the joy of decimation and death, evil radiates from Zamir the elder's voice. "Your brother and son look alike, sound alike, act alike, almost as if they are in truth father and son."

Ochre orbs of sheer evil focus on me, "Hmm... care to share something, little Miranda?"

"Detonate a bomb, it is," Zamir whispers in a scathing tone, a tone surprisingly arrowed in on his father. "Ramsey, take my son back to your quarters, please."

"Yes, of course." Infallibly trusting his brother, Ramsey hoists our son up against his side, leaving me to defend myself.

Jasper is braver, made of sterner stuff, feet dragging across the rug, hesitant to leave me to my own punishment.

"Son?" Zamir cautions, eyes connecting in order to silently communicate with each other.

Satisfied with what unspoken assurances he heard, "Okay." Jasper stands on his own, then walks right out the door, not bothered by the way his grandfather crowds him on the way by, with Ramsey right on his heels.

"Allow me," Zamir the elder says with a flourish, grabbing for the doorknob. "Privacy is needed, I suspect. I'll await you in the corridor, little Miranda."

The way that devil of a man wraps my name around his tongue makes my skin crawl, the darkest of shadows in the back of my psyche attempts to billow forth to unveil a truth to haunt me.

"You can relax, my queen." Leaning forward, Zamir places his work on the low table in front of him, tone no longer mocking.

Around the time I stopped being an emasculating teenager, Zamir started to address me with respect, affection even, which has always conflicted me. Because the time I stopped being a teenager is when I became a mother, and my husband began respecting me because I tricked him on the night of Jasper's conception.

"I've known," leave it to Zamir to be the one to actually detonate the bomb. Leaning back in his chair, arms trailing along the arms, fingertips relaxed. "I've always known. Did you honestly believe my brother wouldn't have a spark of guilt and tell me?"

"Why didn't you say anything?" Gutted, completely gutted, a foreign sensation makes my skin heat, causing the pit of my stomach to twist as if ill.

"I think the real question to ask is why didn't you say anything, Miranda?" Yet again, Zamir is calm, relaxed even. Ego not bruised in the least, and this discombobulates me. "Your reasons are important to me."

"Very well." Righting myself, I situate on the mattress until my behind is firmly planted and my feet are hooked on the support rail near the floor. "Hope. I didn't say anything due to hope."

"Hope?" the upward inflection rises as high as those inky eyebrows, ochre eyes revealing nothing but curiosity. "I know you think me a monster, Miranda... and I am. But I have long ago decided to act like a human being around you. If you manage it, why can't I?"

*Nothing would have spurred me to be honest more than that comment.*

*"Hope. I didn't tell you because I didn't want you to be upset with Ramsey. I didn't want to be upset with myself because I couldn't resist Ramsey. Hope, because as long as none of us know the truth, you could hope Jasper was your son, Ramsey could hope Jasper was his son, and I could see Jasper as the son to both of you."*

*"You, a doctor, never tested our son's paternity?" Even knowing I lie like it is air to be breathed, Zamir isn't calling me out on it. He is genuinely surprised.*

*"No. As I said, I didn't want to know," is the honest truth, not even me lying to myself. "As far as similar looks or personalities, that's not how genetics work. You're more likely to take after an uncle than a father. Just as siblings with both parents usually don't looking similar, one taking after one parent more than the other. One looking like an aunt or uncle on one side of the lineage. So your father taunting you means nothing other than he was being malevolent. He tried to take me that night, after I was with you both, a sick desire to conquer both me and your seed."*

*"I'm aware of that as well." For a few suspended moments of quiet contemplation, Zamir watches me. "I'd like to alter the terms of our union, if that is alright with you? I'd like to state my case first, put it all on the table."*

*"Very well." We're both being uncharacteristically polite, reminding me of negotiation with a rival or equal. The king and queen, equals within our Oikos, negotiating terms, after we were baited to strike against one another.*

*"You don't think me attractive—"*

*"No—"*

*Hand raised to halt me. "Allow me to finish, Miranda," is spoken in a controlled voice, even and patient. "My brother is the epitome of male beauty, and Cyrus is the epitome of masculinity, and I accept that they are who you desire. However, I do think we are intellectual equals on differing fronts, and I think we would suit."*

*With a sharp jerk of my chin, I nod. "I agree."*

*"No one compares to the proficiency I have at work. However, my masculinity comes into question when my wife regards me with distain in public. When my son is now eight*

years old and we have not had more children, which leads me to be ridiculed. A cuckhold. My potency is brought into question. My virility. The size of my manhood. The fact that I am softer than most men."

Now it's my turn to halt my husband, the give and take of a productive conversation.

"If you would allow, I'd like to do a full panel workup on the hormones in your system. I believe that you have a genetic predisposition to some of the insecurities that plague you. I could accurately diagnose that you have high levels of estrogen, which convert sugars to fat as a way to store more estrogen in the body. You most likely have low levels of testosterone, which affects your sex drive, the size of your member, the shape of your body, and the amount of semen you produce."

"It wasn't just the size of my dick and my disinterest in using it that drew me to sadism, Miranda." Leaning forward, Zamir rests his forearms on his thighs, hands dangling between his knees. "The hunger runs in my blood now."

"The sadism isn't the issue when it comes to the negotiation table, Zamir. You worry over how others perceive you. If we meet halfway, we might discover we like each other, which will help your social standing. If you do the blood panel, discover you need to take testosterone therapy, it will help you retain the muscle mass you attempt to build, spark your interest in actual sex, maybe even provide you with minimal growth. The men would take you more seriously, would they not?"

"This is what I propose." A new glint of light flares in his eyes, excitement not centered on making another scream in agony. "For the rest of your childbearing years, every five to eight years, we need to have a child. It needn't be ours, but you must have a child. It will be a cause for celebration for our people, and it will lend to my virility."

Realization dawns, and I'm not sure I am ready, but it was better than the alternative as to how this conversation could have gone, with me lying in a pool of drying blood.

"You wish to try tonight?"

"Of course, I do, Miranda." Lips quirked in a queer smile, Zamir turns uncharacteristically sheepish. "I enjoyed our time together… I said what I did–"

"It was nearly ten years ago, Zamir. We were young, and I just came to your bed with your brother's seed inside me, hoping to trick you. Whatever you said, it was well earned."

A hand brushes my comment away, Zamir suddenly seeming very real to me. Human. "I said that bit about women unable to climax, not because I thought it was true– as I said, you have my beautiful brother and your potent Cyrus at your beck and call. I was saving face in case you didn't climax for me, not that I expected you to. The fact that you did, it blew my mind, actually."

The feverish trail of laughter reminds me so much of Ramsey, that it causes me to do a double-take. At the same time, an odd feeling wells inside my chest, an ache that can't be soothed. Zamir and Ramsey have more in common than I realized, but whatever happened to Zamir altered his personality.

"I wish to change our terms, Miranda." Rising from his seat, Zamir makes his way toward me, going slowly as to give me time to react. Heart racing with anticipation rather than fear, because I too enjoyed our time together... the last time, never the first.

Behind settled on the mattress next to me, Zamir is never anything but brave, reaching out to hold my hand. "I would like to experience the softer nature of intimacy, Miranda. Touch each other, find what feeds our needs. I was angry when I struck out on our wedding night–"

"With good reason," I quickly interrupt, thinking of how poorly I treated Zamir when he and his family arrived, especially when I urinated on him.

"I baited you incessantly, my queen. I was intrigued the moment I laid eyes upon you, as you manipulated a man to commit suicide, as if it were for his own benefit. But then you laid eyes upon my baby brother, and all hope was lost. I knew I was incapable of sexually gratifying you, but that sealed it."

"We're both at fault," I go for the middle ground. With all negotiations, both must gain and lose. "Let's agree on that fact."

"Both at fault, but my actions are unforgiveable, Miranda." Fingers clenching in mine, Zamir draws my hand into his lap. "I irrecoverably harmed you. My father taught me to use the sleeve, showed me how it was a way to get a woman to submit. Reinforced through punishment how all women were to submit. But you are not a woman who should submit. You are my wife, and it took me this past decade to realize I needed you to be stronger, not weakened to feed my ego. I hope to apologize."

Moving on instinct, my hand is drawn from his, and I can feel Zamir's rejection beat within my own chest. Instead of pulling away, I use that same hand to palm the back of his head, drawing his lips down to mine.

An alarmed cry of shock hisses from his lips between mine, palms cupping my hips to draw me across his lap. Biting at each other's mouths, hand gripping and releasing anything they can reach, an undeniable hunger demands to be fed. It's a struggle, pulling my skirts up between us, while attempting to tear open Zamir's fly, needing to feel our flesh touch.

Panting roughly in jarring gasps that quake my chest, I push Zamir down on the mattress. Startled eyes gaze back up at me, in this moment submitting to whatever I desire.

While Zamir's libido might be compromised, mine isn't, rivalling that of a man in his prime, belly always empty to the point of starvation, always hungering to be fed. A monster riding just beneath my skin, waiting for willing victims to pleasure me.

There's an air of desperation when rutting on one another fully clothed, the frustration amping up the desire. Zamir's deft fingers impatiently tear at my blouse, thread tying the collar snapping from the force, breasts freed to open air.

"Gods!" Zamir shouts in a rush, ascending lips snaring my nipple, only to elicit a deep drawing suck. The startled yelp that flees my mouth has Zamir sucking harder and harder, bruisingly so, drawing as much of my tit into his mouth as humanly possible, at least half of it.

Hot and hard, dampness floods between us, some of it his, most of it my slick oil. Zamir worries over his size, but it feels exquisite ground against my erect clit, head roaming over and over it in a rolling rhythm.

Close to the edge, Zamir's mouth latched onto my breast, our nether parts pressing and releasing in a fevered rhythm, the juicy sound adding to the moans raising into the air. Grabbing for his wrist, I wrap his arm around me, then underneath the back of my skirt, pressing fingers into me from behind.

"Never doubt my need for you," is a rough rasp against the top of his head, hair tickling my chin as I rock back and forth over top of him. "Feel the slick oil dripping from me– you caused that." A potent clench causes a breathy moan to flutter up my throat. "I can lie about all things except this."

Falling over the precipice, too lost to sensation to maintain speech, all I can do is suffer the erotic wave as pleasure crests over me. Writhing in jerky stops and starts, Zamir's name pitches high from my throat.

"Did you feel that?" Reaching back, I pull Zamir's fingers from my slit, drawing it in between our faces. My oil drips freely off his fingers, running down the side of his hand. "Did you feel how my body sucked yours into me? No woman can lie enough to force her body to flex those contractions."

Lying against the bedclothes, Zamir's gazes back up at me in stunned silence, face flushed and eyes bright with awe. Fully clothed, only the glistening flesh of his manhood revealed from his open fly, much more semen than our last time together.

Struggling to draw breath, chest rising and falling rapidly, my husband is trying to form words that won't release. "My queen," escapes its trap. "Witnessing you undone is a gift... being the one to undo you is a privilege. I owe you two truths for how you just honored me."

Leaning back upright, sliding my clamshell against Zamir's softening flesh, I retie the cords to close my blouse, hiding my damp and bruised breasts back where they belong, suckle marks branding me for weeks to come.

"My father will attempt to take you from the corridor," is said without emotion, Zamir hiding what he truly thinks. "If he succeeds, he will take you to his quarters, rape you, and seed your womb, attempting to impregnate you. He believes himself better than I, leaving Ramsey alone because they share no similarities and he is second born. Father is envious of his sons, wishing to always best us."

A shudder weaves its way down my spine, experiencing blind terror when it's not an emotion that I generally feel. Fingers quivering, I adjust my skirts around us.

"Miranda, my queen," Zamir breathes softly, attempting to soothe my nerves. Palms settle on my hips, fingers clenching. "Father has far more guards than you believe him to have. To be safe, I have Jax and Ayres waiting outside in the corridor, having alerted Cyrus and your entire cadre of guards. Father will not come against you this night."

Drawing in a lungful of air, I release it as a heavy sigh. "Thank you."

"No need to thank me, for it is my duty," is said with far more honor than I expected from Zamir. "You need to get heavy with child, Miranda. Tell father you're needed at the facility and take Cyrus with you. Do anything you have to do to ensure that you're pregnant before you return to this villa."

The fact that Zamir gives no thought to his ego, going as far as to beg me to use another man, it is utterly terrifying.

Leaning upward, Zamir cups my cheek, eyes focused on mine. "You are safe," he vows, and I believe him. "I need to ease your worries, Miranda. You speaking of hope, it pleased me how you truly meant to give me and my brother hope. But you needn't fret, because Ramsey and I tested against Jasper shortly after his birth, because we needed to know as men."

"I–" at a loss, I stumble off Zamir's lap, nearly falling off the edge of the bed. Once my feet are firmly on the floor, skirts swirling around my body to shield me, I reach out to grab the bedpost, supporting my weight. "I always assumed a mother would know who fathered her children, but that never clicked within me. I truly have no idea if Jasper belongs to you or your brother. Playing the odds, I could guess–"

"Because Ramsey is a fully grown male with a perfect cock?" Zamir is teasing me, not a tinge of self-deprecation in his tone. More playful like his brother. "Because I release so very little? Because he pumped load after load of seed into you, young and virile and filled with a need to be claimed by you?"

Refusing to lie to protect Zamir's feelings, "Those odds, yes."

Sitting upright, spent cock lying limply in his open fly, Zamir's maddening laughter echoes around the king's quarters. "Never gamble against me, my queen." Brilliant smile eclipsing his face, the resemblance between Zamir and his brother is unmistakable now. Beautiful. "Jasper is my son, both through name and seed."

That sharp intake of breath ricochets around the king's quarters.

"As much as I'd love to appease my ego this night…" is trailed off as Zamir tucks his cock back into his trousers and buttons up. *"Gambling with my brother is one thing, since our internal chemistry is probably nearly identical. But I'll never gamble against Cyrus. His seed will always conquer anyone when held within your womb."*

Blinking out of a dream, stunned mind struggling to deal with this new reality.

*"Good luck this evening, my queen."* Zamir unfolds from the bed, then returns to his chair to resume his work. *"I will be pleased to give Cyrus's child my name— a strong brother or sister for our son, a playmate who will love Jasper like Ramsey adores and entertains me."*

*"Good evening, my king."* With a nod, I straighten my shoulders as I walk toward the door. *"Until tomorrow."*

*"Tomorrow."*

With a large draw of air, I fortify myself as I step from the king's quarters into the corridor. What I witness is not a surprise, but it does create a foreboding sensation to niggle at the back of my skull, not only because of the oppressive vibe filling the corridor.

Contained violence is riding the air, a match struck would spark to ignite and burn this entire villa to nothing but ashes on the wind.

Fanning out along the wall on the same side as the doorway to the king's quarters, Cyrus, the villa's guards, our personal guards, and Zamir's two personal guards are having a faceoff with Zamir the elder and seventeen of his personal guards. However, we are not senseless, we know more are hiding in the shadows.

The poisonous serpent and his venomous spiders, scurrying along the walls, currying favor and terrorizing the natives, deriving sick pleasure over how frustrated we become because we cannot seem to exterminate them.

If a war descended upon this house, we would be decimated, leaving no one save a few alive. That is not a cost any of us are willing to make this day. What sense is it to be in power when there is no one left to rule?

Zamir the elder is far too cunning to strike where so many lives would be the cost for his sinful desires. He'll act when we least expected it, when we are most vulnerable, and when the only cost is our lives personally, so that he may enjoy the spoils of war as he conquers those loyal to us.

*Not for the thousandth time, I ask myself why Father, after ninety years of survival, nearly a century of surviving, allowed this snake to slither into our nest.*

*"Cyrus," is spoken in his direction, system attuned to where he is located without the aid of sight to confirm. Walking down the corridor, I expect my people to fall in line behind me as I pretend I'm not fleeing.*

*"Jax and Ayres, your master awaits you in his quarters." Continuing to walk with my head high and shoulders back, for the first time I feel as if I'm playacting the Livas Kyrios, and this realization disturbs me. "I'll be at the facility if needed."*

*One day, Zamir Elezi the elder will no longer hold this Oikos hostage. It's only a matter of odds on whether or not it's because he is dead or because he now reigns supreme.*

# GIFT OF LIVING

The clank of spoon against porcelain rouses me. "I said quietly," is a fierce whisper, causing my lips to curl up and my eyelids to flutter open. For a few minutes, as I arose from a fitful sleep, I was transported back decades to when I was a small child, Laverna's admonishments doing little to curb my behavior.

"Try not to jostle your mother as you fix the tray," Laverna cautions in a calm tone. "That's it. Steady." A slight depression on the mattress has my eyes clamping back shut, allowing my children to believe they're surprising me, spoiling me.

While not biologically related to Ramsey, the twins are natural caregivers. Their need to pamper those they love feeds their souls. Mother was a gentle soul as well, giving and kind. Like seeks like, her best friend, the woman who essentially reared me and who is now helping to rear my children, was of a similar disposition.

"Like this?" Oona's soft raspy voice has my eyelids flashing open in a heartbeat. "This good and stable?"

"Let me do it for you." Oscar is getting impatient, sounding more like me than of the ever-patient Cyrus.

"Come now," Laverna cautions, and it's easy to imagine her palm lightly landing on small backs, ushering them to the side, after an entire childhood of experiencing the same. "Sit with me on the cushions– I'll teach you how to pour tea."

Lying on my back, with my head cradled on a pillow, a breakfast tray is situated over my lap. Laverna teaching the children a lesson allows me time to drink them in. The memories have been cascading for days, leaving only a partial memory hidden in the framework of my mind.

If my mind were a window, these memories have fused back within me without any confusion. Standing before a window, hand on the draperies, you instinctively know what's outside the windowpane, as you've seen the view repeatedly over time. But you still have to pull the drapery back to reveal the view.

I've pulled the draperies back, and the view is nothing short of breathtaking, spectacular, and heartwarming. No confusion. No uncertainty. Calming yet refreshing, and as familiar as looking at my own reflection in a mirror.

Before me, seated on cushions around the low table in the center of my quarters, my nursemaid is teaching the children how to steep tea.

While impossible for male and female fraternal twins to be identical, my children are as close as it comes. Inside my mind, it's as if I haven't laid eyes upon them in a few days, a week at most, as I wasn't able to make and retain memories over the past six months. Expecting to see them as they looked before, only to realize they've grown exponentially in those months, as children their age always do, that is more discombobulating than anything.

Their baby soft features are sharpening, more mature. Bodies identical, tall for a child of eight, with slim builds and wiry muscles. Androgynous, wearing similar genderless clothing, protecting their identities– which was a suggestion made by Zamir for their safety, as no one would be able to target either, either to take out a male heir or kidnap a female to join our families through a noncontractual union.

Both reaching for the teapot, movements calculated but smooth. Thick black hair bladed sharply to swing along their jawlines. Unnaturally large peridot eyes dominate their entire faces, rolled to gaze out the fall of their hair. Button noses have grown sleek and narrow in the past half year, promising to become a replica of their father's most prominent feature.

A sense about her, Laverna knows I'm awake, gifting me this precious time to acclimate myself before I'm bombarded with touch and speech. Seated opposite my children, our nursemaid is motherly soft, even though she has never bore children of her own.

Drawn toward the female persuasion, Laverna resided here with me, until she met the cook's daughter. A widowed educator who often visited, her children nearly grown at the time. Laverna and her wife have been together for nearly two decades since.

Weeks before the strike against us, Zamir the elder tried to use Laverna to weaken me. I sent her and her family away to protect myself from their loss, protect my children from the loss. My father-in-law knew exactly who to strike to destroy me.

Body immobile to not alert my children to my inner pain, tears seep out the corners of my eyes, absorbed into the pillowcase. Heart fractured, I'm unsure how to move forward through all this pain. Suffering other than physically is as new to me as all the other emotions I'm experiencing.

If blinking and my children are six months older, imagine experiencing loathing then love then loss in the matter of days, leaving me lying distraught in this bed, mourning the loss of my husband.

The pragmatic ghost reflected in the mirror strengthens me from the inside out. I still experience the barrage of emotional pain, but I'm able to function, to do the things that need doing, and to appreciate the gift of life I was given.

Fingers blindly seeking the robe draped across the bedding next to me, I slowly transfer the breakfast tray out of the way. Laverna speaks louder, drawing my children's attention, so I'm able to clothe myself without their notice.

Once I'm on my feet, an episode of dizziness descends. Understanding that I have no idea how long since I nourished my body, I reach to grab the tray, then make my way over to the seating area. Kneeling down, I place the tray on the low table next to the tea, then settle onto a cushion.

The children and Laverna look to me, expectantly waiting to see what I'll do next. In my sleep, I heard catches of conversation going on around me. Cyrus and Ramsey, then Laverna, explaining to all three children why my emotional state is so fragile right now, because these things happened moments ago for me, not half a year ago.

"Is Jasper avoiding me?" is spoken softly as I reach for a fork. "I felt his presence in the bed, but he's gone now." Spearing a piece of melon, I thoughtfully chew, gaze locked on the identical children seated across from me.

Their silence to my question is answer enough.

"This is hard for me." Settling the fork on the side of my plate, the melon moistening my mouth and throat, taking away any discomfort I felt over having foul breath. "Even gazing out the window, the landscape is different than when I last saw it. Dormant in the dead of winter, when in my mind it was at the height of its life. You both look so much older, and it's discombobulating."

With a heavy sigh, both hands reach out to cup cheeks that feel different beneath my touch. Less baby soft cherub cheeks, more mature. Those twin gazes to my own are less carefree playfulness, where they trusted resolutely, more reserved and cautious– haunted.

"My body and mind, it expects to go shower, dress, check in with my staff at the facility, then come home to sit in the king's quarters. Listening to the two of you chatter aimlessly over your studies, Jasper speak of his fiancée, Ramsey pester Zamir as he works, Cyrus playing Chinese checkers with Jax and Ayres, leaving me to watch you all as my favorite source of entertainment. But that life doesn't exist anymore, and it's left me feeling both more secure but equally disquiet."

Hands dropping, I spear another piece of melon, using it as an opportunity to order my thoughts. "You've all been given the opportunity to move on, grow without me, grieve, and slowly acclimate to a new life. Overwhelmed is the predominant emotion I'm feeling. Anxiety. A deep sense of mourning, and not just for Zamir."

More silence, the gazes of my nursemaid and children never staying from my face.

"I feel pressured under expectations." Folding my palms on top of the table, I just gaze back at them, emotionally bleeding from every pore. "Everyone has expectations of me, expectations I have no knowledge over, and I fear I will disappoint or act in a way that upsets any or all of you. You were given six months, I need at least a few days, treated with extra patience as I try to understand this new version of reality."

A harsh intake of breath from the adjoining doorway to Cyrus's quarters has my eyes jerking in that direction. The rapid flash of ochre, followed by nearly soundless footsteps, has me shouting out in alarm.

"Jasper!" Palms landing on the low table, I leverage myself to my feet, only to have Ramsey rush into the room to push my behind down to the cushion. "Don't insult my intelligence by trying to feed me a lie by saying that was you ghosting in the doorway. A mother senses her children."

"Yes." Settling next to me, Ramsey reaches for the platter in front of me, picking up the fork. "Our son was eavesdropping, as was I. Cyrus is at work, but one of us had to be here in case this became too much for you."

"We're just happy to have you back." Oona wiggles helplessly on her cushion, trying with all her might to be a good girl and not overwhelm me.

"It was too quiet around here," Oscar pipes up next to his sister. "Someone needs to teach me how to properly hold a blade. Jasper won't do it."

A sharp jerk wracks my body, the veil between my subconscious and conscious mind thinning.

"Let's not speak of such things for a few days, Oscar." Ramsey stabs the fork into an olive, then brings it up to my mouth. "Jasper is only doing what is in your best interests–"

"Whenever anyone uses that phrase, it's generally leveraged as a means to control." Leaning forward, I punctuate my statement by biting the olive off the fork, brininess a perfect balance to the sweet freshness of melon. "While well-meaning, it leaves the patient with a sense of powerlessness."

"Fair enough." Another olive is held out to me as a peace offering. "You have half of a memory left. The worst, most tragic moment of your entire existence. Trust your son for his reasons to delay that until you are strong enough to shoulder the burden."

"Jasper is my trigger?" Mulling that over, I pluck the fork out of Ramsey's hand, then quickly stab a piece of melon and another olive, popping it all into my mouth at once. Gesturing at Laverna, I ask her to pour me some tea.

As my children fight over who gets to serve me tea, with Ramsey monitoring every bite I take, the fight or flight reflex surging in my veins slowly dissipates, allowing me to relax and enjoy the gift I was given.

Another stab to the platter, spearing another bite of food that is tasteless, the action mimics the searing pain radiating inside my chest. The hollowness never able to be refilled. Father was a loss on an intellectual level, because he was already in his eighties when I was born, always living on borrowed time. What little I remember of Mother, it's with fondness, something I strive to achieve with my own children, blessed to have had seventeen years to share with Jasper, and eight with Oona and Oscar.

Zamir...

This first taste of grief, it hurts beyond imagine, not because it's foreign to me, but because I doubt this pain could be duplicated. The grief had been riding me the entire six months I was housed at the facility, draining my progress. A grief I thought was due to the loss of Cyrus, because the amnesia removed the memories of Zamir, all of them painful in different ways.

Tears dripping down my cheeks, I continue to eat until the platter is emptied, draining three cups of tea, affording both my children and Laverna the honor of serving me.

"We three now have the same hairstyle," is murmured wryly as I wipe both my mouth and my eyes. "We should have Ramsey sketch us," is said with a playful air I didn't think myself capable. "Three sketches, one for each of our sleeping quarters."

"Oh, I think that is a splendid idea!" Laverna claps, then rises to her feet, her face brightening. The tea set is placed on my tray, then lifted from the low table. "It will give you four the chance to sit and just commune with one another."

"I agree." Smiling brightly, most of it genuine, my head butts against Ramsey's shoulder. "Let me dress, then we'll find a quiet spot that has good lighting. I'll braid Oona's hair while Ramsey sketches."

"Miranda!" Laverna exclaims, eyes glistening with unshed tears. "You remember, don't you? Remember how your mother braided your hair when you were small."

"Her name was Oona too, wasn't it?" My daughter is practically vibrating with excitement. Oscar wearily looks on beside her, because whatever Oona has done to her appearance, he does as well.

Laverna takes care of the tea set, seeking her in-laws in the kitchen. While Ramsey and Oscar run down the corridor to fetch the sketching set. This gives Oona and me the opportunity for a few moments of mother-daughter time, where she picks out my clothing and helps me dress.

A spark of her femininity flares, when she asks to wear a silky chemise beneath the shirt that is a match for her brother. Someday, Oona will rebel against her androgyny, and thanks to those who saved me, I will be there to help dress her.

# LIKE FATHER LIKE SON

The hours passed slowly and with great difficulty, then there were moments that passed by in a blink of an eye, mind wandering and heart lost to grief. Even still, it was a pleasure to get to know my children again, because their little personalities were shaped by the events that took place when I wasn't here to witness it.

The renewed emotions within me make me nearly a stranger to my own children, while the passage of time made them a stranger to me.

After some argument, Ramsey backed off when he tried to hold me hostage within my own quarters. Undoubtedly there are guards ghosting my every step, but I need to reacquaint myself with every inch of the property without an audience judging whether or not I need to be sedated again.

Lasting no more than three minutes outside, I immediately sought the interior of the villa. In the dead of winter, the vegetation is sparce and the vines are lain dormant. It's too harsh of a change for me to grasp, when the last I remember it was nearly harvest time, when the land was ripe with abundance.

This villa has stood since Father built it nearly eighty years ago, after the death of his first wife and sons. Not a single stone laid in the floor, nor a single thread in a tapestry, nor the configuration of the rooms have changed in those six decades. I am comforted by the familiarity, able to accurately map the contents of my property within my mind.

As I walk the corridors, I pass servants of many types, all sharing well wishes and words of welcome. It's a relief to see how pleased they are with my return, but more so because they have not changed. The younger you are, the faster you change. Six months means very little to a mature adult, who will remain the same for vast portions of their lives.

Feet slowing, I weigh the risks as I approach the king's quarters.

Do I wait longer for the finale of the memory to reveal itself, hoping I'm strong enough to survive it? Or do I trigger it myself, effectively ending this period of statis?

Then there is the grief. Do I poke the wound, drain the abscess, even though it will hurt in the moment? Or do I ignore it, allow it to try to heal on its own, body absorbing the toxins, festering, where there is a greater potential to go sepsis?

The ghost in the reflection in the mirror, she is eager to get this over with, knowing all answers lie within the king's quarters.

It takes me all of three heartbeats to realize the ghost is me and I am her, so therefore I am eager to finish this once and for all, so I may move forward again.

With a fortifying breath, my toes breach the threshold into the king's quarters. Last I was here, it was a happy memory. A decade of happy memories. Happy memories for the entirety of Oscar and Oona's existence.

…and then.

Less than a week of lucidity, but I think it matters naught. A decade from now, my mind will still conjure Zamir sitting in his favorite chair, files scattered about near his feet, spilling over onto the low table in front of him. The expression of total concentration on his face, lips taut and intelligent eyes missing nothing. The button on his collar undone, revealing sparse curls beneath. Sleeves rolled up to his elbows, ink staining the side of his hand.

As both feet cross the threshold, *"My queen,"* echoes in welcome within my head, in the same cadence used when spoken from his lips. Hand flashing out, fingers finding purchase on the chair rail running along the wall, knees weakened by such a visceral, lifelike memory, as if Zamir were still with me.

That voice. The dry cadence of it, as if Zamir wasn't merely mocking me but himself as well. That phrase, once used to insult me, shifted to a tone of absolute respect and adoration, affection even.

An automatic response, *"My king,"* whispers through my mind, no longer the sarcastic sneer but one taking on the same vein Zamir used with me. Love.

Bypassing the edge of the bed, where I sat night after night, entertained endlessly as the children and Ramsey sat on the sofa, with Cyrus and the guards seated on cushions while playing games on a table, with Zamir permanently fused to his favorite chair.

Breath hitching, I torture myself further. In this, my mastery of the human condition is a curse, understanding all the facets of why I am experiencing these specific emotions in this moment. Understanding what hurts the most will also heal me the fastest, I settle into what will forever be known as Zamir's chair.

From this vantage point, I view the world as Zamir saw it, as the king of his family.

The door to Zamir's front, never caught unaware from the corridor. The edge of the bed fully in his periphery, able to watch me seated there from the corner of his eye. Just the same, Zamir was able to entertain himself by watching his brother and children out of the corner of his other eye. Across the way, fully visible, envy was most likely the driving force as he watched his closest friends play with Cyrus.

As I sit, awaiting my son's return, other heartbreaking revelations sharpen into focus. Our son has changed nothing, perhaps to allow me this moment of closure. Decorating the walls before Zamir's chair, Ramsey's sketches of the family are proudly displayed. But it's farther up the wall, a painting is showcased, one in which I wish my children never laid eyes upon, especially kept in the room in which my eldest son sleeps.

Sprawled in its life-sized glory, embarrassment floods my cheeks as I truly look at the painting for the first time. No son should see his mother in the light his father viewed her.

Asleep in my bed, flesh flushed from a post-coital glow, exhausted after no less than two dozen orgasms, the sheet is covering only the necessary parts between my thighs, rosy-tipped nipples kissing the air. Inky locks trailing along the bedclothes to spill to the stone floor. Ribbons fluttering from the bedposts, one still loosely wrapped around an ankle, as if I passed out mid-struggle to free myself.

"Zamir," is a chastising whisper, a nervous chuckle slipping past my lips. "Now I know why you always covered the painting every evening before the family arrived." Eyes flicking upward, I spot how the blind has been removed, no longer able to rise and lower to cover the painting.

If Ramsey is proficient with a charcoal pencil, Zamir was a master with a paintbrush, an art he explored outside of his father's sadistic control. Intelligent mind able to conjure up a moment in time, then paint it, without the subject having to sit for hours on end.

"I always assumed the painting was sadism-related," is murmured underneath my breath. "Wondered if it was Sephira beneath the blind, and here you were respecting me by not flaunting it in my face."

Palms scrubbing over my tear-damp face, I try to will the embarrassment away. "Why would you unveil this, Jasper?" No son should see his mother in that light, ridiculously visible from every corner of the room, especially from the bed and this chair.

Hours pass, my intuition always on high alert, especially after what happened in the end. Every person who passes by, my mind notes them, even if my eyes are glazed in tears. A few friendly faces check in, none catching my attention, leaving me to grieve and wait in peace.

Long after the bell tolls midnight, time creeping by, my son finally drags his weary bones inside the king's quarters. "Mother, what are you doing in here?" sounds accusatory, but that is to hide the quiver of worry lying beneath.

"Waiting for you," is barely out of my mouth, already across the room with my hands cupping my son's face. "I would have waited an eternity if need be."

Jerking his face to the side, Jasper stalks across his space, then lands behind-first on the edge of the bed. Rejection would be the natural reaction, but this is my son, Zamir's son, so I understand Jasper's reactions and actions more than my own most days.

"Delaying the inevitable will not make the truth hurt any less," is softly breathed as I track my son across the room, footsteps silently padding across the rug. "Nor does you visiting me after I'm asleep."

Before me, those ochre eyes flare up at me with open defiance, challenging me to trigger the memory. For the life of me, I don't understand why Jasper is the trigger for the rest of it. Why my son?

"Maybe it's the absence of six months of my life, or the fact that to me it was only days ago, or maybe it's the grief speaking, but you have never looked more like your father."

Hands cupping Jasper's cheeks, fine whiskers tickle at my palms. "I barely see me within you." Moving my hands, I turn my son's face to the side and back again, examining the differences six months makes.

"These eyes, the hair… that voice," is whispered in a shuddery breath. "Dry, but not in a sarcastic way. But different because you're confident in yourself. The build of your body. You're everything Zamir would have been had he been given hormone replacement as a teen and older."

"Had my evil grandfather never laid a hand on him, don't you mean, Mother?" Another challenge, those eyes held wide open, begging and pleading and demanding I end this.

"Why the painting, Jasper?" Dropping my hands, I step away, with my son's disappointment flavoring the air. "It's inappropriate for you to see me that way, son."

With a quick jerk of his head, Jasper rises from his bed, then stalks past me, grabbing my wrist on his way. Pulled across the room, my son tows me to the sofa cushions. Settled side by side, Jasper turns slightly so we're having a face-off.

"Who was hired to take the place of your father?" is a question that has plagued me since I became aware. "It's important, Jasper. Not to be taken lightly. No one but your father was as proficient at keeping our investments secure."

"You needn't worry, Mother." A palm lands across both of my hands, which are being wrung together in my lap.

"It's important, Jasper," is seethed from clenched teeth. "I didn't appreciate how you've been speaking dismissively to Cyrus, nor how you're treating me. Have you suddenly forgotten who I am? Not just your mother, not just your queen, but the Kyrios of the Livas Oikos. Your supreme ruler."

"Are you finished?" flows in a calm and calculating voice, ever patient and dry enough to be tinder. "You can't do everything, nor are you fit to do so right now, Mother. Are you going to fight me every step of the way for the rest of our natural born lives, making life a battlefield? Or are you going to trust me to do my job as your king?"

"I–"

"And before you say I'm too young, just remember that you were named queen at birth, and took over the Oikos when you were younger than I am… and you were not reared by you nor by my father. Gods forbid you run out of your cat-like lives. Who do you believe will take over your position, mother? Perhaps it's not me you don't trust but your competency at rearing me."

"You are…" utterly speechless. I am rendered outright speechless. How could I ever forget how utterly frustrating my son can be, exceptionally worse the older he became. "You are my Karma, aren't you?"

Chuckling without humor, the hand over mine clenches. "I am perfectly competent to decide who would take over which positions, and everything has run perfectly smooth, no differently than how Father had run everything for the past twenty years."

Shoulders slumping, heart pounding, a flash fire sweeps over my skin, leaving a sheen of sweat behind. I need to control something because I am unable to control the emotions rampaging inside me.

"Relax," is a whispered breath, sounding so much like his father that my heart clenches. "All is well. Just concentrate on yourself, because we need you to be strong."

"I can do that– I can try at least." Huffing a humorless laugh, head shaking at how uncomfortable I feel, inside and outside my own skin. "I have no idea how, but I can try."

Gaze rooted on that painting, "I don't want this hanging in here if you're sleeping in here. Either take it down and hide it somewhere or place it in a bedchamber you and the twins will never enter. It's inappropriate for you to see it."

"I realize my behavior seems perverse, but honestly, Mother." Sighing heavily, Jasper's gaze is rooted on my life-sized, erotic form, and it makes me beyond distressed. "I'm not looking at you and seeing you. I'm trying to understand what Father was thinking and feeling in the moment, and how he felt about you as he watched you sleep. I look to understand, and I know you can appreciate that."

"If this were a different medium, and this were an intellectual discussion, I could understand and appreciate a mentally stimulating debate with a fellow intellectual. But you have a life-sized erotic painting of the woman who gave birth to you hanging on your wall, painted by your father, featuring a private moment shared between them, and said mother is seated next to you while you look at it… a teenage boy, with an erotic painting of his mother, hanging in perfect view from his bed. You do Oedipus proud."

Tons of eye action, refusing to back down, challenging the new master of the villa to explain himself. Just as stubborn and expressionless as me. Just as determined as Zamir. Meanwhile, I've lost all emotional cool, running blistering hot since I awoke.

"I'm trying to understand how you can love more than one person, Mother." Slumping to rest his back against the cushions, Jasper releases a heavy sigh. "I'm trying to understand how both Father and you were able to touch others. I'm trying to understand how Cyrus and my uncle can share themselves and you, and how you handle it."

Instead of allowing the flames of my emotions to ignite, I take a step backward and think. I rely on the parts of myself that made me a master of the human condition.

"Did I do the wrong thing by betrothing you to Rica at such a young age?"

"Mother, no." Frustrated with me for not being deep inside his head to pluck his thoughts, Jasper's palms clench into fists, fingernail scratching me slightly. "I know you and Father's marriage started off poorly."

"Understatement, that… seeing as how I just got out of the facility after a six-month stay, all because of that marriage. But I would survive it all again, just to have you seated beside me."

"Mother!" Exasperated by me being emotional, Jasper rolls his eyes and swats at my hand. "Don't make this about you and your supposed failings as a wife and mother."

"Since I've never discussed these insecurities with you, dare say you must believe–"

"Just stop." A palm settles over my mouth, clamping my lips shut. I'm half serious, half toying with him– Jasper must realize this.

"You and Father did the right thing by Rica and me. We met when I was twelve, and we courted until recently. She's aged older than me. Neither of us plan to marry until after thirty, because as soon as we marry, everyone will expect children or think something wrong with us. So we're holding off on marriage, focusing on our education, then our careers, not caring if they think we're dragging our feet, and Rica will drink the tea."

The tea.

The children didn't drink any tea this morning. Only one cup. The tea steeped by Laverna. Tea served every morning by my nursemaid until suddenly the flavor changed, which coincided with Cyrus being snipped.

Sucking in a deep breath, yet another choice taken from me, even if it was for my own good. The powerlessness would not be felt if reasoned with logically and allowed to make the choice myself. I offer more autonomy to eight-year-old twins than what is being offered me, treated as less than a child.

If offered and asked, I would have consumed the tea. With both a fertility regained Cyrus and Ramsey vying for position in my bed, the tea is necessary. Before, with only Cyrus and Zamir touching me, if I ended up heavy with child, it would have been a blessing bestowed upon a married couple, with Zamir's seed the contribution.

"Love is more complex than can be explained," I begin, refusing to allow the rage to overpower my good sense. This is a private discussion between me and my fellow female, not to be shared with my son. "People are more complex than can be explained. No one is the same, reacts the same, emotes the same. Your father's sadism had a different flavor than his father's–"

"Father said that his father would press a trigger within him, he called it a bomb, and then he would be unable to think properly until he fed the sadism hunger planted within him."

*"Father, are you here to detonate a bomb you have hidden inside my quarters?"* Zamir said in the past, voice dry and sarcastic. I had thought him being witty and amusing.

The bomb wasn't inside these quarters– it was implanted within Zamir himself.

Then Zamir the elder shut us both behind a locked door, expecting Zamir to abuse me, break me, and leave me as easy pickings for the vulture lurking in wait just outside the door.

The tears flow, on the verge of weeping at the devastating loss– the loss of being able to support Zamir. To help him break the conditioning.

"Father felt worse about himself afterward, and we both know he didn't regard himself with high esteem in the first place. Grandfather could suffer no competition, especially from his own sons. Father explained the sadism to me, but never the way he loved you."

Jasper gestures at the painting overhead, trying to find the answers to the universe hidden in the brushstrokes. "Rica and I love each other. I've tried to understand how you can love more than one person. The thought of touching another, or learning Rica allowed another to touch her, or sitting in a chair and watching as other touched her, or her sitting in a chair as others touched me, I just cannot rationalize it, no matter how hard I try."

"My father was married five times, having children with all of his wives." This is a topic where it's impossible to explain, where you either instinctively understand or you don't.

"I was born of his final wife, as his final child. I could have allowed my ego to become bloated, because Father said I was the only one he called queen." Hands parting to gesture around the king's quarters.

"It was the fancy you tell a small child to make them feel loved and cherished, because she had lost all the mothers and siblings before her. A dark tragedy, not a fairytale befitting a child. Not that I doubt for a second Father's utter devotion to me. None of his wives were named queen, for their own safety, yet they resided in the queen's quarters."

"Your quarters?"

"Precisely," is muttered with pride, all of it directed at my first born. "Our family consisted of Father, Cyrus, and me. Not once did I believe Father loved me more than his lost children. What kind of monster would it make me to luxuriate in such loss?"

"My paternal grandfather was a monster," Jasper breathes nearly inaudibly, causing a shiver to walk down my spine.

"That will never be up for debate," is muttered in an emotionless tone.

"Father grieved every single day of my existence. He loved his children and his wives. Losing them didn't lessen the love, nor remarrying lessen the loss. Father didn't love any of his wives more than the others, where he would agree to lose one if it meant to bring back another from the dead. Father's love for his children was similar to his love for his wives, where he loved them differently, because love is about the person, and no two people are alike, so therefore the love is different."

"I just—"

"No two people are the same," is not uttered unkindly, hand falling to land over top of the one clenching where Jasper is clenching his own thigh. "Some are only able to love one person with great passion, intimacy, and romantic love, and that's okay too."

Eyes flicking to gaze up at the reflection of myself, the version Zamir saw when he looked at me, I truly try to explain this to my son, fearing he resents me or thinks me disloyal or thinks me a poor wife and mother, else he would have never made that comment. Twice.

"Cyrus is fashioned from my soul, and I fear if I lose him, I will lose my balance. Would I survive? Most certainly, but I would never be the same. Vertigo, staggering through this world lifeless. Ramsey is the light in all of our lives, all incapable of not loving him. We've only been intimate a handful of times, always distancing myself in fear of hurting someone I love."

"And now he's your husband."

"And now he's my husband, and those who would be upset have a voice, and they never voiced a word in over twenty years, so it's too late now," is murmured wryly, shoulder nudging my son.

"I had thought my avoidance of Ramsey was for Cyrus's sake, but as the memories unfold, I see them in a different light. Your father's ego couldn't handle me touching his younger brother, livelier, more befitting of society's standard of beauty. I say this with compassion and understanding, not a judgment on Zamir's self-esteem. I only brushed the surface of the trauma his father inflicted upon him."

"You said your piece about Cyrus and my uncle, and you keep weeping over Father, but you've yet to explain how you felt about him."

Eyelids slipping shut, shuttering the painting sprawled across the wall in front of me, a mournful sigh escapes my lips. "In a different world. With different parents. Parents who allowed Zamir and I to meet when I was only twelve and he was sixteen... where we were allowed to court one another, get to know one another, without insecurity getting in the way, without machinations moving us as if we were powerless to stop them until it was too late."

"Like you and father did for me and Rica?" Jasper muses more to himself than to me, and all I can do is nod in assent.

"Cyrus and I wouldn't have been intimate yet, and the introduction of Zamir would have enlarged our world outside the two of us. I wouldn't have seen Ramsey at the cusp of his prime, still a gangly boy with an older brother more befitting my advanced hormones and education... in a different world, I think Zamir was meant to be my soul mate, and that is not the fancy spung to appease a child when reality is too dark. Fairytales aren't real, Jasper, but that doesn't change the fact that fate cannot be thwarted, where I fell in love with your father, where a day will never pass that I am not in mourning."

"But we don't live in a different world–"

"But we don't live in a different world," I echo my son, the veil inside my subconscious mind cracking, where I'll need privacy soon, or my son will witness his mother breaking.

Standing from the sofa, I press a kiss to my son's forehead, the scent on his skin slaying my soul. "You have until daybreak to remove the painting from your wall. If you wish to keep it, never let me know where you've stowed it."

Shuddering from an influx of information, mind and body and soul unable to handle the brutal burden, I have to get somewhere safe before it floods and takes me down, drowning me beneath my own memories.

"But if you could," Jasper asks the hypothetical question I hoped he would avoid, the musings of a boy who just lost his father, wishing his mother to be miserable to prove her undying devotion to his father. "If you could, would you switch out Cyrus or Ramsey with Father?"

"I am not a god, nor will I pretend to have their power." Blindly fleeing the king's quarters, terror clinging to my skin like a shadowy cloak of darkness, my voice carries to my son's ears. "Who am I but a mere human to question fate?"

Leaving my eldest behind, my youngest tucked in their beds, and Cyrus joining a playful Ramsey in his quarters for the evening, I sprint to my quarters. Grabbing a blanket and pillow on my way by the bed, I lock myself in the closet. Pillow pressed tightly to my face to absorb any sound attempting to escape. Blanket cloaking me in darkness, I allow the evil to pour into my soul.

# DIE OR OBEY

Blunt head nudging me from behind, so desperately attempting to join the one currently filling my passage. Cyrus is still beneath me, fighting the undeniable desire to thrust upward, while Ramsey is curled over my back, rough pants eliciting pleasure-sparked quivers to radiate through my entire body.

Peering up at my husband, using my gaze to communicate, I reveal to Zamir how unquestionably I desire him, how badly I wish to share this experience with him. He is no outsider looking in. No voyeur seated in a chair, living vicariously through the cocks attempting to breach me.

As Zamir hums a soliloquy featuring his favorite of my breasts, I reach for the fly on his trousers, eager to have his taste between my lips, his needy groan ringing in my ears. Leaning upright, fingers hooking his zipper, I gaze up at my husband, feeling as if everything is suddenly proper and just in the world.

Happy.

Instinct overpowers me, an instinct born a lifetime ago. The order in which the events occur, I'll never be able to unscramble, because they all happen at once, within a singular heartbeat from one another.

My elbow is hitching backward to connect with Ramsey's temple, a sickening clack mixing with the air-filled gurgle flooding my husband's mouth, as a rain of crimson surges from above, drenching us in lifeblood.

With a shout of alarm, I move as fast as I can to catch Zamir as he falls. Acting in conjunction, Cyrus is off the cushion and grabbing Ramsey beneath the armpits, just as I catch sight of the arm wielding the knife yet again...

Yet again it makes contact, a scream of pure terror lodged deep in my throat. My husband dying in my arms, slit from nearly ear to ear across the throat. Cyrus half on and half off the cushions, his lover's feet just sticking out from beside the sofa... the knife lodged deep in the side of Cyrus's neck before I have time to react, too laden down with Zamir's dead weight.

"Allow them through to collect the fallen!" Zamir the elder commands the guards at his back. Too lost in our passions, Zamir's back to the open door for the first time, we didn't see the strike coming until it was too late.

Scuttling backward on my hands and feet, bare behind slick across the stone floor, Zamir is lifted off me by two guards I've never laid eyes upon before, just as the pairs are removing Ramsey and Cyrus from the king's quarters.

Backing up and backing up, palms and heels slipping in the cooling blood, causing me to fall and clank my elbows on the stone floor. Before me, a blockade of guards removes all forms of escape, closing off the door and the corridor beyond with a wall of bodies I've never seen before.

"You will now learn your place, little Miranda." Stalking toward me, the serpent hisses my name from his forked tongue, poison dripping around the way my name is spoken.

"You just murdered your own son," is a gasp of disbelief. Body nor mind nor heart nor soul, I cannot believe it. If I don't believe it, it didn't happen. I'm officially experiencing shock for the first time in my life, the psychological version.

"He was of no use to me any longer— you broke him, little Miranda." Zamir the elder crouches down to my level, vile lips sliding into a smug smirk, knowing he has incapacitated me because my brain refuses to help me out of this situation.

"He was my greatest accomplishment," is said with a hint of regret leaking through. "Softer than Ramsey ever thought of being, nowhere near as manipulative or calculating. Pretty too. Competition for me, I tried to chemically castrate him when he was still suckling at his mother's teet, but I guess that failed, since Jasper lives."

Stark terror floods my system, urine trickles down my thighs to mix with my husband's cooling blood. There is no escape. No escaping this. Fight or flight reflex is defeated and confused, warring within me, until I'm unable to move. Shocked senseless.

*"Destroying his manhood didn't break him. Cruelty couldn't break him. His guilty conscious couldn't break him. No, the love of a woman did." Lashing out, Zamir the elder grabs my wrist, and I'm ashamed to admit that I'm incapable of fighting back, let alone screaming.*

*Heart racing, lungs pounding so forcefully I begin to feel faint. Bladder empty. Mind nothing but swirling chaos. Zamir the elder proves he's always been badder, stronger, and in charge.*

*"Hold her," is issued to guards I hadn't sensed were in the room, let alone at my back. "Grab her wrist. I want her to feel the glory of the sleeve once again."*

*A terror-filled chanting rises to a fevered-pitch, accompanied by the clattering of teeth, and it's coming from me.*

*"You took my sons from me, so I demand payment." Crouched before me, handling a length of flesh fashioned into a muffler, with bits of bone and teeth embedded to gouge and destroy the victim from the inside out.*

*If the Devil wore jewelry, and if bone and teeth were jewels, the sleeve is a product of pure evil sent straight from Hell, worn by its favorite disciple. "You recognize this, don't you, Little Miranda–"*

*Skipping down the corridor, the tippy-tappy sound of my shoes on the stone always makes me happy, so I shorten my skips so I can hear it more. The sound always alerts the servants their queen is coming. It never fails to draw a smile to Mother and Father's faces.*

*"Cyrus goes around the cypress tree," is sung as I tap my way to the queen's quarters. Mother isn't the queen– I am, and she*

sleeps with me. "Slipping on a root and banging his knee." Giggles fluttering up, my skips get longer and longer.

"Oh!" the shiny flutter of wings distracts me, body pressed up tightly to the wall, trying to reach the windowsill. Straining and straining, even on my tippy-toes, I cannot reach the butterfly taunting me. "Drats!" is exclaimed as my bottom lands on the stone with an oomph!

Scuttling to my feet, I give a twirl, always entertained as my skirts swirl 'round and 'round me, going 'round and 'round until my head feels dizzy and I batter from wall to wall before landing on my bottom again.

Where was I going again?

"Oh, Mother!" Skipping my way, shoes singing their happy tippy-tappy song, "I should tell Cyrus about the butterfly. He's tall enough to reach." I flip around to go whence I came, only to be hit with the dizzies again, so around I go and around I go.

"Father wanted me to fetch Mother." Bopping on my feet, I skip the rest of the way down the corridor, singing silly songs about big boys who think they're so much better because they're taller and can reach the sweets jar.

Skipping short steps, hitting my heels just so onto the stone, I announce my arrival to Mother, wishing nothing but to please her and earn a smile as reward. Standing on the threshold to my quarters, I blink and blink and blink, not understanding what I see.

Acting on instinct, I try to be brave as I was taught, because I am queen and this is my Oikos, and Mother is mine. Fingers quivering so poorly, I can barely locate the tiny pocket in my skirts. The brush of cool metal, the tip poking my thumb...

Lunging forward, I strike the interloper above the knee, as far up as I can reach. His shout of alarm doesn't stop the bad man from harming my mommy. Slinking forward, blade centered before me, I try to step without making my shoes tap, but it's no use...

The stuck man falls like fresh-cut timber, the landing rumbling through the stone floor– a manmade earthquake.

Mother is lying on the stone near our bed, her body is bent funny, arm wrenched between her back and the floor. The breast I suckle in bed at night is lying in open air, resting on the rug near misshapen fingers.

The tips of my shoes are covered in red. Blinking and blinking, I step around timber earthquake man, trying to get away from it, only it draws me closer to Mother.

"Ah, little Miranda has decided to join us, Oona." Without thought, I rush toward that slithering voice, because he's speaking to my mommy. "Whatever shall we do?"

"What are you doing?!" is a shout of outrage, a part of this bad man is inside my mommy, and it's grotesque and nothing at all like what dangles between Cyrus's legs. "Get out of her." Lunging forward, I stick the bad man in the side of the neck, able to reach as he kneels between my mommy's legs.

"Little Miranda, why did you have to go and do that?" Patient and calm, the bad man plucks the knife from my fingers, cutting my thumb as it slides by. "I'm an old friend of your mother's."

As the bad man speaks, he rises, his body pulling free of my mommy. A torrent rushes from between her legs, red and yellow and brown and clear, whooshing across the floor to stain my tappy shoes.

Mother doesn't move, her insides are on the outside. My nursing nipple is lying on the rug. Those fingers that braid my hair at night are no longer connected to the hand.

Standing over me, blood and darker things oozing off his member, the bad man pries something from his body, struggling to detach it, revealing his member is no different than Cyrus's, only it's man-sized.

The fleshy sleeve is slipped down his forearm, reminding me of the armor on display in the gallery, only there are weird bits impaling the outside.

"Thank you for the use of your knife, little Miranda," the bad man hisses, reminding me of the snakes slithering around the vines. Leaning forward, his back conceals what he's doing to my mommy.

Her body jerks as he grunts from the effort, but it's the unnatural movement of death– Cyrus has a comic book called the Desecrated Corpse.

My mommy is the corpse. I don't know what that means. But the bad man is desecrating her.

"Gimme my knife back!" is a commanding shout, hands pummeling his back, feet kicking him in the rear.

"If you'd please stop that," is said over his shoulder, ochre eyes glowing with annoyance. "I'm almost finished." Several more grunts and more tugging, the bad man finishes his task and turns back to me, more blood dripping from his wrist.

"Oona stole my heart when she decided it was more prestigious to become the Livas queen to their dying king."

"Mother isn't queen– I am!" is another commanding shout, voice echoing and echoing around my bedchamber. "This is the queen's quarters. Mine!"

"I believe you," is murmured with a sly smirk. "You are queen now, my sweeeettt little Miranda," is hissed like a snake. "I'll be back in a decade or so to become your king. Until then." He turns and places something large into a bag.

"What's that?!" I demand, stomping right up to his body. "You stole my knife. You turned Mother into a corpse. You put that spiky thing inside her. You desecrated her corpse. Now you're stealing something else, you thief!"

"I'm only taking back what's mine." A gift is presented to me, dripping with blood to spatter my skirts. Fleshy and oddly shaped, almost round, with shorn tubes connected to it. "She stole my heart, I just came to take it back, little Miranda."

Blinking over and over and over again, I don't understand what I'm seeing.

"I'll add this bit to the sleeve." Using my knife, the bad man carves something near the top of the gaping hole in Mother's chest, then returns to present it to me. Jagged and sharp, the white of bone, with ribbons of flesh and blood dripping off it.

"I'd have you make a wish, little Miranda, but humans have no wish bones. Wishes are lies, my sweet little Miranda." The bone is placed in my palm, the palm that is out to clasp my returned knife. "Jab it into the sleeve for me, would you? I can't very well use the hand of the arm I'm trying to impale."

With a vicious lunge, I slam the shard of bone into the sleeve. "You could just carve your fingers off your hand and use those instead."

The laughter is instant and riotous when I was not making a jest nor performing mockery.

"Oh, little Miranda, I will count down the days until we meet again." My knife is flipped, hilt landing in my palm. "Careful now, wouldn't want you to cut yourself with it." Now I know this serpent of a man is making a mockery of me.

"You will learn your place when I become your king," the bad man promises, hurrying past the timber earthquake man to disappear out the door to the corridor.

"Mother!" Shouting in a rush, I drop to my knees at her side, sliding away from her, the blood as slick as ice. Shaking and shaking her. "Wake up, Mommy! Wake up!"

When I get a booboo, Mother always puts a plaster on it, but I don't have a plaster big enough to cover the booboos on Mother's body. Working fast, all the while chattering at Mother to wake, I press my pillow between her legs, because that hole is bigger than I am. Then I grab for my nightgown, pressing it into the hole in her chest. Then I cover where the nursing nipple is supposed to be with my body, because I ran out of linen to use as plasters, and I cannot take off my blouse– Mother said not to unless it's bath or bedtime.

"Mommy, you should wake up," is whispered in a rush, trying to rouse her. "I'm not ready to go to sleep yet. You shouldn't sleep without me. MOMMY!" All that red is cold and sticky, drying on my arms and making it itchy.

Mouth         open         on         a         bellow, "MOOOOOOOOMMMMMYYYYYYYYYYYY!"

Guards come running in twos and threes, their king unable to keep up. They try to pull me from my mother's body, but I hold on, because she doesn't like to sleep without me. The hilt of the knife clutched in my hand, I swipe and swipe and swipe, keeping them away from my mommy.

"Miranda?" Father approaches, a guard on each side holding him upright as he tries to lower himself to my height. "Put the knife down, please." Hands raised, Father tries to get closer, so I lash out with the blade, slicing open his palm.

"You're safe–"

"Mommy's not," is punctuated with another slash, voice as edged and cutting.

"Mommy needs help, my sweets. Let me help her."

"I'm helping her."

"Are you a doctor?" Father tries to reason with me, and that has the knife pausing mid-slash.

"I could become one."

"No doubt, my sweets. But you are not a doctor today, are you?" Father slides to his knees, red splattering up to dot his trousers. "Today you are a little girl–"

"I'm your queen," is a pronouncement in an emotionless voice.

"You are," Father agrees, getting closer. "A protective queen, my sweets. But Mommy doesn't need protected against her king, does she not? Mommy needs a doctor, and you said you're not a doctor."

"Not yet."

"Exactly. Not yet. So you can't help Mommy right now, but as your king, I can find someone who can." Scuttling backward, I try to drag Mommy beneath the bed, the place where she told me to hide from monsters.

"Use your logic, my sweets. Mommy is not in danger anymore, because Mommy's gone. You're protecting what will become ash displayed in the mausoleum."

"Mommy's dead?" rises on an upward inflection, panic and terror breaking through. Father nods, so I repeat it. "Mommy's dead." Flipping the knife, I jab it into the hidden pocket of my skirts, then scuttle underneath the legs of the guards, leaving my dead mother with Father.

"Where are you going?" Father demands, voice forceful and commanding, halting my footsteps.

"Cyrus will help me hunt the bad man." Scuffing the tip of my shoe on the rug, I try to get the blood off it.

"In due time, you and yours will avenge our whole entire Oikos," Father vows. "But that day is not today, Miranda. You are still a little girl. You will learn to become queen, just as you could become a doctor. But you are not a huntress yet, my sweets."

"Logic over emotion," I whisper to myself, finding peace. But my next words bring me pleasure. "He is a walking corpse."

Unintelligible sounds flowing from between clattering teeth, body vibrating on the stone floor, arms and limbs jerking at odd angles, *tongue trying desperately to seek refuge in the depths of my throat, seizures overpower me.*

*"Hmm... I needn't assistance after all," Zamir the elder calls his guards off. "Since I have plans for you outside of this moment, how would you like to feel your mother inside you?"*

*Slyly smirking while petting that sleeve comprised of human flesh and bones and teeth and terror, Zamir the elder slowly rolls it inside out, a calculating air wafting from his pores.*

*Completely vulnerable, unable to help myself, body revolting as my mind shuts down, there is nothing I can do as Zamir the elder slides the sleeve up my forearm on my dominant hand.*

*"As my possession, you needn't this arm, as you will no longer wield a blade." The voice is soft, almost a purr, the words jarring. "We will wed after you heal. Then I will lock you in the queen's quarters, where you belong."*

*The ochre disappears in his eyes, pupils eclipsing the irises to pitch-black. Hands crank around the sleeve, then drawn downward with slow cruelty. Scream shattering the glass trinkets in the room, an agony like none other overpowers me, yet I do not find the blissful abandon of unconsciousness.*

*Without my dominant hand, with my legs thrashing on the rug, I cannot protect myself, leaving me open to as much torture as this master of cruelty can administer.*

*"How does your mother's bones feel inside you? Have you learned your place yet, my little Miranda?" Again and again, hands clamp down on the sleeve and pull, repeating until my screams are lifeless, balancing on the precipice of unconsciousness, black dots sparking within vision that is sightless.*

*"Women should be seen and not heard," is muttered to himself, as Zamir the elder tosses the sleeve and retrieves the blade used to murder both his son and Cyrus.*

*A whimpered sob escapes before I can halt it.*

*"What did I just tell you?" Zamir the elder lashes out, slash after slash, my mind unable to process what he's carving from my chest. The agony so sharp, vomit fills my mouth, threatening to drown me.*

*"This was my son's favorite tit, if I remember correctly." A slab of hot flesh lands on my face with a splat, blood dripping to*

mix with the vomit filling my mouth. "This will silence you, won't it? I had warned you, yet you didn't listen."

The flesh is pressed into my mouth, soft and supple. Fingertips keep pressing, shoving it partially down my throat, something hard and pointed abrading the roof of my mouth. Vomit rises again, making its own exit through my nostrils.

Coughing and choking, I can hardly keep track of Zamir the elder, struggling to survive but unsure why.

The blade slashes and slashes around my head, so numb that I don't even flinch, sheering off miles of inky strands. All around us, my hair flutters in the air, landing on my splayed arms, sticking in the blood.

"I will use you and use you," Zamir the elder dehumanizes me until there is nothing left. "Once my seed has taken root, I will pass you around to all my guards as favor. Honored to take a turn on the Livas queen, the most worthless position ever. Your only job is to lie still, be quiet, hoard seed in your womb, carry and nurse children, and repeat until you're barren. Once worthless, I will toss you off the cliffside to the rocky shores below. That's all women are good for."

Jerking from the force of a knife struggling to cut my skirts from my body, the flowing movement disturbingly familiar to rocking a baby. Searing pain radiates everywhere, to the point I'm unsure of its origin.

I've failed.

I've failed my mother, my queen.

I've failed my father, my king.

I've failed Cyrus, my soul.

I've failed Ramsey, my light.

I've failed Zamir, my heart.

I've failed my people, my purpose.

I've failed my children, my life.

I've failed.

"Once Oona is of age, I'll lock her in her quarters as well," the patient words flare a burst of terror through my veins, body pumping adrenaline. I put up a fight, but my limbs are worthless, my body weakened by bloodloss, as my system begins to shut down from entering shock.

"Women are not meant to orgasm. It makes them flighty and hysterical. It breaks men, look at my son." The renting of fabric ricochets around the room, body jerking roughly as it's torn free.

Lifeless legs parted, a palm smashes down with brutal force, and I don't even have energy enough to scream. "I should have castrated you the first moment we met– my fault. Never fear, I'll take care of Oona this night. No woman should have the audacity to walk around with a bundle of flesh that was to grow into a cock. You are not men."

Gods! Imagine if Zamir the elder learned how his precious shaft started out as a clit and his testes began their journey with the potential to become ovaries. They're the same parts, hormones and genetics altering them.

Mind flying high. Brain detached from my body. From above, I float, staring down as my lifeless body is mutilated. The first slash has my body jerking from the force, a soundless scream arcing the spine, opening the throat, agony pouring out.

"You should take no pleasure in sex." Another slash and another slash, witnessed from above. "Your reward is the child. Why should you get extra when men do not?"

Dangling a piece of flesh before my face, Zamir the elder taunts me, the evil laughter freezing my soul. As the piece of my womanhood pass his lips, vomit ejects out of my nostrils. As I watch from above as he swallows my flesh, all hope is gone.

I will never leave this room alive, soon to become ash displayed in an ornate urn within the mausoleum, if Zamir the elder honors me with that at least. Perhaps I'll be dropped from the cliffs to wash out to sea.

Impossible to stay detached, floating from above at the ceiling, I'm thrust back into my body with the penetration of a blade. "How does it feel, little Miranda? First your mother's bone penetrating your flesh. Now your husband and lover's combined blood is coating your insides."

Jerk of his elbow, over and over Zamir the elder penetrates me with the blade. Shredding. Slicing. Cutting. Butchering. Gutting. The fiendish light glowing from those demonic eyes, he takes pride and joy in his work.

The only consolation is that I now understand what my mother's final moments were like, as well as understand the depths in which I failed my father and the Livas Oikos. I was never meant to be laid under siege, held hostage by the Devil himself. I was meant to avenge their deaths from the inside out.

Trousers are yanked down, and I'd rather have the knife. A cock is pressed inside a hole gouged out, nearly gutting me from belly button to tailbone.

"My first step will be to slit your sons' throats, just as I did their fathers', then I will take little Oona into this room and castrate her myself. As we needn't her getting any ideas in her empty head over seducing my guards for her safety. On the joyous event of her first menses, I will seed her. I will seed mother and daughter together in the king's bed, until both are rendered worthless."

Grunting and rutting above me, my fingers wiggle, or at least I pretend my fingers are wiggling. Pretend the hilt of a blade is resting in my palm.

"Every son born will be pitched into the sea. Every daughter born will be added to my stable. Seeded by my guards. Married off to influential competitors. Once barren, not even worth the cost of the food to fill your bellies, not even deserving of air."

Rocking in the ocean, a pool of blood flowing to cover me. I cannot even find the space where I float to the ceiling. I no longer feel anything but movement. Neither heat, nor cold, nor pain.

"You have no one to thank but your precious mommy, little Miranda," the serpent hisses above me. "To have a king steal your intended, that is the highest honor paid. To have that king gift his daughter to my son rather than I, that is the highest insult paid. To have a worthless woman reject me, question my manhood, that deserves the cost of every single female in her bloodline, for generations to come. Generation after generation, my guards will propagate your females, breed them, sell them, seed them to begin anew. Execute the males for the audacity of being born... and you have no one to blame but your precious mommy, little Miranda."

Releasing a victorious grunt above me, Zamir the elder empties himself inside my body. Orgasm cresting with an arc of blood raining down from above. As the head of the snake rolls across the rug, fierce ochre eyes glare down at me, mirrored from the face of my son.

Reaching down, Jasper picks his grandfather's head up from the floor, holding it by the artificially colored inky strands, blood and viscera dangling down. With a swift kick to propel the headless corpse off my body, he turns to face the doorway.

"I am your king!" is bellowed with command, decapitated skull raised high above his head. "Obey or die!"

*Around me, the stone floor rumbles with celebration and battle, and I finally let go... drift off into nothingness, until Miranda Livas no longer exists.*

# 6 MONTHS OR 6 YEARS?

Coming to within the closet, hours or days or years later, I have naught a clue. Punching my way out of the blanket, stumbling over the pillow, I scurry from the closet.

Once in my room, I'm unable to stand. Crawling on my hands and knees, sightless eyes staring blindly in front of me. Moving by touch alone, the pattern on the floor guides me. Smooth stone. Wool rug. Wool rug. Wool rug. Smooth stone. Smooth stone. Wooden threshold. Smooth stone.

Crawling through my bathroom, I lean over the basin, retching until what little was inside my body is now out, most of it the bitter taste of bile. Crawling still, I slide on slick stone, worried what little strength I have will die out before I make it inside the shower. Reaching and reaching, fingertips slipping off the tap, only to reach out again. Over and over, minutes pass as I struggle, exhausting myself, until finally blissful cleansing rain falls from above.

Strong, insistent hands cup my armpits, pulling me from the water. "No!" weakly lashing out, I slap and hit. How dare they take me from where I need to be. A towel is wrapped around my body, a hard chest pressed beneath my cheek.

Next I know, I'm swaddle in bed, fierce arms gripping my tightly, reminding me of how hard I tried to protect my mommy but was too small, too weak. Too little. But the one holding me is big and strong, all the attributes I am not.

"If anyone so much as steps near this bed, I will break their hands," threatens a voice so familiar to me, one that murmured to me in my sleep. One too young to be the one I mourn. Arms squeeze me tighter, dragging me farther and farther up the bed, reminding me of when I dragged my mommy beneath the bed to protect her from the monsters.

"We have to do what's best for your mother, son," Ramsey's voice rings clear as a bell. My eyes attempt to open, but they're swollen shut for some reason. "We're following Miranda's protocol."

"No!" is fierce command, punctuated by another protective squeeze, hauling me farther and farther up the bed until we're wedged at the headboard. "I won't allow you to do this to her again. My mother is strong enough to survive this, but you always sedate her just when she's about to break through. We can't do this again. None of us," is choked off on a sob.

That firm chest is vibrating beneath me, feral noises are rising in the air, and I realize they're coming from me. "If you sedate her, I will snap her neck and be done with it, because to sedate her one more time is to kill what little strength and sanity she has left."

"Ramsey, back off!" Cyrus orders, booming voice brooking no room for argument, yet breaking at the end. "Jasper truly means what he says. If you love Miranda, you'll back off."

"I warned, this is the third time– I'll do it." A palm travels to cup the front of my throat, fingertips wrapping around the side. "It would be far more humane than the torture you're doing to her, forcing her children to watch it, and you call it love and healing? How many times do we do this? Until the end of our days?"

"I don't know what else to do!" Ramsey shouts in a panic, sheer terror warping his tone. "All I can do is what Mira listed before any of this happened."

"Exactly," my son rasps, voice heavily laced with rage. "All you can do is follow protocols my mother put into place before she was harmed, and you have the belief of a zealot they will miraculously work, when she had never been in this position to know what needed to be done to heal herself. Over and over again, why don't we ask her how long ago this happened?"

"Six months," is a hoarse breath, incapable of making much sound.

"Six months. Do you hear that, Ramsey? Six months. Do we keep lying to her, having the same conversations as the first time? Insanity is the mark of repeating something over and over and expecting different results. How many times has Mother gone through the sedation at the facility? Three times getting this far at the villa, and it's harder to keep the lie. I'm sure in her head, it's time to visit Sephira and give her the garnet choker in honor of my father."

"I was planning on it– she's heavy with child," is a soundless croak, voice not carrying enough to be heard.

"Let me reveal a memory we have no luxury of time waiting for you to remember, nor should you suffer the indignity of reliving the trauma anew. You simply need a reminder to spark recollection, not dive right straight back into hell."

Shuddering as if cold, for once I wish I were numb, because I'm experiencing everything at once, and I doubt I could survive living through another tragedy in the here and now.

"You did visit with Sephira, Mother." The palm cupping the front of my neck smooths down the column to rest at my shoulder, bracketing me tightly to his chest.

"You visited her, you shared memories of my father, grieving together as a wife and mistress should. She told you how my grandfather had gotten to her earlier that day while you and Cyrus and Ramsey entertained my father. How he raped her and tortured her and seeded her belly, laying claim to something that belonged to his son."

"Nooo," lips quivering, the entire bed begins to shake, and I fear we're to have an earthquake. The arms tighten, hands attempting to soothe me, and suddenly the earth stops shifting.

"Sephira begged you to take her child once it was born, because she wasn't fit to raise her. You instantly agreed, saying you loved the girl's brothers– it needn't matter who sired her, she was yours. On a beautiful spring day, you were holding a newborn of two hours, while Sephira dived off the cliffside to her death."

Vault in my psyche flying open, revealing this as truth, my body unable to handle the tragedies, experiencing them as if they all happened this day.

"That's why this isn't working, Mother. Your body is going into shock, so therefore Ramsey is brandishing a syringe to sedate you– for your own protection, of course," is murmured with disgust against the shell of my ear.

"But then we do this again and again, torturing you with the most painful of memories, as if they are happening to you at once, and not spread out over a lifetime where you can heal before being bombarded again. Over and over, torturing yourself anew with the worst life has to suffer, in an endless cycle, where they think you'll magically get better this time, the next time, perhaps the time after that. No more!"

The feral bellow echoes around the chamber, reverberating from the walls, bounding off the glass panes, pummeling in the face. My son releases a sound more befitting an animal, one wounded and lashing out yet trying to sound fierce to scare the predators away.

"Go get little Sephira," Jasper orders, and my heart picks up in speed, hoping it was a lie. If she's here to be brought to me, then she didn't harm herself. If I had known the pain she was in, I would have helped her survive. "She needs to be held by her mother."

Confused, I attempt to look around, sight hazy around the edges. Shadowy dark spots eclipsing my vision. The foggy outline of Ramsey holding a hand up in protest catches my eye, Cyrus's palm landing squarely on his shoulder to stop him.

"Come with me– we're doing it our son's way this time." Voice grave, body bowed, Cyrus attempts to pull Ramsey away from the bed.

"So glad to see that you'll stop giving him everything he asks for. How he enjoys pampering and healing my mother in this endless cycle, because it gives him unadulterated time with her, when she wouldn't give him that if she were lucid. So glad you've finally discovered your balls, Uncle, and stopped being dick-whipped."

"Enough!" Cyrus shouts, dragging Ramsey with him. "I'm only retreating because the protocol hasn't worked, and it's time we try something new. You're as stubborn as your mother, so if anyone can will her into good health, it is you."

"I don't understand–"

"Of course, you don't," is not said unkindly, voice dry and firm, fluttering fingertips along my clavicle soft. "How could you? They've played this game with you, toyed with you, warped you, doing so because they felt it was for your benefit. Believed it would help you because they love you, but you don't need love right now, Mother. You need logic, and reason, and strength. You need the truth spoken to you as if you can grasp it, because you can. You are not a child."

"How long? I... what I just remember as happening moments ago, I was in the king's quarters, talking to you, ordering you to take the painting off the wall."

"That was six years ago, Mother–"

"I remember braiding Oona's hair while Ramsey sketched us."

"That was four years ago, Mother. It was two years and four months after the attack, and they continued to lead you to believe it had happened only six months prior, because that was the last time we had come that far. The children looked older to you, older than six months' passage. The landscape looked wrong. It was difficult for you to comprehend, because your mind was conflicted on how it was being told one thing but instinctively knew it was another. That is what has destroyed you."

"And my talk with Sephira?"

"Six years ago, Mother. Six months after the attack. You lasted three months that time. Three months of memories made, of us having our mother, of your lovers having you in their bed, of you endlessly mourning my father, of your happiness to hold the baby, and it all was wrenched from you when Ramsey injected you with a sedative, because you were inconsolable after witnessing Sephira jump to her death."

"I could have helped her," flees my lips, the same thought that passed through my mind as she swan-dived off the cliff to fall to the rocky shores below. I see it now, a film playing inside my head.

"I could have saved her, if only I knew. She told me she was leaving– I assumed she meant to move away, because seeing her rapist reflected in her daughter's eyes was too much to bear. Seeing the loss of Zamir reflected from the baby's features was incomprehensible. That's why I built the facility in the first place. It's why I enacted the protocol, to help those who cannot handle the traumas their physical body survived, leaving their minds and souls fractured."

"Ramsey didn't understand that it was a blow to your professional capacity to not save someone in distress, and yet another loss of something directly tied to Father. You would have healed from it if left to mourn properly, not taken the easy way out that only ended up being tragically more difficult. This torture would have ended back then, losing only six months to the protocol, had Ramsey not injected you. Six years later…"

Mind reeling, stacks of memories attempt to reorder themselves, but it's next to impossible. What I just remember experiencing this evening, it happened six years ago, another memory I thought happened earlier that same day was actually two and a half years later. What just happened in the bathroom and in my closet, that happened moments ago, right?

Right?!

"Truth." Fingertips skate down my arm and create a bracelet around my wrist. "I am twenty-three now, Mother. The twins are fourteen. Little Sephira is six. You're forty-four. It's impossible to keep pretending we're children, allowing your mind to be harmed as you look at us and know instinctively how we are not the age we say we are."

"I do remember thinking that, at least," rumbles past numb lips. "If I calculate it correctly, the memory was when the twins were ten, right? And I was told they were only eight?"

"Just turned eleven, correct." That dry tone is filled with rage, thankfully not directed at me. "My fiancé wishes to marry and have children earlier than we planned, but we cannot while we have this madness swirling around the villa in an endless cycle of torture for all involved. Truth."

The fingertips braceleting my wrist draw my hand up, but only a few inches. "Do you remember gazing upon yourself in the mirror, Mother?"

"Yes, as if it were yesterday. Logically, I realize I've probably looked at myself in the mirror at the facility thousands of times. But that first time, the first time the ghost in the reflection begged me to never take the sedation again, to do everything in my power to stay lucid."

"Your hair was how long?"

"Chin-length. In my memory, the ghost in the reflection, the hair swung around our jawline and it felt all kinds of wrong."

"The progression of children and the length of hair, no one can dispute it a proper indicator on the passage of time, correct?"

"Yes." While confused, I'm no longer hysterical, speaking to my son in the same calm and even tone he uses upon me.

"I wouldn't allow them to cut your hair to the length it was after the attack. You needed to see the passage of time, so you could swim your way out of the dark seas of your mind, rather than drowning again and again."

Fingertips settled against my hip, my son moves my hand, positioning it so... and then I feel it. Feathering between my fingers, wrapping around each digit. Grabbing a handful, palming it and bringing it up close to my face.

The darkest of strands, a few lightning strikes of pure white, telling the story of the passage of time. No confusion could compete with such irrefutable evidence. The chaos swirling in my mind calms, it's comforted by the truth, with the thirst for knowledge sated.

"Make me a promise, since the one you made to yourself was out of your hands. You begged like an animal, reduced and dehumanized, never to be sedated again. You felt terror over the prospect... and Ramsey always got to you when I wasn't around to stop him. He didn't do it with malice, honestly believing he was doing as you wanted, the Miranda before his father harmed you. Loyal to you. Ramsey saw me as a hysterical boy who couldn't understand. If you make me a promise, I'll help you keep your promise to yourself."

"I would very much like to keep both my promise to myself and the one to my son."

"That's my mother," is trailed by a bark of joyous laughter, lips pressing a kiss to my temple. "If you stay with me, Mother. With us. I will never allow Ramsey to sedate you again. You need to promise to heal yourself, and on the tenth anniversary of the attack, I will give you a reward. A secret only I know exists."

"A reward? What am I, a child? Will you give me a dish of berries and cream, even if I don't finish my supper? I'm the mother here. My absence has given you a false sense of authority."

Our combined laughter– Jasper's elated, mine sardonic –is cut off by the arrival of a little girl, the sweetness and light, the epitome of Ramsey, and the sum total of everything Zamir was fated to be. Pale brown ringlets falling to her behind, the only remnant of her birth mother– everything else, from the shape of her mouth to the color of her eyes to the mischievous expression glowing at me, Sephira is all Elezi.

The draperies open.

The view outside the windowpanes change.

The organization of memories right themselves.

The memories return in a way that does not hurt, nor harm, nor offer confusion. It's simply whispers through me, known as truth. No differently than a name forgotten, spoken aloud, sparking a cascade of truth, until the name and all it encompasses is remembered as if you always had access to that knowledge.

This is how the protocol was supposed to function, not the adulteration that I've traveled. With Sephira's death, I should have never been sedated again, the six months of treatment and three months of normalcy would have afforded me the strength to survive the devastating loss.

"Daughter!" opening my arms, she flies to the bed, wrapping her arms and legs around me. Her sweet voice chattering, a sound I heard even in my unnatural sleep, remembering the times we spent together at the facility. "My sweets, Sephira."

"Did my nephew promise you sweets?" Nuzzling her cheek against mine, she sticks her tongue out at Jasper.

"Nephew?" Snorting, Jasper crawls from the bed. "I am your king, little one. You don't call your daddy Brother, do you? So don't call me Nephew."

"Someone's pride is bent," Sephira fires off, tongue sticking back out. Saucy little personality, it's easy to see how she adores teasing Jasper. "No matter how much older than me you are, I'll always be a branch above in the family tree. Mommy says so."

Ignoring the obvious bait, "See how calm she is?" Jasper directs to the two figures casting a shadow across the floor.

Cyrus is braver of the two, immediately stepping forward, eyes slanted in annoyance at my son. Ramsey is only brazen when he's being denied, so he says nothing but situates himself on the mattress next to me, in direct challenge of his nephew's rule.

Intellectually and instinctively, I comprehend how Ramsey must feel right now. Head lowered, shoulders bowed, a tragic expression of immense guilt etched across his features. He honestly believed he was doing my bidding, honoring my orders, remaining loyal to the woman he loved, even if it set me back years and could have possibly cost me my life.

Then there is Cyrus, who reaches out to draw fingertips through my hair. He fought. He fought both Ramsey and Jasper, neither listening to him as they decided my fate. Neither my husband, nor my king, honestly never understanding that the only one who ever had authority over me was him.

Both of my men are ashamed, their actions should be unforgiveable, but the reasons they made those decisions means there was never a second of doubt as to me withholding clemency.

Those decisions were made out of love and loyalty and emotion, never logic and calculation and knowledge.

There is no one to blame, no one to forgive, except the evil that descended upon our Oikos, but the serpent is already long gone, slithering back to the darkest of hells, leaving nothing to fight, no outlet for the suffocating sense of injustice and rage. If there is nothing tangible to blame, one begins to blame themselves, and if they are cowards, they begin to blame everyone but themselves.

Reaching out, I grab each of their hands. Cyrus slotting with mine as naturally as breathing. Ramsey's familiar touch a comfort. As my daughter clings to my front, continually teasing the master of the house, just because it entertains her so, which means it entertains us all as well.

"If I go back to work, you promise not to do anything irreversible, correct?" My son has taken over for me, respecting me enough not to demand the title Kyrios, but we both know that crown rests irrefutably upon his head.

Jasper is capable, logical, grounded with a deep sense of right and wrong. He saved not only me that night, but our entire way of life for all the generations to come.

The title of Kyrios is not a reward, nor a curse. The responsibility for the lives of all those you rule, it is a sacrifice that only the strongest can bear.

"Mother knows what she needs to do," is directed solely at Ramsey. "Trust this version of her, not the unknowing one who hadn't experienced any of this from nearly a decade ago. Mother is not that sociopathic Miranda Livas. This woman is an emotional mother of four, your lover. Simply known as Mira."

# 10 YEARS POST

"So then I told Oscar to go pound salt." Dancing around me, skirts flaring in a kaleidoscope of colors, Sephira reminds me of the little girl I once was and lost. At nine, she's yet to shed that infectious sense of whimsey, and we will all mourn its loss the day it comes.

"What did he do this time?" Weaving around the vines, we go off the beaten pathway, trying to find a few grapes that ripened early in the heat of the sun.

It needn't bother me that I had no other children, as Sephira is child enough for ten, with the promise of grandchildren on the horizon. Forever underfoot, an insatiable need for knowledge, except it all centers on joyous experiences, and she demands I join her. My constant companion offering endless entertainment, warming my heart on the coldest of nights, keeping the shadows at bay when they threaten to swirl and overpower my sense of self.

"You know how Oscar can be," is muttered in a telltale grumpy tone. A stick picked from the earth, only to be tossed several rows of vines away, releasing pent-up frustration.

My eldest brought peace to all. The quote featuring love and fear is unnecessary, as Jasper is both equally respected and feared, and not due to inherited cruelty. Follow-through. Rules without gray areas. All know what path they must walk, and if they stray, they understand the consequences. There is comfort in that, even if at times if feels as if we're being parented than guided.

Safety and security, those who would creep in to take advantage of our weakened state, they now respect Jasper because they fear he always acts on his promises. They keep their distance and behave, knowing what they hope to gain is not worth the cost.

"Ah, you didn't want Oscar to go away to school, I take it?" Hiding my smirk behind a still expression, Sephira doesn't take mocking well. Just as her brother didn't– Zamir was incapable of understanding the concept of healthy teasing, thinking we were mocking him.

"No, Mom," is a lie if I've ever heard one. "He was just being highhanded and bratty."

Jasper was an adult when Sephira was born. During that time, I was experiencing a loop of madness, pulling all of us along on the journey.

Oscar never bonded with Sephira as a sister, not even as family, as they are not blood related. More adversarial tension than an incessant pesterer for a baby sister. Oscar has spent large portions of his eighteen years abroad at learning institutions.

So very like Ramsey, Sephira cannot be denied. She cannot be anything but adored by all. It's a thorn in her paw that Oscar doesn't give her the time of day, calling her a child in a snotty tone, reminding me of how Cyrus lashed out when I got in his hair when we were children.

"Oscar will come home again," I remind Sephira as I have every other time he leaves. "He's incapable of staying away for long."

"But this time…" trails off as my daughter ducks beneath a vine trellis, then pops out the other side. Keen eye spotting a ripe grape from a distance. "Oscar will come back a grown man."

"Ah!" a flirty giggle echoes down the pathway, footsteps padding in our direction. "Still pining away after Oscar, are we?" Oona's shaved head comes into view, smile encompassing her entire face. "You're too young to care about crap like that, little rabbit."

Practice-hewn arms catch her quarry dashing through the vines, girlish laughter ringing loudly to the clouds, released from both of them. Oona carries her sister like a giggling log, hitched up at her hip.

"Lookie what I found." Pretty shoes covered in soil are dropped to the ground with an oomph. "Caught me a little rabbit this time, Mom." Unnaturally large peridot eyes gaze down at me with amusement from the height she gained from her father, victorious smile always eclipsing all other features.

Oona didn't go the path of her brothers, no desire to become an intellectual. Towering and powerful appearance entirely passed down from Cyrus, her strength and determination were inherited from me.

Drawn more toward physical endurance, cunning and strategic, my little Oona is now a fully grown woman, half her head shaved with the other covered in tight braids, more than capable of protecting the back of even the most reckless master.

"Not difficult to snare little rabbits, seeing as how they can always be found in the midst of mischief." Reaching over, I pluck a leaf from Sephira's coiled locks. "Oscar will come home a grown man," is murmur in a serious tone, removing the smiles from my daughters' faces.

"The ability to age is a blessing," is accompanied by a few tears of grief escaping.

Mind drifting to nearly thirty years in the past, yet again I regret how Zamir and I lost the first decade of our marriage, too immature and easily manipulated by the snake holding us hostage— the division between all of us was for the snake's benefit, once we presented as a united front, he panicked and rushed his attack.

But at least Zamir and I had nine amazing years together, for that I will eternally be thankful, to experience unconditional love and acceptance.

Hands reaching out, I cup both of my daughters' cheeks, one slightly more difficult to reach. "Slow down and experience life, daughters, because one day you will be past your midlife, full of regrets and grief and wishes to change the past. Never wish– *do*, because humans do not have wishbones."

Pacing away, hands dropping, I gaze out over the landscape Father made our home. Those traumatic memories still hurt, but they're not debilitating anymore. The rage is ever present, the sense of violation and injustice. The frustration of being targeted and victimized when I did nothing wrong. My only choice was to let it all go, a choice I have to make every time a memory stirs or resurfaces.

"You will become a grown woman someday soon, my sweets." Turning to Sephira, a joyous grin eclipses my features. "Women have many weapons in our arsenals. The day Oscar comes home to witness such a sight as a devastatingly grown Sephira, that is the day you will finally bring a man to his knees without the aid of a blade."

"But that day is not today, little rabbit." Oona reaches out, snaring a giggling Sephira. Little sister clasped to her chest, Oona easily stalks off with her. "I have me a rabbit to skin and eat for supper... but Mom needs to go check out the view by Tortoise Rock– Jasper left you something. A reward for a promise kept."

"I do, do I?" Huffing a laugh, I behave, infallibly trusting my daughter. Weaving along the vines, keeping my feet off the pathway, I spot a few ripe grapes that burst with the taste of pure sunshine on my tongue.

With the help of the adults, the children named all the craggy outcropping of rocks along the cliffside. Not only was it easier to give accurate directions, it was an entertaining afternoon, arguing over which creature the rocks resembled, teasing how they should be named after each other.

This isn't the first time, nor the last, that Oona ordered me about. She and her brothers are known for leaving gifts and prizes and trinkets, sometimes making a whole day into a scavenger hunt. After the misery I endured, and with none of us truly trusting my mental stability, everyone goes out of their way to keep me happy, finding pure joy in entertaining me.

By Gods, I've earned this small slice of tranquility.

Curving around Mountain Goat Outcropping, I bypass Sly Fox Stone, headed toward Tortoise Rock in the distance. Hidden in the shadows as the sun slinks behind a cloud, there's a figure up ahead, facing the sea, back toward me. Even from this distance, the posture is relaxed, hands plugged into trouser pockets.

As I approach, my soft footsteps announcing me, the man turns to gaze upon my face. Captivating ochre eyes, a witty dry tone, a scar bisecting his throat, and a smile bleeding with anticipation.

"Miss me, my queen?"

# MY KING

## Zamir Elezi

Shaven scalp reflecting no light, leathers the same tawny shade as her flesh, shadows swirling around her as if she produces the darkness herself, Oona reveals herself just as her big brother closes the door at his back. She must somehow mask her presence to others, because I can always feel her lurking nearby, using my sixth sense.

Placing the papers on the low table before me, a pleased smile breaches my face. "My dearest Oona," easily slips off my tongue, pure affection wrapping around the words as a caress. "Thank you for visiting me."

"Zamir." Steps silent, form moving as fluidly as a predatory feline, the young woman does her parents proud. Stealthy. Sneaky. Spirited. "Gods! I hadn't realized my brother could talk and talk and talk." The whites of her eyes roll, peridot irises sent to the heavens. "I didn't think he would ever leave."

"Well, yes." Smiling up at the girl, I present her my cheek for a kiss. "Jasper does seem to enjoy scolding me, doesn't he? Speaks down to me as if I were the child and he were the parent. Taking all the credit for my hard work."

"I don't know how you put up with it, honestly." Falling heavily onto the scattering of cushions located across the table from me, Oona proves she has to work at being stealthy and silent.

Oona's father was never comfortable enough in my presence to be lumbering, as I suspect Cyrus can be quite lumbering indeed, with the sheer mass that body of his takes up in every space it occupies. Our youngest, the twins are comically different. Oscar is an academic, smaller in stature like his mother, while Oona is formidable in form, much like her father. As for my son, Jasper is the embodiment of both of his parents, which means he is the punishing sort.

"My son holds my leash, you know that," is muttered wryly in my daughter's direction. I find the children all so entertaining. The older they age, the more entertaining they become.

As Jasper speaks down to me... if only he could hear the monologue running through my thoughts at the time. My son would learn just how little he controls me. I was his age once, believing myself all-knowing. Gods! I was a moron, as is my son on most things. Age brings wisdom, having a little shit talking down to me is more amusing than insulting most days.

Lean fingers tap at her chin, pretending to contemplate something nefarious. The girl needn't pretend too hard, since she is a rather nefarious creature. So proud of the woman she's become.

Shadowing her big brother, Oona came upon me half a decade ago. Always knowing where her brother is located, with an uncanny ability to sense when I do or don't have visitors, Oona drops by unannounced several times per week, bringing the most excellent gossip with her.

I've lived two lives– under Zamir the elder's control, post Zamir the elder's death.

The former shaped me, provided immense wisdom to embrace the latter.

My son rescued me from the clutches of death, and when I was at my lowest, he manipulated me into staying in the dark. For my own good, of course. For the good of his mother, of course. For the good of everyone, of course.

Of course.

Sometimes sarcasm cannot be helped.

Other than a not so little Oona, which my son doesn't know about, I was allowed to retain Jax and Ayres as my companions. Other than medical appointments, where I'm seen hours from here under an assumed name, I do not leave my tiny slice of property. I perform the same official tasks as always, my son taking the credit as our figurehead. Hidden in a cottage at the edge of the vast property surrounding the Livas villa, with the song of cresting waves hitting the cliffside heard from every open window.

A peaceful life, the blessing outweighs the boredom. The monotony seen as a fitting punishment. On days where I feel I'll go mad from a lack of contact, the wind catches my scream of frustration, where I berate myself for feeling as if I deserve anything more, a fitting punishment to lighten the burden of guilt I'm taxed with continuously.

With no more bombs to detonate, with a son who thinks himself omnipotent, I am not allowed contact with our family, nor with a female in any capacity, fearing the evil Zamir the elder instilled in me will rear its ugly head.

Behaving like an angel, mind dying from boredom, tongue withering from disuse, sex angry to be holstered now that it is fully functional. The days roll by, age slowly creeping up as the most ironic of gifts, and here I sit… a good boy awaiting his reward.

Even if I have to wait another ten years, and another after that, I will behave, as I want my family back. I need my wife back.

My son, far more intelligent than his own parents, he has us both held hostage, no differently than Zamir the elder held us hostage, only it's for our own good.

Sigh.

While Mira heals mentally, emotionally, and physically, while mourning me as if I'm dust in an urn, I sit here on my best behavior. Jasper truly believes I wouldn't be healthy for Mira's rehabilitation. Honestly, I think on a subconscious level, our son is punishing his mother for not taking out Zamir the elder the instant he stepped into the Oikos.

I've mulled over the reasons why a Kyrios would invite such as man as my father into its midst. Why a calculating man who lived just shy of an entire century would wed his only living daughter to the son of his tormentor. Why a Kyrios would invite the very man who slaughtered his wife and fractured his daughter. Why he would allow that man to take one breath of shared air with Mira. The ailing Kyrios set the Elezi family up for failure, expecting his daughter to evoke the memory she had blocked, not realizing Mira's loyalty to her father, her need to do his bidding, blinded her to the truth.

My father was invited to his own funeral, gravely insulted when I was asked to wed Mira and not he.

I've come to the same conclusion our son has.

Mira was set up to kill all Elezi, make an example of us, with an entire grand hall filled with their people as witnesses. The slaughter would have had the Livas people fear the small, sixteen-year-old girl, when there were whispers of needing wisdom to rule, wisdom that only a man could provide.

Mira failed, the Livas people looking to Zamir the elder with fear and respect, thinking Mira a false Kyrios... and we allowed his reign to continue for two decades and almost lost our lives in the process.

Our people respect Jasper. Wise. Male. Having earned his position by taking out the tyrant who held us all hostage, while fostering the woman who was delusional enough to believe she led us all.

Then there is me, leash clutched tightly in my son's fist. Jasper is angry I didn't assassinate my own father to protect us all, only Ramsey or I allowed close enough to take the bastard out. Believe me, I tried, no matter the conditioning I'd survived. But Father was too crafty to not sense when his imminent death was near.

My reward isn't simply contact with Mira– it's regaining my life. As long as I behave, the prospect of being resurrected from the dead is on the negotiation table. The boundaries of good behavior are drawn hard. I keep to my cottage, take no lives, interact with no females, and do not practice sadism.

I've found a loophole for two of those boundaries. I assume conversing with my own daughter doesn't count as female interaction. As well as visiting the villa doesn't count as leaving the area surrounding my cottage, seeing as we inhabit the same estate.

Loopholes.

Our son is holding both of our leashes, and he might deny it, but Jasper enjoys the sense of power and control it provides, as any good ruler always does.

"I must behave," is followed by a heavy sigh, back pressing harder into the cushions.

Smile broadening, that finger drops away from tapping her chin. "You could visit Mother again." An eyebrow waggle, braids jittering on half of her head from the movement, shaved half glinting in the sunlight cast from an open window. "She honestly believed your last visit was a dream."

"It seems cruel," is spoken down at my clasped hands. Cruel for both of us. "I have so many blessings to be thankful, so many things I took for granted in my previous life. I don't wish to upset the balance of Mira's life."

During every visit, Jasper informs me how his mother is better off without his father.

"Mom pretends to be happy, ya know?" A flash of the insightful woman Oona is destined to become etches across her features, gone as quickly as it arrived. Overwritten by pure mischief. "I could tell you myself… or you could visit her in a dream, remind her it's only a dream, so therefore she's in control, and then she will be open and honest with you, since she lies to everyone else, including herself. Mom never lied to you."

I take the bait. "What do you think she lies about?"

"Love." Wiggling on the cushions, Oona palms the floor, preparing to rise and leave me. "Mom lies to herself about love, fearing we're all just tolerating her." Ghosting to the door on silent steps, the girl senses someone may visit me soon and we needn't get caught.

Palms pressed to the casing, Oona leans back into the door, smile huge and naughty. "I'll invite Sephira for a sleepover in my quarters tonight. Be there early. Hide in the closet like you pretend you don't do on a nightly basis."

"Brat!" is bellowed with nothing but pure affection.

"Notice you didn't deny it!" flows on the wind, a girlish giggle tugging at my heartstrings.

Witnessed through the cracked door, Mira is exhibiting a level of restlessness she hasn't felt in ages. Ghosting in the closet is a nightly ritual of mine, waiting for Mira and Sephira to dose off before I soundlessly peer at them from the edge of the bed, before taking my leave for the night.

Creeping in my wife's chamber would assuredly be placed in the misbehavior column, but I just cannot help myself. Mira grieves for me, but it would be infinitely worse if you knew the love of your existence was alive and breathing yet you weren't allowed contact.

A nightly glance has been enough to stave off the starvation, endless information with daily anecdotes, but the craving is never satisfied.

The shriveled muscle in my chest throbs with agony, only the prospect of regaining all I've lost keeping me inside the closet as Mira paces a trench before her bed. Jagged nail bitten, eyes flicking to and fro, the frenetic energy Mira is unleashing is worrisome.

Ramsey and others still fear Mira having a mental breakdown. Whereas I was never one to believe Mira a harm to herself or others, finding the sedation process detrimental. Mira merely needed to process the first time around, not experience it over and over as if for the first time.

They call me the sadist when that was the worst torture I've ever encountered.

"How do I get out of it?" is muttered beneath her breath, hair flaring out as she completes a circuit, turning on her heel. "I cannot share their bed– I cannot."

From the open doorway to the corridor, "My love?" flows from my brother's voice, causing every muscle in my body to go bowstring taut. "Aren't you joining us tonight? Little Sephira is sleeping with her sister." Softly padding into the chamber, Ramsey casts his gaze around, unsure what is causing Mira's distress.

"Have you taken ill?" Hands land on Mira's shoulders, halting her pacing. "Should I call a doctor?" sounds like more of a threat than a question of concern, causing Mira to jerk back as if struck.

"Ramsey," is a feral growl from clenched teeth, Mira at her wits end. "I am not a child," she lashes out, lines of rage marring her beautiful face. "Do not talk down to me as one. I'm allowed to feel emotions. Being disquiet is not uncommon. Evoking threats every time I exhibit an emotion is cruel."

"Mira–"

"No!" is bellowed loudly, the veins in Mira's neck throbbing from the force. "You need to listen to me, Ramsey!" Fingers curled to palms, she forms fists at her side, frustration clear to my eyes, witnessed through a cracked door.

"I was loyal to my father, held hostage by his needs and wants. Held hostage by the needs of an entire Oikos. I was held hostage by my father-in-law, his reign of evil two decades long. For the past decade, I've been held hostage by my own mind. But what makes it all worse, is how someone who purportedly loves me uses my own emotions as leverage."

"What is that supposed to mean?" Hardly ever losing his temper, Ramsey takes two steps back, hurt and rejection warring on his handsome features. "Are you picking a fight for some reason? Why?"

"No, dammit!" Mira is losing it in the most human of ways. "If I'm not agreeable, if I don't automatically do as you wish me, then obviously I'm having an episode. If I don't react as you think I ought, I'm obviously having an episode. If I show even a variant of personality, one that doesn't benefit you in some way, then you threaten to call a doctor, which is a code for calling in a therapist. Forever holding me hostage to the threat that I can and will be sedated if I don't toe the line."

The glare that is hotter than the hottest of suns, Ramsey stalks forward with purpose. "None of that is true." Beneath the seething, I hear the very threat Mira just voiced.

"It's true because it's how I feel!" Mira bellows into Ramsey's face, jerking her shoulders from beneath his curled palms. "You don't get to dictate if what I feel is true or just. It's how I feel. It's how I perceive the situation. It. Is. How. I. Feel." She articulates slowly, making sure she is heard.

Stalking away, now her glare could incinerate everything it its path. "It's been three years since my last episode, Ramsey. You need to stop walking on eggshells so I may stop as well. The pressure is killing me, but you refuse to hear me."

"I'm listening." Attempting another advancement, my brother is left with empty hands and a pissed off wife halfway across the room.

Flipping around to snarl in his direction, "But you're not hearing me," is stressed heavily. "No, I don't wish to join you and Cyrus in bed. Never once have I seen you interact intimately, hiding it from me, which makes me wonder why it's hidden. This makes me feel as if I'm the third wheel in your relationship shared. It's been nearly three years since we have touched sexually."

"Because it was hard to shift from being forbidden fruit–"

"Because it was no longer exhilarating for you because it was no longer forbidden!" A verbal lash strikes Ramsey directly in the chest. "You only wanted me because I was your brother's wife, because I was your Kyrios. You didn't want me– you wanted me to want you! Once I was neither your brother's wife nor your Kyrios, it felt as if you wanted me out of your bed because I was dominating Cyrus's attention."

"None of that is true!" Fury crawls its way kicking and screaming from my brother's throat. That charming creature, his manipulation, jealousy, and calculation are on full display.

"It's all TRUE!" is a bellow of pure rage, voice cracking from the force. "You don't want me! You only wanted me because someone else had me, because it would feed your ego to be lusted after by your Kyrios. You wanted me to pick you over your elder brother to bloat your self-worth. Once it was no longer forbidden, where I wasn't kept under your care, where others had access to me, suddenly I was in your way."

"I notice you haven't been fucking me yet still fucking Cyrus." The possessive, nasty monster unfurls from beneath the surface, showing the less favorable parts of my brother.

"I noticed how you purposefully only heard what you wanted to hear, then made it about Cyrus," Mira mutters wryly, tone humorless and disgusted. "I haven't touched Cyrus in over a year, nothing but affection between us," Mira stresses hard, gaze hammering into Ramsey.

"Don't make me voice the underlying truth screaming inside my head as to why you were always so eager to sedate me just as I was on the brink of a breakthrough. Divide and conquer. With Zamir the elder gone, Zamir the younger dead, Ramsey Elezi managed to hold me hostage in yet another way, under the guise of care versus how the father was blatantly honest in his quest for evil, never pretending to be a good Samaritan like his baby boy. Gatekeeper to me with Cyrus all to yourself."

The irrationally enraged expression etched across my brother's face is reminiscent of our father. "Cunt," Ramsey snarls at the implication, revealing a nasty side of himself I've never witnessed. A side that rings Mira's claims as truth.

But this is not news to me. The fighting over Cyrus is news to me, but not the assumption that Ramsey had less than honorable intentions for keeping Mira sedated and under his control.

Jasper and I have discussed this subject to death, my son quizzing me to determine if these are Elezi traits coming out of his uncle, traits causing his mother harm. We both agreed that Ramsey was not sedating Mira to help her. However, I felt it was subconscious on Ramsey's part, used to keep her under his care, while my son felt it was entirely conscious and entirely over Cyrus.

Seems we were both correct, my son and I, while the subconscious-conscious implications are still up for debate. It was entirely necessary that Jasper take over as an advocate for his mother's care.

My brother is a good person, all of us subject to the nastier plagues of the human condition. This just so happens to be Ramsey's affliction. Maybe it's my affection for him, but I do not believe Ramsey did these things with purpose.

"For you. I have pushed off Cyrus's advances. You had Cyrus all to yourself when I was ill. Almost seven years, and the twenty before that where it was just you and him. Just random bursts of interaction between us, where it fed your ego to have me isolated with only you as the go-between. Once you got what you wanted from me, you magically never came to my bed."

"Because you use little Sephira as a shield between us!" More than frustration bubbles up from my brother's throat. "You use the excuse that since we are not her biological fathers, how it would be unhealthy to rest in bed with you both. I'm not some pervert– I'm her biological brother, raising her as my own. Yet she is a girl of almost ten, no longer needing to sleep with her mother. You use her as a shield."

Falling lax to the nearest chair, head in hands, Mira is closer to me than to Ramsey, and I can sense that she is silently weeping, tears not visible from a distance. "I'm forty-seven, Ramsey," is whispered as a grave secret.

"As am I," is breathed back, Ramsey treading very carefully, behind falling to land at the foot of the bed.

"Isn't it time we stopped playing pretend then?" Mira has perfected gutting a man, verbally eviscerating him while he's down. "I have never wanted to be loved out of duty nor obligation, so I surely do not wish to be loved out of pity. We're months shy of knowing each other for thirty years. Don't you think it's time to be honest about how you feel? How you feel for Cyrus? For me? Don't you think it's time to stop playing pretend? We're too old to be living a lie anymore."

"What are you suggesting?" The affront is an act, the confusion even more so, Ramsey knows exactly what Mira is suggesting, refusing to acknowledge that it is a suggestion at all but a fact.

"You act as if my emotions are debatable, as if you can deem whether they are true. Yet when I shove facts in your face, suddenly it dwells in an ambiguous gray area of emotion. You cannot pick and choose how we view something, only when it benefits you."

"I think we need to take this evening to digest this conversation." Coward that he is, Ramsey slowly backs away from Mira, never coming forth to comfort her, to ease her insecurities, to tell her she is wrong.

As soon as the door closes at my brother's back, Mira is rumbling underneath her breath, as if she senses me watching from the cracked closet door, when I realize she's just talking to herself.

"My emotions are wrong until they are right, then Ramsey runs away like a little boy, back to Cyrus." Scoffing at herself, pure disgust etched across her futures, Mira stalks off into the bathroom to get ready for bed.

Jasper had warned he felt something was simmering beneath the surface, one of the reasons he mentions the reward with every visit. While I do believe my son altruistic, everything he does benefits him, similar to how his uncle operates.

There's a reason Oona begged me to ghost in the closet tonight. Not that I believe she set them up to quarrel, but that she knew Sephira taking leave of this chamber would cause words to be said that have been locked up for the little girl's comfort.

Being introspective and patient are my greatest gifts. However, tonight it feels as if every second lasts an eternity. Mira is one to fall easily to sleep, especially with the little girl snuggled up against her chest.

Tonight, it takes eons for Mira to slip off to dreamland.

Ghosting from the closet on silent footfalls, a soft glow is cast from a lighted lamp, Mira not breaking a habit started for the comfort of Sephira when she wakes in the night to use the toilet.

Only one other time did I dare do anything but gaze down at my wife, far back in the first weeks after she made her return to the villa, almost a decade ago.

Mind still altered from the trauma, while her system tried to digest the last of the drugs sluggishly drawn through her veins, Mira believed me nothing more but a dream. Cyrus and my brother were bedded down together in the adjoining quarters, our sons were in their own quarters, as I sat on the edge of the bed and watched Oona and Mira sleep. Mira thought me nothing but a dream, while Oona has since informed me that she knew I was reality.

I had visited Sephira, my friend, that night, saying goodbye, as I knew exactly what she would do once she birthed her daughter. There was a reason Sephira and I matched well, a sadist and his masochist. The same reason why when we tried anything sexual it turned into a nightmare. Sephira was not a sexual creature, more asexual in nature, intrigued and confused when she watched Mira with my guards. Us both having been raised by sadistic fathers, Sephira couldn't handle the sexual aspects of life, rather seeking pain as an outlet to release the agony of the past.

What my father had done to Sephira broke her. The night we said our final goodbyes, made peace with one another. We both knew what would occur after Sephira birthed my sister. I could have told someone, but I didn't. I understood Sephira better than anyone, how she was only sustaining her life as it sustained her daughter. Sephira found it to be the ultimate release into oblivion, and I couldn't take that peace away from her by alerting anyone to her plans.

The women in my life, how they've all been such different creatures. How I've made it my lifework to understand them.

Fingertips outlining Mira's foot from a hairsbreadth above, wondering if she can feel the displacement of air as I move, my words are barely an audible breath of sound. "You're dreaming, my queen."

As she stirs slightly beside me, sheets rustling with the movement, I slowly crawl up the mattress, until I'm lying nose to nose with my wife. "I'm nothing but a dream," is a rough rasp, tone taking on a dreamlike quality.

"Zamir?" is slurred in confusion, lips plush and inviting a kiss. Unable to help myself, I slowly lean forward to brush my mouth against hers.

The first time she kissed me, Mira meant it– it was my undoing. A shock to the system was my first kiss. I've never kissed another save Mira.

"Take comfort, my queen. You're dreaming of me."

"I dream of you, even when awake," is whispered against my mouth, undoing me just the same as that first kiss did. It's tempting to pull her to me, forgetting all about behaving to our son's standards.

Why do I have to earn my life back when I could just take it?

Jasper's voice echoes inside my mind. *"It's to prove you're nothing like your father."*

Touché, son. Touché.

"What makes you so restless, my queen?" Unable to help myself, I must touch my wife, but I do so lightly as to not disrupt her to the point of dragging her from a dreamlike state. Slowly weaving the white streak of lightning painted in her onyx hair, I hum underneath my breath, finding it fascinating.

"I cannot stop grieving you." Mira's admission harms as much as heals me, as she carries a loathsome tone of mourning in her voice. "If things had been different, Ramsey and Cyrus could have admitted they were in love with one another. Admitted they were partners. No need to pity me by playing pretend."

Heart clenching, Mira honestly believes what she says. "They both love you."

"I know that," is a fierce bite with a defensive edge. "I know they love me, no differently than I love them. But it's not the same."

"What's not the same?"

"Once you love someone with all your soul, crying out for them with every heartbeat, you recognize the different types of love. None more important than any other, but the loss of your soul is debilitating. I fear it's one of the reasons I've never gotten better, because there's a vital part of me I lost when I lost you."

"You're getting better," is murmured against the side of her cheek. Unable to stop myself, I snuggle in deeper, attracted to her heat and her scent and her presence. "There was nothing wrong with you to begin with. You're just now refusing to accept anything less than what you desire."

"Well, I don't desire to be pitied," Mira grumbles against my cheek, a saucy tone causing me to smirk. "I love them, Gods know I do. I am insanely attracted to them since they've aged like fine wine. But I don't want to come between them. It's the emotions it makes me feel. I hate it."

"Hate feeling reality?" Smirking slightly, the warmth I feel throughout my entire body cannot be duplicated. I've missed the connection between Mira and I. The intensity. How we would sit for hours in companionable silence, yet at other times, we would talk all through the night, baring our souls, never lying, especially to each other.

"What do you think?" As soon as the words are out, Mira chuckles to herself.

"What?" is slurred with a smile, intoxicated by the sound of her uninhibited laughter.

"Well, if you tell me what you think, you're actually just voicing what I think, since this is my dream." Dream Mira rests her dream palm on my dream hip, and I just about keel over dead for real this time.

"Or I'm telling you what you assume I would think, even if it contradicts how you feel." Chuckling, this conversation is going to blow my brains. "Ramsey and Cyrus both desire you and love you. Their duty and loyalty to you makes it suspect."

"Exactly," Mira drawls out slowly, fingernails biting into my hip. "There are reasons one doesn't get involved with their authority figure. The power imbalance. The one in authority can never know if they are loved for who they are or if the other person is reacting out of loyalty and duty."

"Until it becomes an area so gray that neither of them knows where the love stems," is mused beneath my breath. "My thoughts… not yours," is murmured wryly, a smile in my voice. "It must be easy for them to love one another, be in love with one another, seek each other out in bed, without the veil of duty. There is no misinterpretation when it comes to their feelings with each other."

"They've never touched one another with affection in front of me, barely been flirty." Mira just spews all of her misgivings, trusting this dream version of me, since it's therapeutic, similar to speaking to oneself. Even if I were here in the flesh, she would still speak openly, so I only feel mildly guilty.

"I question why they behave differently when I'm around. Why they hide how they feel for one another. Why Cyrus appears guilty for touching me. That was the last time I initiated anything sexual between us, that flash of guilt on Cyrus's face when Ramsey waltzed in killed me."

Heart clenching, hearing the insecurities in Mira's tone, my emotions turn chaotic.

"You've always been one of the most sensual people I've ever met. Such a strong desire to seek and give pleasure. A libido riveling all others. What do you do now that you refuse them in your bed?"

"I refuse to initiate." The agony in Mira's voice is a treacherous landscape, the pain a palpable thing lying between us. "I refuse to use my stature as a means to receive pleasure. If I asked anyone, they would feel dutybound to touch me, same as I fear with Cyrus and Ramsey."

"That doesn't feed the cravings." Voice thick, body arching toward hers, I cannot internally scream loud enough to curtail my erection– it's pleased to be in the vicinity of the one it most desires, it can't possibly control itself.

"I have fingers," is murmured with a flirty little chuckle, causing a groan deep from my chest to expel. "I have a shower, a hidden cubby, and a basket filled with blown-glass phalluses. I feed my own cravings."

That groan crawling its way from my chest is painful in its intensity, the imagery painted in my mind, there is no way I will not return to my cottage and paint that scene with one blistered hand yanking my cock.

My bedroom is a gallery, nothing but life-sized canvases featuring Miranda Livas as my only muse. The bed is centralized to see every brushstroke as I fantasize the paintings coming to life with every cock-stroke.

"The difference is between porridge and a five-course meal," is murmured with empathy. "Both sustain you, but only one is truly satisfying."

"I'm forty-seven." Mira was always one who saw age as a gift earned. Evidently not in this regard, judging by the peevish tone in her voice. "If anyone initiated intimacy with me, I'd automatically think it suspect. That they wanted something from me."

"Yes," is murmured with a lust-filled chuckle. "They'd want orgasms from you. You're forty-seven, not dead. I'm fifty-one and my cock has never been harder."

"This is such a bizarre conversation," Mira muses. "We were always uninhibited with one another. Raw honesty, especially if we felt it a flaw of ours. But you saying you're fifty-one with a hard cock is not something my dream self would envision."

"Are you so sure about that?" trails with a flirty little chuckle, missing the ability to banter back and forth with my wife. As natural as breathing, it feels as if we just spent last night in bed beside one another.

"Yes, because you were immortalized at age forty-one. Forever that age, forever looking as you did in those final moments. I would never envision you at fifty-one."

"Perhaps this is you wondering what it would be like to speak to me in the present." I skate far, far away from the truth. "Perhaps you're projecting how it would have been between us. This is something a fifty-year-old me would say after my hormones were leveled, thanks to my poisoner being dead."

"You were being poisoned?" The fact that Mira sounds surprised means our son and daughter have been keeping distressful information from her. She almost sounds as naïve as Ramsey.

"Weren't you?"

"Excuse me?"

"The tea?" is a prompt to remind Mira. "The fact that you only got pregnant twice in your entire existence, someone beyond fertile. The first time was because you weren't engaged in sexual activity with anyone who had motile sperm. The second was at a clinic, artificially inseminated when your nursemaid was nowhere nearby."

"I was... I was being poisoned?"

"If you call hormones poison." Sighing heavily, I try to keep my emotions in check, fearing if I became upset, Mira would become upset.

In reality, she knows damn well I'm here in the flesh, but it's easier to think me dead than deal with reality. We've all learned the lengths Mira's mind will go to protect itself.

"Laverna," is a harsh snarl, nails digging deep into my hip, only the fabric of my trousers keeping the bloodshed at bay. "I thought it tasted off at times, but it hasn't in many months. Laverna is serving my daughter tea now."

"And her mother-in-law was serving me food." Dead or not, I still have spies all throughout this villa, Oona the most proficient among them. Oona pretends to drink the tea, not that our daughter is keeping company with the male persuasion. Not that a daughter would admit that to her father, but mine enjoys keeping my confidence.

"Not that I believe Helga meant me harm. She thought it special vitamins and minerals to keep me healthy, provided by Father."

"Laverna controlled our conception," Mira murmurs in abject horror, betrayal laced deep. Mira never felt more like a woman than when she was pregnant or nursing or caring for young children. "What was your father attempting to do with you?"

"Slowly kill me?" is muttered with a shrug. "In all honesty, Zamir the elder was torturing me, no differently than he had since my birth. He loathed women, yet feared his sons being better than he. Zamir the elder tried to change my gender from my birth."

"Hormones?" That scientific mind calculates what my father would give me. "This is a very odd conversation. Is it because I pressured you to have your hormones checked but you refused, thinking it a mark on your masculinity?"

"Remind me to kick myself in my shrunken nuts for not taking you up on the blood panel offer," is muttered without humor, because it's true. Many a night I've lain awake, enraged at myself for wasting so many years in the dark, because my pride got in the way. "My mother said my father tried to bribe the man performing my circumcision to cut too much off by accident."

"But—"

"Yes, I realize I'm not circumcised," rumbles deep from my chest. "The man thought the request odd, especially given that our religion was not one that utilized the practice. Once that avenue failed, my father began drugging me with female hormones."

What I don't vocalize, none of this was evident during my three-week stay in the hospital. A miracle, my father had missed the major artery in my neck. Mostly this was due to the fact that I sensed the movement behind me. As the knife sliced, I was leaning backward, the blade not cutting deep enough to kill.

The bloodloss was life-threatening. My son saving me in the corridor. While the battle raged on, Jax and Ayres bound my wound and took me to the villa's physician, then I was transported to a hospital for numerous transfusions, where I was pronounced dead by my son.

"Once Zamir the elder could no longer poison me, once I was away from the cook and her need to nourish me, strange things began happening to me."

"Like what?" For someone thinking me a dream, Mira sure does sound eager. Fingernails dragging me closer, a song of surprise fleeing her throat once she feels my much larger erection press against her belly.

My queen is playing pretend, knowing damn well I am her reward. No one survived all she had, my intellectual rival, and could possibly be that naïve. She must know, perhaps mourning so deeply to make whoever is keeping me away feel horrid.

Mothers and daughters have tight bonds.

If Mira didn't spy me by her bedside herself, then Oona would have shared this information with her mother. At the very least, the few times little Sephira's eyes opened to cast her gaze upon me in the middle of the night, she has never screamed in terror.

The women know– they know, because they stick together.

On the very night I was ordered to visit by Oona, Miranda has a fight with my brother, knowing I would be listening, knowing I would join her on the bed.

I feel played.

I feel proud.

Touché, wife. Touché.

Mira plays the game our son created better than he plays himself. No doubt Jasper is beside himself with guilt watching his mother mourn the loss of his alive and well father.

Well played. Well played.

"Do you still menstruate? Do you still feel desire? A tightness in your belly. Your body empty and clenching?"

"Yes," is a breathy moan. Body rocking the mattress beneath us, Mira presses her soft belly against my erection, rubbing and circling to pitch my need higher. I haven't touched another person since those last fateful moments nearly a decade ago.

With a grumpy grumble, my palms curl around her shoulders, tugging slightly to make space between us. No rejection felt, because Mira could feel how my cock jerked, too close to completion.

"As the weeks passed and I began to regain my strength, this undeniable urge overpowered me. Not the urge where I funneled my insecurities and desires into delivering pain, since my sexuality was essentially poisoned from me. This incessant itch, where I had to masturbate day and night. It never subsided, no matter how many climaxes I reached. There were days where I would lie in bed, hand calloused, staring up at my paintings, a fantasy playing out within my mind. I masturbated around the clock, and it confused me. To the point our son dragged me to a physician, fearing I had descended into madness."

"Puberty?"

"Yes." My wife has made this her lifework, of course she understands. "The urge. My body changed. I had more energy. Voice deepening. Hair thickening. Muscles firmer. Hip and belly fat melting away. I ate twice as much, and it fueled my body instead of being stored inside my body."

"Did you ever find out what your father was feeding you?"

"A spy located the vitamin stash in the kitchen so it could be analyzed." The spy was Oona, and Jasper was the one to deliver it to the lab, not realizing his little sister was the one to fetch it. "The drug regimen for a male to transition into female, administered my entire life because my father loathed women but feared men more."

"Men require sons to pass on their legacy. I loathe that I know deep down my father wished I had been born male, just for the respect I would have automatically received. It makes no sense as to why Zamir the elder wouldn't be proud to have two sons."

"Ramsey was second born, a softer demeaner– neither a threat to Father's manhood nor to his dynasty. From my first breath, I was a threat to both. Father needn't to pass on a legacy, as Father always said he was immortal, and after so many attempts to end his life witnessed, we believed him."

"Jasper proved otherwise," is said in the most bloodthirsty tone, causing my cock to jerk and release a few spurts of cum. "The world celebrated the day that devil died. If I could resurrect him, I would kill him a thousand times over, simply for poisoning you."

There's the fierce Miranda Livas who bewitched me when she was only sixteen, skirts covered in blood. She was everything I ever hoped, a spark of lust felt for the first time, and then she set her sights on my baby brother and my world careened to the depths.

"It took months, but eventually my body went through full puberty, hormones leveling out. My ah... my cock grew," is muttered barely audible, shame flaming my cheeks. "Nothing impressive. Ending up five inches when fully aroused, but it's a rare joy to have long strokes on my cock."

A curious hand cups between my legs, squeezing and fondling to the point I fear I'll stroke out. "Mmm... I guess we both went through a second puberty, didn't we?" Voice deeper, a seductive tone that causes moisture to bead out of my slit. "I want to suck this length of flesh," is punctuated by a strong squeeze.

Suddenly, Mira's head cocks to the side. An instant later, she jerks up from the mattress, ears seeking something I cannot hear. "Go back to your closet and escape to the balcony– I won't lose my reward."

Well played, wife. Well played.

Miranda Livas is as sane as any of us. My daughter helped lure me here tonight. I am no man visiting a woman's dreams... and someone is about to enter Mira's chamber and take our fun away.

Feeling as if I'm a young buck about to be caught in a girl's bed while her father is turning the doorknob, an inaudible snort fires from my nostrils as I bound from the mattress, bare feet soundless as they land on the stone. With a single lunge, my body makes it inside the closet just as the door to Mira's chamber creaks open. A heartbeat later, the rest of my leg is safely tucked inside, no longer visible inside the bedroom.

Tempting, beyond tempting to press my luck and watch from a crack in the door, instead I decide it's safer to merely listen in on a private conversation. Back pressed to the wall on the hinge side of the door, so if it were to open, the door itself would shadow me. I strain to listen.

"Miranda?" is a fierce whisper, one meant to wake the dead without alerting anyone in the corridor. "Are you awake?" Cyrus pretends he doesn't wish to disturb her.

"I am now," is filled with annoyance, which works in our favor, as it's annoyance at being disturbed from our conversation, not from her being roused from sleep. "Are you here to fight Ramsey's battles?"

"Ramsey is Ramsey," is muttered sheepishly, followed by the sound of the mattress springs depressing as his lumbering frame lowers itself down beside her. Brave man. "I don't want us to quarrel."

"Forever the peacekeeper." The endless exhaustion is obvious to anyone who listens to Mira. "Never making the tough decisions because you needn't wish to hurt feelings."

"Ramsey warned me you were in a mood," is grumbled dryly, the whisper of sheets as Cyrus plays lion tamer by crawling into bed next to Mira. "What do you want, Miranda?"

"I want us to be honest with one another," instantly fires. "I want you to be honest with yourself. I want you to know should you decide to fully commit to Ramsey, I will be perfectly content on having a relationship built on trust, loyalty, and mutual affection, one that does not have to include sexual contact."

"I enjoy our sexual contact," comes from a stiff voice, poor Cyrus being slaughtered from the inside out. "I enjoy it very, very much."

"The point you seem to be ignoring, Ramsey does not enjoy our sexual contact. He was fine with me touching him as long as it fed his ego, but he is not fine with you touching me." While I can't see into the bedroom, I can envision the loaded look Mira is no doubt flashing Cyrus.

"Ramsey is Ramsey. Charming. Spoiled. Sweet. Caring. Manipulative. Ramsey gets what he wants, or he pouts and throws tantrums. I can survive not touching you sexually. What I cannot survive is dealing with Ramsey's resentment, mechanicians, and tantrums. We were already under siege by his father. I will not be held hostage by yet another Elezi throwing himself like a child due to a bent ego, my son included."

Soundless chuckles rumble deeply in my belly, that last dig no doubt meant for my ears alone.

"Maybe if people in the past had not given into Ramsey's demands, we wouldn't be subject to his tantrums in the present. Perhaps we should stop now to curtail them in the future." Cyrus makes an excellent point.

"Perhaps that person is you." Mira follows it up with another excellent point. "In the interim, I suggest you not crawl into my bed, leaving your lover to stew in yours."

"Maybe I cannot survive not touching you." Voice pitched low and intimate, I can picture Cyrus sliding across the sheets to touch Mira. A slap echoes around the chamber a heartbeat later, the picture in my head springing to life.

"You need to come to terms with what is a need and what is a want, Cyrus." The shifting of the mattress sounds as if a herd of elephants have moved in for slumber. "In all honesty, this isn't me being an impossible woman, forcing you to make choices. The person you need to be discussing this with isn't me. Talk to Ramsey, actually listen to what he's not saying, and we'll go from there. Just know, I can survive whatever you decide. But I cannot survive this limbo I'm living."

Drifting away, I leave them to their privacy. When I entered this Oikos nearly thirty years ago, I always knew Cyrus was permanent in Mira's life, in all capacities. In the beginning, I promised petty threats, my ego bent thanks to my father. But never once did I force Mira to make impossible choices with the one person who has had her back since her birth, shouldering the burdens through every trauma.

This is an important lesson my brother should have learned all those years ago. More and more, as time passes and I'm out from beneath the umbrella of Ramsey's charisma, his faults and flaws become more apparent. I'll forever love my brother, but it's times like these, when listening to two people who love each other so greatly discuss the boundaries of their relationship that should have none, that I'm not entirely sure I like my brother.

Since I cared for Mira's contentment, her happiness, and her need to seek release to slough off the stress being who she is creates, I learned to accept that Cyrus helps with those impossible tasks. What Mira shares with Cyrus has nothing to do with me. Cyrus was here before me, he's still here, and will possibly be here after me, and I respect that.

Hopefully my brother will understand this in regard to his lover, as Cyrus will be miserable contained within the boundaries Mira is setting. The only one who can release Cyrus from that prison is Ramsey.

This truly is a discussion that Mira shouldn't have to have with either of them, as it is fully between them.

Padding barefoot along the dirt path between the outer row of vines, I mull over how best to help Mira. For a moment, I think to enlist our children. Oona and Jasper are the voice of reason to both Cyrus and Ramsey, but then I think it best to let it go.

Ghosting down the path to my cottage, the wind forever billowing to whip my hair across my face, the cliffside imposing to the depths beneath. I walk these paths barefooted, enjoying the cool dirt beneath my feet and the soundless transport it offers. A rare joy I discovered nearly a decade ago, wishing to travel undetected from my cottage to the villa and back.

Face lifted to the wind, a smile on my face, peace settles over me like a comforting blanket.

ÆE

Tinkering around my homey kitchen, pots hanging from the ceiling, herbs drying on the windowsill, open shelves lined with goods, not for the hundredth time wondering when my son will make a reappearance. Cucumber in hand, I meticulously shave peels into a discard bowl, eyes peering out the window at the sea below.

*Jasper knows* whispers through my mind yet again.

My son is a pesterer, micromanaging every single detail of life. The fact that he has been scarce in the week since I last spoke to him makes me wonder if he didn't learn of my misbehavior.

In the past week, as penance, I too have avoided the villa– the longest stretch since I began this new life.

My guards and their families have made random visits, Oona popping in unannounced when I'm alone. A messenger has made his twice daily treks to bring and take work, a task my son used to make.

Curiouser and curiouser.

Isolation is a blessing– total isolation is a curse. Mind mulling over what will happen should my son push me from his life, I make my way outside, the discard bowl clutched to my chest. The sun shining high overhead, I tilt my face to the wind, nostrils pulling in the scents around me.

Most would find this simpler life a punishment, while it suits my personality.

The solitude.

Pitching the scraps and peels in the compost pile, I check on a few plants in my garden, finding tending the earth rewarding, especially when I consume all of what I grow.

Stepping back into the stone cottage, I appreciate the journey from seed to belly, controlling one of the most vital acts. After learning I was slowly being poisoned for my entire life, I began tending seeds, growing plants, fertilizing with organics, harvesting the crops, then preparing and cooking the meals myself.

Hormones and insulin go hand in hand, both affecting the way our bodies store, conserve, and expend energy. When I was being pumped with female hormones, they tend to create fat stores, since female hormones eventually run to an end with menopause– a failsafe system to ensure those hormone stores exist when they're needed most. I'm neither female nor going to experience menopause, so my body was fighting the influx of hormones that my system didn't create.

Balancing my system has taught me many lessons. As I was growing up, I struggled to maintain my weight to the point of starvation, yet not a single ounce was lost, no matter how hard I exercised. Instead of larger meals, I now graze when I'm hungry, a greater understanding of what hunger truly feels like. Smaller meals at specific times during waking hours.

Arranging a platter of homegrown vegetables, organic fruits, and smoked and cured meats, I take my midday meal outside, intuition sensing my son will visit. Just as my bare sole touches sun warmed stone, I sense Jasper at my back.

"Good afternoon, son." Placing the platter on a low table, I return to the kitchen, bringing two glasses of wine back outside. "I was beginning to wonder if you were avoiding me," is muttered down at my only biological child.

Brooding and grumpy, Jasper is hunched forward over the table, dark hair covering his eyes. Legs folded beneath him, ass planted on a cushion, elbows rudely plugged on the tabletop, my son is dragging homemade pita through a bowl of hummus.

After watching the children act as pigs at a trough, something they picked up from Uncle Ramsey. "No double-dipping," is a warning issued as I lower a glass of wine in front of his face, wiggling it to gain his attention. "What has you in a mood?"

"Your brother," is snarled down at the food I provided. I'd be insulted, if it weren't for the way my son attacks the spread, a starving animal angry with his kill. "You know how Ramsey gets."

Ah!

Cyrus is being proactive after all, deciding to put Ramsey in his place. There would be no need for a tantrum if Ramsey got his ultimate wish of Cyrus all to himself. Cyrus had made the comment that someone should have stopped Ramsey in the past so we wouldn't have to suffer in the present. Mira hit Cyrus back with how that person should be Cyrus.

To be a fly on the Villa's wall right now…

"Don't we all." A sardonic chuckle trails off as I take a seat on a cushion opposite my son. Unsure what direction this conversation will take, I decide it necessary to make a meal of wine. "Why have you been avoiding me? Sending me busywork via messenger as if I'm a child."

That animalistic gaze peers out at me through the fall of his hair, Jasper a younger, more virile replica of myself, had I not gone through hormonal warfare. Toned and firm, muscles corded with frustration. Dark skin flushed with rage. That gaze, reminding me too much of my father's, has the breath hitching in my lungs.

"I would hope we were past lying to each other, Father." Nary a blink, stare pinning me to my seat. "Care to explain yourself?"

"Care to not talk down to me as if I'm the child," flows back without hesitation. "Ordinarily I find your controlling ways highly entertaining, but not this afternoon. How about you ask questions, not demand answers to unvoiced accusations."

"Fine." Stabbing a cucumber slice with the tip of a blade, my son pretends it's my flesh. "Did you ask Mother to cut Cyrus loose?"

Eyebrows hitched high, there's a lot of information to unpack in a singular question. "Does anyone ask your mother anything?"

"Father!" Leaning back on his cushion, Jasper just grabs the bowl of hummus and declares it all his, double-dipping and triple-dipping, using a fingertip just to infuriate me more.

"I hope Rica enjoys garlic breath," is murmured with evil intent, a smug smirk breaching my entire face.

"Still sadistic as always, I see." Just to be an ass, a nearly thirty-year-old grown man licks the bowl.

Fathers and sons, the battle of enemies and allies fought since the dawn of time.

Not taking the bait, "I'm glad you enjoy the food I prepare." Smirking against my glass, I take a small sip, enjoying the bouquet of wine made right here from our lands. "Your mother and I, we made sure you and your siblings didn't have the same upbringing as we suffered. We felt we would be respected and cherished unto our old age for treating you as we had."

That glare could melt the ceramic held within his palms. "Such a wonderful childhood as it was."

Another sip, followed by another sip, trying to drown the words crawling from my throat. "My earliest memory is of my mother holding a newborn Ramsey at her breast." Making sure I hold my son's undivided attention, I take one last sip before placing the glass on the table, then I lean back, body at repose as my mind wars with itself.

"Mother had a sweet, mischievous disposition. I was just an eager, happy boy, who crawled onto his mother's lap, her arm held out in welcome to cradle me to her chest. She offered me her breast to nurse alongside my newborn brother. Blissfully warm and comforted, before my lips made contact, I was flying across the room, backhanded by my father.

"Resting on my belly, stone floor knocking my noggin, I witnessed my father backhand my mother, forcing her to fall off the cushion and onto her belly. One arm was supporting her weight to ensure she didn't squish my newborn baby brother. Ramsey was squalling, tiny body landing on the punishingly hard, frigidly cold stone floor. Mother attempting to take the brunt of the impact, though she was taken unawares.

"That was the first incident over a lifetime." Staring my son dead to rights, an onlooker would see an elder and younger version of the same man warring within himself.

"Seated across from me as you are now, I respect you as my equal. When you, for a moment, think your childhood harsh, recall how I've never touched you with an angry hand, nor mentally nor emotionally abused you. I've comforted you, loved you, educated you. We've spent a lifetime by each other's sides, never lying to one another, connecting on a deeper intellectual level. We have the relationship I should have had with my father, which is why Ramsey is so spoiled by me."

Reaching forward, Jasper snares his wine glass from the table, draining half of its contents in a single mouthful. Gulping to clear his throat, "You've never spoken of this before. Why now?"

"Because I've endured nearly a decade of you asking me the same questions during every visit." Pitching my voice, I pretend to take on the snide tone my son employs on me. "Have you been near any women, Father? Have you practiced any sadism? Have you masturbated?"

Eyeing my son, I show just how very much I do not appreciate those interactions and interrogations.

"When I turn the tables on you, asking if you masturbate, if you fuck your fiancée standing up against a wall, maybe choke her a bit just as she climaxes, you think me a pervert, when I'm simply attempting to prove how gravely inappropriate you're being with your father. Our relationship is based on honesty and open communication. Had I asked my father those questions, insinuated what you were insinuating, he would have gutted me before half a sentence was uttered."

"You know I ask those questions to gage your mental health. You've behaved poorly in the past, and I cannot allow you to continue that behavior." Never has Jasper sounded more like a little boy, honestly believing it's my fearing his disappointment that keeps me on a leash, not my own morals and self-control. "Why haven't you told me?"

"Perhaps I was saving you from the torment?" Head cocked, I hitch an eyebrow, wearing the same expression of supremacy the Elezi males are infamous. "I do not envy you. I see your accomplishments as an extension of mine. The better you do, it informs the world I reared you well. Even when you fail, you entertain me. Succeed or fail, I am proud of you."

"Do fathers and sons honestly envy one another?"

"I don't know…" is murmured wryly. "Is Ramsey holding the villa hostage to an epic temper tantrum right now." My son's deep chuckle is answer enough. "This was the relationship a father and son should have. I'd appreciate it if you'd treat me with the respect I afford you, stop playing games, stop treating me as a child. If you'd self-reflect, you'd understand that I've humored you for the past decade because it entertained me. I was always going to do what I'm doing, with or without your permission, as I am a grown man."

"Could you–" Cutting himself off, Jasper leans against the table, hand connecting with mine. Lips rumbling a nearly inaudible whisper. "Could you tell me what not to do? There are things you and Mother did that I don't agree with, but I need to know how else it could have been done."

"Tell me your reasoning, then I'll decide if you deserve the knowledge over the darkest period of my existence," is a harsh rasp, eyes flashing around to take in my joyous solitude, the healing peace I needed to survive what had been done to me and the heinous acts I've committed.

"Rica is pregnant." That secret revealed from a terrified father-to-be is all it took to convince me.

Palm flipped, I squeeze my son's hand. The two of us are not cuddlers, yet that didn't mean we didn't touch, even just enjoying the comforting weight as we leaned against one another while others chatted around us. Our connecting touch evolves, as I know what I'm about to say will haunt both Jasper's waking hours and nightmares.

"When I was nine, Father called me into his chamber." Gaze going fuzzy, I stare at nothing and everything, transported back to a time and place I wish could be erased from history. "If Father called, we came.

"Stepping into his chamber, I found a woman bound and gagged, belly pressed to the mattress, with Father rutting between her legs. The grin he flashed me as he turned, pulling his length from her body. Cock covered in blood, still obscenely hard."

Shuddering, suddenly thankful that I only ingested wine…

# ÆE

"Son, welcome." Zamir the elder's smile was one of pure evil, a flash of cutting teeth. The impact of that smile was more forceful than a backhand to a fractured cheek. I'd learned years prior to fear a smile such as this, as what comes next would destroy me.

Stalking toward me with a swarthy stride, obscene cock waggling with every step, dripping blood and other nastier stuff to the stone floor beneath. I couldn't help but stare, not realizing men were fashioned as Father. Ramsey and I were shaped the same, even though he is years younger than I.

Father proves I wrongly assumed all males had the same size cock, forever that shape and size, no matter if babes or old men.

Moaning on the mattress tears my gaze away from Father's display, the woman's pale hair tinted pink with blood. Gouges dent deep at her wrists and ankles, the cordage harsh and rough, tightening as she struggled. Skin painted with a wash of blues, blacks, and purples, splotches connecting across ruddy flesh. The muscle in the back of her thigh is so taut, it can be nothing if not cramping. Then there is the mess beneath her rump, the area where babies are born.

Mother had bled and tore from there when Ramsey came screaming into the world, bled when the babies after him died within her womb and came out as grotesque forms. I haven't knowledge of how babies are placed into wombs, only that women must bleed when they're placed within, when they die within, and when they are born alive.

"Lesson time, Son." The feral quality to Father's voice has my muscles quivering, skin tightening, and my bladder warning how if I do not get control of my emotions, it will empty itself to my mortification and eventual brutal punishment.

"What do you wish me to learn, Father," flows in an even voice, nine years of lessons teaching me to hide my terror.

That grin notches up in wattage, Father revealing how I am not as proficient at hiding my emotions as I believe myself to be. The more terrified I am of the man, the happier he becomes. That disturbing protuberance from his hips kicks and jerks, plops of white stickiness falling from the tip to create a string to the floor.

I had thought a cock was only for pissing, which is why it was so small and unnecessary. But Father's pride in his cock is obvious, making me doubt my assessment, as men seem to be measured by the size of their extra appendage. That milky fluid Father keeps spilling when his excitement spikes is unlike any urine I've seen before.

"Take your pants off, Son." When I don't move fast enough, only a heartbeat or three of hesitation, the backhand comes, knocking me to my knees. My continually fractured cheek throbs to maddening levels, but it has become muted background noise, the agony familiar to me. I don't remember a time when my cheek didn't ail me.

"You must learn to listen," is a warning only issued once.

Before Father can retaliate once more, I'm stripping my pants off, instinctively sensing my underwear must be removed as well. I fight the urge to cup my manhood, keeping the sac and button safe within my palms.

Standing in nothing but a shirt, I'm relieved that the tormented woman is lying on her belly, face pointed away from me, unable to see my silent shame.

"You still shower with Ramsey, do you not?" Father sets a trap, a trap I do not wish to become ensnared, but a trap I nonetheless have no idea how to free myself. "Your brother is barely five, yet he is inches taller. His cock already taking shape. His sac beginning to fall."

"Yes, Father." Shoulders curled, making me look as small as I feel, when it's the very humiliation Father seeks. Nothing is as bad as being smaller than your baby brother, besides being born female.

"This—" Father bellows in pride, taking his cock in hand, giving mighty strokes, yanking and pulling until his hips are gyrating with the movement. Moans pour forth, causing the woman on the bed to jerk as if struck from behind. More sticky strings drip out the tip.

"This is a cock," Father announces with pride, flesh overflowing his palm. "This is the cock of a grown man. It gets larger and harder when it seeks to enter a woman." Finger pointed down at the tiny button resting lifelessly above the twin pillow, Father sneers at what I've failed to grow.

"When I was your age, my manhood already functioned. Hair was sprouting. My father was bringing me his whores as playmates. Yet there lies your infantile cock, never to get larger as you age. Your brother already far exceeding in growth."

Hand falling heavily to land on my shoulder, Father leaves a sticky residue on my shirt. The musky stench rankling my nostrils. Tugging me across the room to the woman sprawled at the edge of the bed, Father stands between her legs, hands cupping her bottom to pull her apart.

Raw meat is revealed, the stench of stale urine, the coppery twang of fresh blood, and the nose rankling reek of passed wind wafts up as Father displays what a woman has between her thighs. The farther he pulls, the more that is revealed. Red and swollen, the passage inside the woman continues farther than my eye can see.

"This–" Father points between her legs, raw and bloody and ravaged from his obscene cock, until it's impossible to recognize any of it as flesh. "See this small nub?" Father flicks a bean-like object at the top of her sex, causing the woman to jerk in her bindings. "Your cock is the same size as a woman's pussy. I'm going to call what you have boy pussy from now on. You're no son of mine with that dinky, worthless cock, never able to best me. Your mother ought to have borne me a daughter instead, at least she would have had worth when I sold her cunt to the highest bidder."

Silently cascading, tears drip off my chin, this moment of humiliation no different than the dozens upon dozens before it. Only made worse by the fact that a woman is witnessing it.

"You'll never be able to do this." With the jerk of his hips, Father roughly enters the woman, that cock causing her to jerk and flail and make gargling sounds beneath her gag. "You'll never be able to go deep enough to seed a womb. You may as well just bend over the bed and let me fuck you instead."

Body shuddering, my mind is spinning, attempting to figure out where Father intends to enter when I have no natural hole in my body like a woman does.

*"Unless…" Father pauses his movements, pretending to contemplate something he already imagined months ago, perhaps years, simply toying with me. "Since you'll never be able to take a woman as you ought, you have a choice to make. Either you bend over and take a cock like a woman, be treated as a woman, or you can learn to use other means to penetrate a woman."*

*Watching the emotions scroll across my face, Father turns impatient. "Make the choice. Quickly." That hand flexes, prepared to backhand me across the room, fingers twitching with desire. "Either become my plaything or turn women into playthings. There is no in between. You must learn the lesson I teach you, and if you do not continue with your studies, I will bend you over a bed and rut upon your anus until your entrails spill onto the stone floor, as no son of mine will be a worthless woman."*

*Translation: it's me or her.*

*I choose her.*

*"Teach me, Father," is a rasp far more confident than I feel. Gulping loudly, I gaze down at the woman, unsure what Father could possibly need me to do next.*

*"This cunt here–" with a heavy slap to her buttock, Father causes the woman to roll on the mattress, her binds digging deeply into her wrists and ankles to draw a fresh wash of blood. Beneath the gag, the woman releases a silent scream.*

*"Women deserve to be punished, especially every female in this cunt's line." Another slap, this one far harsher than the last, Father's nails scratching deep furrows down the length of her buttocks. Deep enough that it takes seconds before blood wells to fill the trenches.*

*"Why, Father? What has this woman's family done?" Realizing I spoke out of turn, how the punishment Father is employing on this woman could easily be turned and employed on me, my mind scrambles on how to right the wrong. "What has occurred, other than she is a worthless woman who deserves any punishment you see fit."*

*"Nice save, Zamir." Father smirks at me as if proud, forever telling me how my body and cock are a disappointment, but my quick mind will help me survive him. "Her sister left me."*

*"When?"*

*"Four years ago."*

"But what of Mother?" tumbles out before I can capture it and swallow it down, not understanding the ways of men and their wives. I earn a backhand for the insult, but the hit is pulled because I saw the error of my ways before Father could punish me.

"A woman is to have but one man, while men are not held beholden to that concept, not that it will be an issue for you." Sighing heavily, as if eternally disappointed in the first son Mother bred him, Father smirks down at my button-sized cock.

"Her sister, Oona, she thought herself better than a woman. Thought she had a choice. Ran from me and married an ailing octogenarian– a king among his people."

Waiting my reaction, Father inspects the emotions flashing across my face. "To be rejected for a common man would be a grave insult paid. That he is a king–"

Clack!

Wrong answer, I find myself halfway across the room, cheekbone radiating a fiery explosion of agony. Rational thinking is not part of my education at Father's hand. Father must come first, everyone bowing down to his commands, all women must find him the most masculine creature on the planet.

"Had the king chose her, I could understand." Spittle flying, Father is lording over me, imposing form curled down to shout into my face. "That would have been the highest form of flattery, a king demanding possession of my woman. Oona chose him after refusing me. No woman has a choice! The fact that she left me and propositioned him is why every ounce of her blood will be eradicated from this earth."

Using my elbow as leverage, self-preservation gives me the strength to come to my feet, movements sluggish from yet another hit landing. "Then we must punish this woman, Father. Since we cannot punish her sister, she must be the proxy."

Frozen still, I stare up at my master, fearing I gave the wrong answer. Blood drips from the corner of my eye, vision blurry– the sting causing tears to build then fall. But I don't brush the tears nor the blood away, fearing Father would find it a sign of weakness.

Just as offering this innocent woman compassion would be a weakness. Explaining to Father how Oona has a choice in who she marries would be the gravest insult I could pay him. Explaining how nothing Father does is rational would leave my body broken and lifeless after enduring unimaginable torture.

Muscles turning taut, shoulders curled back, head held high, I turn to the woman. Cruelty is Father's currency, a currency I must pay to survive. Stomach turning over on itself, as I pretend this is the most fascinating experience of my life, I slide my entire hand inside the woman between her legs, instinctively knowing Father would feel proud for me doing so.

Scorching hot, the moisture clinging to the sides of my wrist, I struggle to fit my entire hand inside the cavity between the woman's legs. Slick and sticky, blood paves the way, coating the sides of my forearm, sucking me down until I'm elbow deep. Once I hit a stopping point, I push in farther, causing the woman to jerk and yank at her binds, deep gouges bleeding anew at her wrists and ankles.

The gag cannot contain the scream.

Focused. Determined. Angry. I do as Father bids, destroying her from the inside out, using my curled fist because I only have a boy pussy.

Either her or me, and I choose me.

Choose me to survive this hellish landscape for being Zamir Elezi's namesake. Because if I do not commit this act, it will be my much smaller body tied to the bed, a hole created where one doesn't exist, and I would not leave this room while still breathing.

"Impressive, Son." Father's praise should not fill me with life but it does, radiating from inside my chest cavity to envelop me with its fiery evil. "Allow me to demonstrate." Fingers curl around my elbow, touch gentle for the first time, then they slowly pull my arm from the woman's body, the sucking sound perverse as I am freed.

With pride and lust and demonic desire, Father stares at the filth coating my hand and forearm. "This is practice for you." Father materializes a vile bracer covered in bits of bone and teeth and drying viscera. "After we dispose of this one's entire family, we will travel to take care of Oona herself."

"Yes, Father," is stated in an emotionless voice, stepping aside to allow Father access between the woman's legs. Beside me, Father is sliding the bracer onto his grotesque cock, the inside smooth flesh, with the outside covered in what used to be housed inside flesh.

*"We shall bide our time, Son."* Sharp teeth gritted, eyes glittering with a jewellike determination of pure evil, Father thrusts harshly with his hips, hammering his cock within the woman's body, the bits of bone cutting her from the inside out.

Panting roughly, Father grins at me as the woman screams behind the gag, body fighting to remain conscious. A fresh wash of urine and blood flows from between her legs. The agony so severe her bowels empty themselves, liquified as the light slowly fades in her eyes.

*"Weak. Women are weak."* Father yanks from the woman's body, bits of her womb clinging to the bracer to splat to the stone floor, the spattered blood burning my bare feet. The stench twisting my stomach.

*"I thought this one would last as long as her mother."* Snickering loudly, Father flips the woman over onto her back, not caring that her left wrist is nearly bisected from the cutting action of her binds. *"Mother dearest lasted for hours, refusing to give me the whereabouts of her daughters and granddaughters."*

Pivoting to the side, Father snares a curved blade from the bedside table, then begins butchering the woman. She has to have already passed unto the fade, because the jerking of her body is caused by Father's movements.

Pale, lifeless eyes stare up at the ceiling, as if she is begging the Gods in the heavens to save those she left behind.

The first cut and the second are her breasts, the flesh tossed to the stone floor with a wet splat, discarded as garbage. The following cut is to slice off a flap of skin running along her sex. Once the curved blade penetrates the opening to the womb, gutting her like a goat, I fly across the floor, curling myself into a ball in the corner. Retching, I vomit down the front of my shirt, piss dampening the floor to spatter against my knees and palms.

A touch to the small of my back has a high-pitched scream pouring from my throat, shrill enough to notify everyone on the estate. Echoing off the walls, bounding out the open windows, my panicked, horrified song escapes because I cannot.

*"Do you wish to be treated as that woman, Son?"* Enraged at my show of weakness, Father swats me so hard I end up righted on my palms and knees. *"Shall I treat you as a woman ought to be treated?"*

The proud, gentle touch from earlier is replaced by harsh movements meant to teach punishing lessons. One. Two. Three.

*Four. Then a thumb. An entire hand fists itself into my rectum, pounding lessons into the fabric that makes me who I am, destroying me from the inside out, destroying any goodness left within me.*

*"You will do to Oona's daughter that which I will do to every female descending from her linage." Another pounding punch, Father demonstrating how he can turn anyone into a whore, even if he has to create a hole himself.*

*"If you do not do as I instruct." With the twist of his wrist, Father has vomit ejecting from my throat, the pain unimaginable as he rearranges my bowels. "The next time will be my cock, and the last time will be the sleeve. You will take the daughter as I will take the mother, the grandmother, the aunts, and the nieces and cousins. Do I make myself clear?"*

*"Yes, Father," flows without sound. "It's them or me and I choose me."*

ÆE

Jasper asks from across the table, our meal gone to the flies. "What happened next?"

"No," is a harsh rasp, my voice raw from the storytelling. Nerves frayed on edge, skin taut and itchy, a buzz is swarming in my belly. I never wanted to relive that moment in time, which has me empathizing with Mira, how she was forced to relive devastating events over and over again, with no compassion nor care for how that would affect her long-term.

"No."

"No?" My son doesn't understand, because if he did, he wouldn't ask. If he understood, he wouldn't want the answer. "No?"

"No. I will not give details on what happened next." As soon as the words breach my lips, I know they will not sway my son, as he is my son. Stubborn and willful, too curious for survival's sake.

"The woman I helped murder, she had three daughters, all of them close in age to me and Ramsey. Do not ask for details on what Father did to them," is a warning that I will never voice the atrocities I witnessed.

The atrocities I was forced to participate in or risk a similar fate.

"Father slit the throat of all the males in their family, because they were chosen by the women when Father was not. Then he hung them from pikes bordering the property line, enjoying the view of crows consuming their eyeballs and entrails as he ate his breakfast."

"Sounds like the sadistic sonofabitch I beheaded," cuts sharp as my son sneers in my direction. "What happened to your mother?"

Eyes rolled in my son's direction, "I cannot believe you had the audacity to ask that, Jasper. I thought you smarter than that." What little wine I consumed threatens to flee my stomach. "Your grandfather murdered both of your grandmothers, your great-grandmother, your aunt and her daughters, along with fifteen males– the grandfathers, uncles, husbands, nephews and cousins. No differently than he planned to do with your mother and sisters."

Fingers tapping on the table before us, mind sparring in many directions, Jasper is frustrated because he doesn't understand the mind of madness. "Why did Grandfather chemically castrate you then humiliate you for it?"

Head weaving to and fro, I simply eyeball my son. "Because Zamir Elezi the elder was evil?" Hands parted, I cannot believe I have to explain this to my son. "Because he was a narcissist who couldn't handle anyone thinking him not as powerful as he thought himself to be. Because your grandmother rejected him and that was proof that the false narrative he wrote within his head was exactly that, false. It was a reality check he couldn't handle, so he made them suffer and pay to prove he was as powerful as he thought himself to be."

"But why did he do that to you?" Jasper muses more to himself than to me. It soothes my tortured soul to see that my son is a good person who cannot fathom why evil performs evil.

"Because half a man would never be seen as greater than his father, as Father had to be the best, most powerful, most virile man on the planet, and his spawn could not outshine him. Because if my cock couldn't rise, your mother couldn't seduce me with a single look." More than a boundary or two is crossed with this admission alone. No son should realize the males in his family find his mother intoxicating.

"Father tried to make me loathe women, so when I met your mother, I would think her inferior to me, believe she deserved pain and punishment for being born female. Feel emasculated that Mira felt she was in charge. Feel insulted when she gazed upon my brother with lust. This was all set up by father. If my cock couldn't communicate, I would still be my father's creature, your mother having no hold over me, which your existence proves false. Another harsh reality that contradicted the fantasy my father erected for himself."

Nodding while chewing on the inside of his cheek, Jasper is rolling all of that over in his mind, finding it unfathomable because he himself is sane. "What do you think Mother's father planned?" Nodding more, Jasper keeps staring at me over the corpse of our midday meal. "That has always plagued me."

"As it has your mother," is murmured across the table. "I believe Mira was meant to assassinate the entire Elezi family the day we entered the Livas Oikos. Your grandfather was ailing, the dusk of his life, leaving behind a young daughter with no protection, one his people would not respect. Mira was supposed to remember who butchered her mother, then appropriately slaughter my father, me, and my brother, with the important members of her people acting as witness for her sheer ruthlessness."

"Grandfather would know it was a trap." More nodding to himself as he analyzes the risk assessment. "He was issued an insult when he wasn't betrothed to my mother. Insulted again when he was passed over for you. Then invited into our Oikos. Why?"

"Because Mira and I were both groomed to kill each other on sight, and we failed both of our fathers, then we spent the next thirty years paying for that failure."

"I'd say that makes no sense because Grandfather rarely makes sense, but..." Shrugging, Jasper reaches for his glass, neck arching as he drains the rest of its contents. "Men have gone to war over less."

"Think of your parents as benevolent, Jasper," is stressed hard, my fingers curling on my thighs, struggling to smother my rising ire. "Imagine your mother and I, both pawns in our fathers' game. The only difference between your mother and I, I knew my father didn't love me, so therefore my loyalty did not lie with him."

Leaning forward, angry that my son forced me to share the darkest of myself to prove I've been a kind and compassionate father, I point directly in his face. "You will respect and honor me as your father, the same as with your mother. You will stop treating me as a child, the same as with your mother. You will stop trying to control me, as if I am a dog to heel with a sharp yank of my leash, same as with your mother."

"Father—"

"I'm not finished," breaks under the force of my power, proving to my son that I am ultimately in charge. "I have left your mother in peace because I felt it just and right, my morals and self-control the reason, not because I am obeying my son as if he were my master. No doubt, your mother has been doing the same. I've found this an entertaining escape but no more. Do you understand?"

"Yes, but I want answers—"

"You may ask." Finger lowering, I'm no longer pointing in my son's face, but he understands how he is walking a tightrope before me now. "But you are not guaranteed an answer."

"Does Mom know you're alive?"

"Yes." I answer with all honesty, this a much more comfortable topic than the previous one. "I have no idea for how long. As soon as Mira was released from the clinic, I have visited her nightly, unless Cyrus was in her bed."

"Does Cyrus know?" That rage-filled narrowed stare is comical. No doubt when levied against a subordinate, they would cower in fear. As Jasper's father, all it does is make me chuckle how the boy honestly believed he was in charge.

"I honestly have no idea." Leaning back on the cushion, I raise my arms above my head to stretch out the stress held within my muscles. "I didn't know your mother knew until last week, the last time I visited. The first time I visited, Oona awoke, crawled over your mother, and then cuddled with me for the rest of the night.

That was the only time until last week that I allowed myself the luxury of touching your mother."

"My sister has known all along?" The betrayal is thick within Jasper's voice.

"Between the two of us, which one is deserving of loyalty, Jasper?" Scoffing, this is the part of fatherhood I find so entertaining. "I am her father, a man presumed dead, her mother's husband. She loved me as I loved her. She sought my attention. Why deny your sister and I happiness and comfort because you feel as if she didn't obey you by spilling all her secrets?"

"She's my righthand!" is bellowed in rage, causing me to chuckle audibly.

Shrugging as if I'm not delighted by this interaction, "Sometimes the righthand must keep secrets because they're protecting their master from himself. Power corrupts, my boy. Oona was making sure you weren't omnipotent with a bloated head, since she knew something you didn't."

"Harsh, Father." Rubbing at his chest as if I dealt a true blow, Jasper leans forward to grab the fattiest substance of our feast, a fistful of crumbled cheese. "That was harsh." Stuffing his mouth, Jasper effectively stops himself from saying more.

"I had visited Sephira several times when she was heavy with child, coming to terms with the way our lives would be led, until we ultimately said goodbye."

"Did you know she was going to take a header?" Being insensitive, as if he's not speaking of someone who was close to me, Jasper nudges his chin in the direction of the cliffside. "You did, didn't you?" Always thinking the worst of me. "You could have saved her."

"I did save her," is a fierce rasp, angered that my son doesn't understand anything that isn't black nor white, the important hues in between where the flawed people dwell within the human condition.

"Sephira was my friend, Jasper. I had firsthand knowledge of what cruelty my father did to her because I'd witnessed it time and time again. Sephira had a difficult childhood, not a sexual being as an adult. What Father did to her, she could not heal, no matter the care or love or compassion dealt. She merely survived to birth her daughter. She made me promise, as I know she made your mother promise. We were to take care of little Sephira as if she were our own, raised as we raised you and the twins."

Openly staring at me in disbelief, my son evidently doesn't understand. "You honestly believe allowing a woman to take her own life was a compassionate act?"

"Yes," is said, brooking no room for argument. "This thread of conversation is closed, Jasper. It's over. Too late. I think what I think and feel what I feel, placing my friend's needs and wants above my own desire to keep her with me. That is compassion at its core."

"So your dead mistress knew you didn't die. Oona has known all along. As of last week, you discovered Mom knows. Who else? Ramsey?"

"No. Not Ramsey. Nor Cyrus." Sighing heavily, I decide it's more important to communicate with my son, to be open and truthful than combative, harping on hurt feelings and betrayals.

"Little Sephira opens her eyes most nights, smiles at me, then cuddles closer to Mira's chest, then instantly falls back to sleep. I'd assume if a girl saw a strange man staring down at her from beside her bed, she's scream like a banshee. But perhaps she remembers me, because after her birth, Ramsey and Cyrus fled Mira's bed, leaving Oona and Mira to take care of the crying child in the middle of the night. As to not disturb them, I would cradle the baby, feed her, change her, allowing the women to rest. I'm just surprised Sephira never told anyone about me ghosting in the room as she got older."

"They're women," Jasper rumbles, reminding me of my father, which has me cringing. But he doesn't mean it as it sounds, because I know he would lie his life down to protect them all. "If one knows something, they all know it. That's how it works."

"What of Sephira?" Musing to myself, I realize I need to add. "My friend– please do not insult her by calling her my mistress, as any attempt at sexual intimacy was awkward and torturous. Sephira was my friend, and she knew I had survived. Do you think the ladies knew that much earlier than I suspected?"

"If one knew, they all knew." Finally relaxing, the edge of betrayal softening as we analyze the women, Jasper begins eating whatever his hands can reach in earnest. "Mom was so hopped up on psychotropics, she could have known and forgot within minutes. Once she wasn't being medicated, it took months for it to clear from her system."

"Someday, I'd love to sit with your mother and discuss how she views the past decade, from an academic standpoint."

"Sure." My thirty-year-old son has the audacity to roll his eyes at me, and here he is about to be a father himself. "Has nothing to do with the reward or anything."

"The reward?" Chuckling, yet another entertaining facet of parenthood. "Do you honestly believe your reward meant anything? We will meet when one or the other initiates, and it will not be with your permission. We are your parents, not your children nor your subjects. Don't be so insulting."

"I'm going to go ahead and assume it will be sooner rather than later, judging by Rampaging Ramsey throwing a tantrum all over the villa. Mom must've cut them loose because she only wants you. You must be as possessive as the rest of us."

"Not in the least." Snorting, I adore that I just baffled my son. Nothing is more entertaining than taking Jasper unawares. "I mean, I'm sure your mother has her reasons for pushing Cyrus and Ramsey away, but it's not my doing. I'm perfectly content with her having contact with one or both of them. I am not the possessive Elezi in the scenario, and your mother is not who Ramsey is possessive over."

"How do you... how do you handle knowing Mom has touched others?" Oh, the expression on my son's face is telling, and I begin to wonder if there are a stack of Rica's old beaux piled up in an old stone cellar somewhere.

"Mira's joy is mine." Shrugging, I know I cannot express this in a way that Jasper will understand, the same reason Cyrus cannot get Ramsey in hand. "After the maltreatment at my father's hand, perhaps some of it is that I don't believe I deserve all of your mother's attention. Or perhaps I understand how our lives have shaped us, how it has forced us to create connections with various people, and how we cannot just erase all of that when we fall in love with someone."

Dark features marred with confusion and frustration, "I'll never understand." My son's tone dips into a whine, sounding more like a little boy than he ever has."

"Thank your mother and me for that," is murmured wryly, yet again entertained by my offspring. "Thank us for raising you with respect for the man you'd become. For treating you as an equal.

For not coddling you yet loving you with our whole hearts. Thank us for choosing Rica for you. Both of you are in love with one another, expecting your first child. It is not for you to understand why your mother or I feel as we do, just be blessed your life is far less complicated than ours."

Back stiffening up from the implication, Jasper gestures around the landscape, from the garden to the cliffside, to the roaring sea below, silently stating, *"Complicated?"*

Eyes glinting with mischief, "I'll assume it's either going to be far less complicated or more, judging by how my brother is reacting from Mira cutting him and Cyrus off." Leaning forward, I issue a warning to my son in a whispered tone.

"They will feel betrayed by all of us, Jasper. Your uncles and your brother, especially when it comes to you, thinking you kept me from them." Sighing heavily, a wane smile curls my lips. "I will take the brunt of the responsibility."

"Why?" My son isn't asking me why they'll feel betrayed, as I believe that is the major reason Jasper has allowed this to string on for so long, fearing Cyrus, Ramsey, and Oscar will feel as he just did when he learned Oona knew all along, only on a grander scale.

My son is asking why I would take their ire when he believes himself at fault.

"Because you're my son," is muttered with a shrug, as if it's just that obvious. "It's what fathers do. Let that be the first lesson I give to the father-to-be. You must sacrifice yourself for your children– your happiness, your wellbeing, and sometimes your life."

Chuckling underneath my breath, I go in for the kill, knowing Jasper's reaction will entertain me so. "Then a decade or so into your child's life, they will begin talking down to you, as if they're the parent and you're their child." Smirk encompassing my face. "I cannot wait to witness this."

"Karma," Jasper murmurs with a visible shudder rolling down his spine. "I'm going to regret how I've treated you and Mom, aren't I?"

Laughter dying on the wind, that is the funniest thing I've ever heard.

## ZE

Nerves on edge as I stare out at the roaring sea below, wind whipping at my cheeks, hair fluttering around my head. Palms curled into fists, plugged into trouser pockets– the stiff fabric foreign to me after so long of wearing nothing but soft cotton pants and shirts.

After cleaning my modest cottage, placing things where they belong, laundering the linens, shining the fixtures, and fixing a light repast, I was prepared enough to make the short journey to Tortoise Rock.

While my surroundings are prepared, I'm not sure I'm mentally or emotionally prepared for Miranda Livas and Zamir Elezi to meet again for the first time, the way we ought to have met almost three decades ago.

Having been at peace, the solitude a healing balm on my soul, the surety that the devil himself can never manifest in the flesh to torment and torture me, even by slipping into my dreams and detonating nightmares.

My life is balanced.

Content.

Almost happy.

Almost.

Heart pounding a rapid tattoo beneath my ribcage, I worry Mira won't be able to find that level of calm, balance, centered contentment by my side. Especially after the two other men in her life realize I've never truly been out of their lives. While I cannot wait to reconnect to my youngest son, Oscar, I do not look forward to the stress and angst a reunion with Ramsey and Cyrus will bring.

This location was important to me, because of the isolation, with me the only other human in the vicinity, no others to gain

Mira's attention. Unlike the first time we met, when my father dominated the scene, demanding all eyes on him, where my charismatic baby brother lured Mira's gaze from mine, dashing all my hope for rescue and a better life at the side of such a formidable woman.

This time it will be different. I'll be able to discern Mira's emotions without any distractions. Mira's reaction will determine the outcome of today's meeting.

Facing the sea, my back toward Mira, I listen to her soft footfalls as she nears closer. Adrenaline and anticipation fire in my veins, eagerness causing a jittery sensation to flow through my muscles, fingers shaking within my pockets.

Turning slowly, as to truly see Miranda in the light of day, after so many nights visible only by soft lamplight, I drink in all the changes, the differences a decade makes. The way a body changes to cope with trauma.

Miranda Livas, no matter how much she ages, she will forever be the most stunning woman I've ever encountered. Soft face beautiful. Wisdom-lined eyes fierce. Sensual curves with knowledge hidden deep beneath. A voice that digs its way beneath my skin, delves to the depths of my soul, and attaches itself for all eternity.

That lightning strike of white hair woven into a cascade of midnight tresses, how I long to lie in my bed, silk flowing between my fingertips, as I gaze at my wife, a smile of contentment spread across her face. I could do that for the rest of my life and die happy, feeling as if I've accomplished all I set out to do in this lifetime.

"My queen?" Turning slowly, I take note of how Mira's focus is on the faded scar bisecting my throat. There is no sense of rejection or revulsion, merely that Mira sees the scar as confirmation.

Yes, I was nearly killed.

Yes, I survived.

Yes, this is not a dream, as we are firmly planted in reality, roots dug deep into the Livas Oikos's soil, never to be unearthed, dying here when our time is called.

"My king?" is a breathy rasp, as if Mira herself cannot believe I'm standing here in the flesh. Perhaps she's lied to herself all this time, thinking me a fantasy sprung to life, much similar to how I think of her when I lie in my bed, surrounding myself with her painted image.

That look.

That look where Mira doesn't gaze away, where she doesn't seek out my brother... where she raises her hand as if to touch the air, hoping to feel a disturbance there to prove I'm real.

That look of hope springing in her eyes.

The love shining brightly at me.

"I was wondering if you'd like to visit my cottage, my queen?" Turning from facing the sea, I give Miranda my total attention, hand raising to seek hers out. "Oona will alert those who need to know once they discover you missing."

"I'd love to visit." Feet soundless, legs moving quickly, Mira's supple form is fitted perfectly against mine in a heartbeat. Her scent and her presence shorting out my mind. Lips reach for mine, seeking a first kiss of sorts– our final first kiss.

"Perhaps I'd love to do more than visit." Gaze naughty, tone seductive, Mira takes hold of my hand, tugging me in the direction of my cottage, as if she instinctively knows the way, proving that between us, she will forever be in charge.

Walking slightly ahead of me, Mira turns to smirk over her shoulder. "Perhaps I'll stay."

"Perhaps I'll capture you, never allowing you to leave," is exactly how a Elezi would reply.

"I'll never be a hostage again," Mira murmurs wryly, but beneath the humor and seduction is an edge of truth. "I do believe I'd like to visit."

Hand squeezing mine, eyes boring into mine, every emotion Mira is feeling is flowing in my direction. Raw and exposed, no barriers between us.

"I'd be honored to stay," is a whispered admission as my stone cottage comes into view. "Perhaps I'll summon Sephira to join us here. They'll have to drag me out kicking and screaming, as I'll never want to leave."

"You'll forever have an invite," is rasped in reply, Mira giving me a sympathetic look, realizing I wasn't just inviting her to stay in my cottage.

Mira will forever be invited into my home, into my life, into my heart, and into my soul. A well of confidence and certainty bubbles up from somewhere deep, since my father is no longer able to detonate my sense of self.

A private smile just for me, Mira's fingers laced through mine squeezing at my hand. Her presence warm and inviting, love radiating in my direction. Acting as reckless youths, we stumble into our cottage, absorbed in our reunion, refusing to leave until our family drags us out– our family the ones doing all the kicking and screaming.

# ACKNOWLEDGEMENTS

A lot of work goes into writing a novel, and it isn't just by the writer herself. **My parents:** for their unconditional support. **My readers**: thank you for reading my twisted words and spreading my books to the masses. For without you, no one would've ever heard of my stories. My readers are my lifeblood. A shout out to the members of the **M&M of Restraint Group on Facebook**: thanks for the endless entertainment and inspiration. **Wicked Reads**: (in all its incarnations) **Angela G.**, thank you for taking over and making Wicked Reads better than I could have done by myself. & thank you for helping promote my work and the work of other authors. Angela? Have I told you lately how much I appreciate you? A huge thank you to the **Wicked Writer's Betas** for keeping me grounded and encouraging me to keep trudging along when I get frustrated. Your thoughts and observations are invaluable. ((Hugs)) Beta readers who helped with Evoking Mira: **Diane | Jacki | Linsey |** Someday, I'd love to meet you all in real life– it would be the experience of a lifetime.

# ABOUT THE AUTHOR

Erica Chilson does not write in the 3<sup>rd</sup> person, wanting her readers to *be* her characters. Therefore, writing a bio about herself, is uncomfortable in the extreme.

Born, raised, and here to stay, the Wicked Writer is a stump-jumper, a ridge-runner. Hailing from North Central Pennsylvania, directly on the New York State border; she loves the changes in seasons, the humid air, all the mountainous forest, and the gloomy atmosphere.

Introverted, but not socially awkward, Erica prides herself on thinking first and filtering her speech. There are days she doesn't speak at all. If it wasn't for the fact that she lives with her parents, giving her a sense of reality, she would be a hermit, where the delivery man finds her months after expiration.

Reading was an escape, a way to leave a not-so pleasant reality behind. Reading lent Erica the courage she gathered from the characters between the pages to long for a different life. Writing was an instrument of change, evolving Erica into the woman she is today– a better, more mature, more at peace thinker.

Erica has a wicked mind, one she pours out into her creations. Her filter doesn't allow all of it to erupt, much to her relief. Sarcastic, with a very dark, perverse sense of humor, Erica puts a bit of herself into every character she writes.

I love hearing from readers. If you would like more information on release dates, works in progress, teaser chapters, and random bits of madness, please visit my Facebook Fan Page: Erica Chilson, my website: ericachilson.com or please contact me via email: wickedwriter.ericachilson@gmail.com

Made in the USA
Monee, IL
10 April 2022

94474468R00144